MATT REES was born in Wales and read English at Oxford before moving to the Middle East to become a journalist. He is also the author of the award-winning Omar Yussef series, which follows a detective in Palestine, and is now published in twenty-four countries.

Visit his website at www.mattrees.net

ALSO BY MATT REES

Mozart's Last Aria

THE OMAR YUSSEF SERIES
The Bethlehem Murders
The Saladin Murders
The Samaritan's Secret
The Fourth Assassin

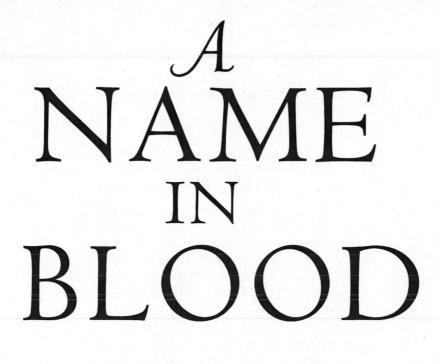

A NAME IN BLOOD

MATT REES

CORVUS

First published in hardback and trade paperback in Great Britain in 2012 by Corvus, an imprint of Atlantic Books Ltd.

10 9 8 7 6 5 4 3 2 1

A CIP catalogue record for this book is available from the British Library.

Hardback ISBN: 978 1 84887 919 5
Trade paperback ISBN: 978 1 84887 918 8
E-book ISBN: 978 0 85789 678 0

Printed in Great Britain by TJ International Ltd, Padstow, Cornwall

Corvus
An imprint of Grove Atlantic Ltd
Ormond House
26-27 Boswell Street
London WC1N 3JZ

www.corvus-books.co.uk

For Mari Carys, my little Madonna

CONTENTS

In July 1610, Michelangelo Merisi, known as Caravaggio, the most celebrated artist in Italy, disappeared. Though he had dangerous enemies and had been on the run with a price on his head for several years, he was said to have died of a fever. His body was never found.

He died as badly as he had lived.

> Giovanni Baglione (1566–1643), on Caravaggio in *The Lives of the Painters, Sculptors and Architects*, 1642

What a good end he makes, who dies loving well.

> Petrarch (1304–74), Sonnet 140

MAIN CHARACTERS

Michelangelo Merisi (called Caravaggio, after his hometown), *an artist*

Maddalena 'Lena' Antognetti, *Caravaggio's model*

Giovanni Baglione, *artist*

Scipione Borghese, *Cardinal, nephew of Pope Paul V*

Domenica 'Menica' Calvi, *courtesan*

Costanza Colonna, *Marchesa of Caravaggio*

Leonetto della Corbara, *Inquisitor of Malta*

Onorio Longhi, *architect*

Antonio Martelli, *Knight of Malta*

Fillide Melandroni, *courtesan*

Mario Minniti, *artist*

Francesco del Monte, *Cardinal, patron of Caravaggio*

Gaspare Murtola, *poet*

Prospero Orsi, *artist*

Giovanni Roero, *Piedmontese nobleman, Knight of Malta*

Fabrizio Sforza-Colonna, *Costanza's son, Knight of Malta*

Ranuccio Tomassoni, *ruffian, pimp*

Giovan Francesco Tomassoni, *Ranuccio's elder brother*

Alof de Wignacourt, *Grand Master of the Knights of Malta*

Prudenza Zacchia, *courtesan*

PROLOGUE
The town of CARAVAGGIO,
in the Duchy of Milan
Things Thought Hidden
1577

The boy sat in the dark. *Watch him*, he thought. *Watch this man lurching upright with his hands to his belly, retching, grimacing, sweating, kneading himself with blackened fingernails.* The sheets stank, but the boy remained on the bed. He wanted to be near the invalid whose privates and armpits were bulbous with the scabbing sores of the plague. This was his father, who was dying.

Across the bed lay the boy's grandfather. Each breath choked the old man, rattling his narrow chest. Perspiration shone on his grey beard. Runnels of sweat glimmered between every stark rib in his heaving torso. Rotting plague weals brimmed out of his armpits like leeches. Bloody urine seeped into the mattress. His face quivered with shame under the sallow shaft of sun from a crack in the shutter.

His father's voice. Would he forget it? He knew he would remember the words: 'Michele, why are you here?' But would he recall the tone? A mellow bass, warped and desiccated in the furnace of the Black Death until it sounded like the futile gurgling of a man smothered by a mouthful of sand. 'Why?'

'To keep you company, Papa.' His own speech. When he was older and alone, he remembered it like the cadence of an ineluctable melody. Lost and innocent, he would hear it in his head. Ah, but never in his throat. That voice – the one that would resonate when he opened his mouth as a grown man – that speech was stripped of all innocence.

'Go, my boy. You'll catch the—' His father heaved and rolled on his side, shivering. He drew up his knees.

The air was sharp with the lime and sulphur his mother said would chase away the disease. It prickled in the boy's nose and his lungs. It made him sneeze. His father lifted his head, a motion quicker than any he had made since the infection had come on. The man's features were taut with horror. A sneeze was the first symptom. The boy twitched a wavering smile to reassure him.

The father's head dropped as though his son's grin had sliced it from his shoulders. He descended again into his own tortures. The boy wondered about the sneeze too, and he reached his thin, pale arm under the drawstring of his calico pants to feel around his groin. No lumps, no buboes. The sulphur scent returned and he realized he had been holding his breath.

His grandfather shuddered, eyes flickering upwards, white and blind. He surrendered his vision to the dimming light within his skull, so that some spirit too refined for living perception might reveal itself to him. When the pupils descended, they were fixed and unseeing and the boy's grandfather was still. His father's tear ducts were dried by the vinegar with which he had tried to wash away the pestilence; the weeping wouldn't come. He struck his brow with his fists as though the tears were merely stubborn and might relent, like a donkey, with chastisement.

The boy stayed with them for hours. His father lay beside the dead man, whispering and incoherent in his fever. That evening he complained that the bed was wet and hot, slid to the floor, stared into the night-black. The boy stood over him.

'You're too young, Michele,' he gasped. 'Too young to see this.'

At first the boy thought he meant that a child of six shouldn't witness his father's parting and so he sobbed, because he already felt what it would be like to be without him. Then he followed the direction of his squint. With eyes unsynchronized and palpitating, he knew his father was looking into the face of Death. The boy could make out nothing in the darkness. The father opened his mouth to explain what he saw, but his jaw fell and his weight slumped against the side of the bed. The boy grappled with his father's head, clinging to the tangled hair, so that it shouldn't be dashed to the floor.

The boy glanced down at the dead man, his brow ridged with pity. Something moved in the darkness and he sensed it, the sudden illumination that comes to those who make a compact with death. The sufferer from disease or the willing sacrifice. The murderer and his victim.

Watch the darkness, it told him. *What materializes from the shadow? What emerges when you stare at things thought hidden? Keep looking and one day you'll see its shape. Your gaze will make a light that penetrates the mystery.*

He stroked the dead man's head. *Isn't that true, Papa?*

I
ROME
In the Evil Garden
1605

1

The Calling of St Matthew

'He's the most famous artist in Rome.' At the end of the nave, Scipione Borghese crossed himself. His hand passed across his scarlet robes, slow and voluptuous, as if he were stroking a lover's breast. 'Do you think you can keep him to yourself?'

Not now that your uncle is anointed as Pope Paul, Cardinal del Monte thought. The appointment of the new pontiff had made Scipione the most powerful prince of the Church in Rome. *He'll force my protégé to sign his letters 'your humble creature'*. 'If you think it's possible to control Caravaggio, my gracious Lord, I shall be happy to introduce you to him so that you may attempt it. He answers to a higher power than you or I.' He gestured to the golden crucifix glimmering on the altar in the light from the high windows. 'And I don't mean the Holy Father, may he be blessed by Our Lord.' Scipione prodded his wrist downwards, his index and little fingers extended like the horns of the devil.

Del Monte grimaced to see such an earthy gesture formed by the manicured hand of the new arbiter of art and power in the papal city. 'From what I hear of his behaviour, Caravaggio's authority comes not from above, but from below,' Scipione said. 'Artists are all rough sorts. I know how to bend them to my will.'

With 200,000 ducats a year bestowed upon you from the Throne of St Peter, I'm sure you'll find a way. Del Monte guided Scipione to the chapel in the left aisle. 'Here they are.'

Scipione shifted his scarlet beret on the back of his head, scratched his jaw, and pulled ruminatively on the point of his goatee. His tongue ran along his upper lip. He was young and delicate, but something in his face made it easy to foresee what he would look like when he became fat. *And this one's certainly going to be fat*, del Monte thought. *The body can barely contain the avarice of the man. Just give him a few years with absolute power and unlimited budget, his stomach will swell and his chins will multiply.*

'The famous pride of the Church of San Luigi of the French,' Scipione said.

The two cardinals passed beyond the green marble balustrade into the Contarelli Chapel. '*St Matthew and the Angel* and *The Martyrdom of St Matthew*, these are wonderful of course.'

'Yes, but it's this one. This is the one.' Scipione turned to the massive canvas on the wall at the left of the altar.

'*The Calling of St Matthew*.' Del Monte opened his hands wide. 'I admit that even I, who recognized his talent before all other patrons, never expected a genius of such virtuosity to emerge.'

'It's revolutionary. Everywhere such darkness.' Scipione spread his feet and rested his hands on his stomach. He worked his jaw, rippling his cheeks, as though he were consuming the canvas before him.

The Calling portrayed five men at a table. Three youngsters wore showy doublets and cockaded hats; the other two were grey-haired. A plain room, its walls dun-coloured; one window, dirty and lightless. But from the right, where a vivid sun illuminated the chapel itself, a shaft of warm yellow and brown tones angled as if cast through a high window into a basement. Just beneath that soft beam, obscured by shadow, his hand reaching out to call his future disciple, the bearded face of Jesus.

'What a brilliant stroke,' Scipione said, 'that Our Lord should be displaced from his usual position at the shining centre of the composition.'

'And yet He still dominates the painting.'

'Quite so, del Monte. The meaning of the work isn't forced upon us by bright skies and radiant angels. We must search. Like St Matthew himself. Search within ourselves.' Scipione pointed at one of the seated figures who seemed to be gesturing towards himself, questioning whether it was he whom Christ was calling.

'When these were delivered to San Luigi five years ago,' del Monte said, 'I knew they'd transform painting forever. In any church in Rome now, you'll see that every new work of art is either a copy of Caravaggio's style by one of his admirers or an angry rejection of it by someone who wants to stick to the manner of the last half-century. Caravaggio is present in every work these days, whether painters admit it or not.'

He snapped his fingers. A manservant came from the rear of the church in del Monte's turquoise livery, bowing low. 'Command Maestro Caravaggio's presence. I will receive him at my gallery.'

'Yes, my Lord.' The manservant genuflected towards the altar and went into the piazza at a trot.

'He paints without any of the usual preparation, you know,' del Monte said. 'No sketches. He works directly onto the canvas from life – from the models he positions in his studio.'

'The moment is simply captured.' Scipione rolled his fingers across each other, like a thief limbering up to pick a pocket. 'As Jesus passed forth from thence, He saw a man named Matthew sitting at the customs house: And He said to him, "Follow me."

And he arose, and followed Him.'

Del Monte watched Scipione's face transform with each detail he noticed on the painting, moving from perplexity to understanding and admiration.

'Look here, do you see?' Scipione touched del Monte's sleeve. 'It's as though when Our Lord lifts his hand everyone holds their breath. It's truly alive.'

The two cardinals left San Luigi, their footmen going before them to part the crowd of Romans passing between the Piazza Navona and Santa Maria Rotonda, the church inserted within Emperor Hadrian's great Pantheon. They crossed the street to del Monte's palace, named after the illegitimate daughter of the Holy Roman Emperor who had been known as the 'Madama'. They climbed the broad stairway.

Scipione paused at the landing so that he might recover his breath. 'This painter didn't train in the town of Caravaggio, I'm sure. I've been up that way. It's a backwater good only for producing the silk in my underwear.'

Del Monte measured his step to the younger man's laboured ascent. They reached the floor where he kept his private apartments. 'He apprenticed with Maestro Peterzano in Milan.'

'Milan, now I see it. You can find something in his work of other great artists of that region. I'm thinking of Savoldo's use of light and dark. But an artist has to come to Rome to make anything of his career.'

Del Monte inclined his head. *Come to you, you mean.* 'It wasn't merely the grey skies of the north that compelled Maestro Caravaggio to quit Milan.'

Scipione opened his palm, questioning.

'It was something to do with a whore disfigured and the wounding of her jealous lover, who also happened to be a policeman,' del Monte said.

Scipione's shrug indicated that such circumstances neither surprised nor perturbed him.

'When he came to live at this palace,' del Monte said, 'Caravaggio was just a Milanese neckbreaker. In some ways he still is. His work changes more than he personally seems to do. There's something sweet and spiritual in his depths, and it's there that he finds his art.'

'He came directly to you when he arrived in Rome?'

'He stayed for a time with a priest who kept him as a favour to his patrons in the Colonna family.'

Scipione's eyes became distant. Del Monte saw that the Cardinal-Nephew was reckoning Caravaggio's place in the calculus of influence and domain that a man in his position maintained at all times. The Colonnas were among the most powerful of Roman families.

'I see.' Scipione's movements slowed, as though he needed all his functions to estimate the political advantages he might contrive through the artist.

'He came to me a decade or more past,' del Monte said. 'I gave him a room and a studio, and a place at table with the musicians and men of science who live at my pleasure.'

'The Tuscan embassy under your direction is renowned as a place of art and of reason par excellence. Does Caravaggio have no other protector?'

Del Monte barely restrained his smile. *He wants to know who else he must brush aside to take possession of Caravaggio? This man's in even more of a hurry than I expected.* 'The Mattei family has commissioned some works.'

Scipione's arithmetic of prominence and prestige seemed to spread across his features as though he sketched out its equations in fresco. 'Cardinal Mattei is—?' He rolled his wrist to suggest the question, as if it would be indelicate to speak it.

'Not an art lover. But his brothers are great admirers of Caravaggio and are inclined to spend money on pleasures the honourable cardinal denies himself.' Del Monte waited as Scipione assessed the connections he might cement with the gift of a painting or whose gallery he might raid to sequestrate one of Caravaggio's works.

I'll allow him to discover for himself just how many other links Caravaggio has built in a dozen years here, del Monte thought. Soon enough Scipione would learn about the commissions from Marchese Giustiniani, from the banker Don Ottavio Costa, from Monsignor Barberini whom many believed would be pope one day. As for the works in the collection of the Lady Olimpia Aldobrandini, he thought it best they remain unspoken. She was the niece of old Pope Clement, whose family Scipione was engaged in denuding of all influence and wealth now that his uncle controlled the Vatican. 'In spite of his range of admirers, Maestro Caravaggio has remained under my ultimate protection.'

Scipione twitched his moustache, as though deriding the value of such security as del Monte afforded the artist. 'He needs you to vouch for him when he's arrested and thrown drunk into the Tor di Nona, I'll wager.'

'He has been known to call upon my guardianship on such occasions. As you said, these artists are rough sorts. His work, however, is incomparable.' They came to the top of the staircase. 'My own collection is through here,' del Monte said. 'It includes seven canvases by our Maestro Michelangelo of Caravaggio. Please, Your Illustriousness, this way.'

He drew Scipione into a wide gallery. The walls were hung almost to the ceiling with paintings. The best were at eye level, hidden behind green curtains to protect them from sunshine and fly droppings. The cardinals crossed the room. Del Monte took hold of a yellow brocade cord to draw back one of the curtains.

A young maid scrubbed beeswax into the terracotta tiles of the palace as a man in his mid-thirties came to the head of the stairs. She sat back on her heels, wiped her forehead and tucked a strand of red-brown hair behind her ear. Her features brooded with a resentment and resignation the man recognized well from his years living in the palaces of wealthy patrons, though he sensed it wasn't yet of the kind that betokened bitterness and collapse. From her olive skin, her sharp jet eyebrows and angular nose, he assumed she was from the south, where the people were descended from early Greek settlers of the Italian peninsula. Grime darkened her hands. Each fingernail was framed by a black halo of dirt.

A statue of Hercules dug out of the Roman Forum guarded the head of the stairs. The man threw the end of his short black cloak over his shoulder and leaned against the stone figure. The habitual set of his face was hostile, forceful and proud, so that when he smiled at her he saw that the girl hadn't imagined it was possible for such features to allow themselves repose or gaiety. His teeth were white between his black moustache and goatee. He took up a heroic stance at Hercules's shoulder, ran his hand through his longish, wavy black hair, cleared his throat, and mimicked the pagan god's noble gaze.

'How do I look?' he said.

The girl laughed.

'Who cuts the better figure? Me or this fellow?' He tapped the statue's muscular upper arm. 'Come on, he's been underground for fifteen hundred years. Surely I don't look so bad?'

'You *do* look a bit sick, though.'

'Yes, well, I was out late with the notable architect Maestro Onorio Longhi, dear girl, and much fun it was.' He touched the tip of his moustache with his tongue and rubbed at the pitted stone

15

of Hercules's hand. 'Poor fellow, his limbs of ancient marble forbid him to reach out and caress the beauty before him.'

'That's a shame.'

His brows drew down over eyes of glowing brown, Indian red lightened with the warmth of russet, and he stepped towards her. 'But I am no hero on a pedestal. I may touch.'

He bent his knees to crouch beside her, smelled the wax on her hands and the old sweat in her rough workdress, which she had tucked up at the side so that she might kneel. She regarded him with neither the stupid incomprehension of an ordinary serving girl nor the lascivious complicity of the whores at the Tavern of the Moor. In her eyes he saw a quiet beauty of such calm that he briefly forgot the seduction upon which he had embarked and wondered what to say next.

A footman came into the corridor and cleared his throat. 'Maestro Caravaggio, His Illustriousness awaits your pleasure in the gallery.'

'My pleasure.' The man recovered his playfulness and winked at the girl. '*My* pleasure.'

She dabbed her brush in the beeswax. He watched her face a moment more. It was a little too wide, but her jaw was fine and it tapered to a chin of great delicacy.

Without looking up, she sensed his gaze and smiled. 'I've work to do. Go and study His Illustriousness instead.'

He crossed the tiles, gleaming with the results of her earlier labours. As he entered the cardinal's chambers he glanced back at her. The soles of her bare feet were turned upward as she leaned forward on the brush. They were soiled in such striations of black, brown and grey that he could taste the dirt on his tongue.

Since Caravaggio's last summons to the gallery in the Madama Palace, del Monte had expanded his collection. A spasmodic Francis of Assisi now adorned the wall beside a version of the same saint by Caravaggio. Across the room an unfamiliar face turned to him, a cardinal, flattening his hand in expectation of a flunkey's kiss. But Caravaggio's eyes were drawn to the new work. The saint's head was thrown back, his eyes rolled up into his skull. His clumsy, stubby fingers splayed out. He seemed to be in the midst of a fit of the falling sickness, rather than the ecstasy he was supposed to be experiencing. A fat cherub gestured towards a crown of thorns, though how he expected the saint to look at it in his present state was beyond Caravaggio. It was just the kind of nonsensical gesture he hated to see on canvas. That it should hang at the side of his own Francis appalled him. *His* saint was breathless, gashed in his side with the stigmata, cradled by an angel who shared Francis's transport of divine love.

'You've noticed my new acquisition from the studio of Maestro Baglione,' del Monte said. 'It's exquisite, isn't it?'

Caravaggio gave a low, scornful laugh. *I might've known this would be that fool Baglione's work*, he thought. It had become hard to tell which of Rome's artists had executed any given imitation of his art, so many of them had committed themselves to thieving his style. None of them knew what was behind his use of light and shadow, his work with mirrors and lenses, the choice of models from among his poorest acquaintances. To other painters, they were just a bag of tricks to make pretty decoration. Men like Baglione failed to see that what Caravaggio did was profound – that he took the things everyone had seen countless times, the bar-room cheats and pretty boys on the make, the martyred saints and even the Lord Jesus, and he made people see them as if for the first time.

'He has captured something of your style, Maestro Caravaggio,' the new cardinal said.

Don't say it, cazzo mio, Caravaggio told himself. *Don't say, 'What the hell do you know?' If del Monte's taking the time to introduce you, this must be someone important.* 'My style?'

'Quite so.' The cardinal's eyes glistened in his long, soft face. 'The light, falling on the most revealing features of the subject. The close, intense focus. The lack of a background. This is your accustomed device, isn't it? Upon which your reputation is founded.'

My ideas, debased for a quick judgement by a man who pretends to be a connoisseur. Caravaggio closed his eyes.

Del Monte clapped his hands. 'So what do you think of my new *St Francis?*'

Caravaggio muttered something behind his hand.

'What was that?' del Monte said.

Caravaggio threw out his arm with disdain towards the painting. 'I said, he needs to get laid.'

Del Monte covered his smile with his hand. The other cardinal rubbed a finger along the side of his nose. 'I, too, have heard it said of Maestro Baglione that he's a virginal man who doesn't give himself to the flesh.' He ran his hands down his front to draw attention to his cardinal's suit of red velvet. 'Do you have something against a life dedicated to celibacy?'

Caravaggio had seen painted streetwalkers come bruised and stumbling out of alleys jostled by gangs of drunken Spanish soldiers and they had still looked more celibate than this cardinal. 'A life of such renunciation is one thing for a man of the cloth. But for an artist? How can you paint skin if you've never touched it?'

'You've painted the skin of Our Lord, as I saw at the Church of San Luigi. Have you ever touched *that*? Or are you going to tell me you've tasted it in the form of the Holy Communion?'

'Skin's skin. Whether it's a bag for my bones or those of Our Lord Jesus Christ – or Your Illustriousness.'

The cardinal watched him long enough to know that Caravaggio, neither embarrassed nor disconcerted, wasn't about to drop his eyes. 'A heretic. I see why you get on so well with this one, del Monte.'

Caravaggio's old patron forced a smile and bowed. 'Maestro Caravaggio, your presence was requested here by Cardinal Borghese.'

The new pope's nephew, the man who now runs the Vatican. Caravaggio touched the pulse in his neck, feeling the charge of adrenaline under his fingertip, thrilled by the prospect of impressing the most powerful art lover in Rome and shaking at the thought of how close he had come to insulting him. He fell onto one knee. With his head low, he took the smooth pale hand which Scipione eased forward from his soutane. He brushed it with his lips. It smelled of calfskin gloves and the ambergris used to scent them.

'The divine Michelangelo used to say of a mediocre artwork that it hurts no one,' Scipione said. 'May we not say so of this *St Francis* by Maestro Baglione?'

'It hurts *me*.'

'Michelangelo's formulation was a way of avoiding offence. I see this isn't one of your objectives. Before an excellent work of art, he used to say that it was painted either by a great scoundrel or a great rascal.' Scipione tugged on the golden cord that drew the curtain back from Caravaggio's *Musicians*. He went close, stilling the swinging viridian taffeta with the palm of his hand. 'Which are you, Maestro?'

Caravaggio hadn't seen this canvas in months. Four youths wreathed in loose white shirts or draped in sheets, their shoulders and hairless chests exposed. Del Monte had commissioned several like this. The young artists and musicians who lived at the Madama Palace called him Cardinal Madama, because of his discreet preference for pale, yielding boys. At the front of the composition, pretty Pedro, the castrato singer, Caravaggio's closest friend when he had first lived in del Monte's palace, now returned to Spain.

Over the singer's shoulder, a self-portrait. He couldn't bear to look at it. He had made himself appear so innocent and wan, his lips parted in a tender, sensuous moan. He found it hard to remember a day when you could have truly read such inexperience and freshness on his face. *Perhaps once,* he thought. *With Costanza and Fabrizio Colonna. In their palace, in my hometown – before they sent me away.*

'A scoundrel or a rascal?' He hooked his thumbs into his belt. 'That depends on the night and how old the girl is.'

'Or the boy?' Scipione tapped his knuckle against the swooning features of Pedro, who tuned a lute at the centre of *The Musicians* as if he were caressing a lover's belly. 'Don't you agree, del Monte?'

The older cardinal flinched.

Well, well, Scipione knows about Cardinal Madama and his little peccadillo, Caravaggio thought. *From the way he wrinkles his lips, I'd say he shares the same predilection. Here's the man who heads the Inquisition, making jokes about effeminate boys, when only last week a baker was burned to death by the Holy Office in the Campo de'Fiori for buggering a street urchin.*

'But this is my favourite, Maestro Caravaggio. Her eyes follow me even through the curtain.' Scipione ran back the material that covered *St Catherine of Alexandria*. 'The face is inescapable. Bravo, bravo.'

The saint leaned against the spiked cartwheel that had been the instrument of her torture and fondled the sword that had dealt her death and martyrdom. Kneeling on a red cushion, she was encased in a billowing black silk dress of intricate embroidery. Her hair was red-blonde and tied in braids at each side. She looked out of the canvas directly at the viewer. *Fillide.* Caravaggio smiled to himself. *She strokes that rapier like it was the stiff member of a high-paying client.*

'Since I saw her, I've barely been able to think of anything else. Her gaze is mesmeric. But why doesn't she look to heaven as the saints do in their moment of martyrdom?' Scipione's voice sharpened and Caravaggio saw that, despite his air of levity, the cardinal was to be addressed with care.

'She stares out at you, because I wished to show that your relationship with the saint is more important than her connection to heaven,' Caravaggio said. 'Her martyrdom isn't a distant suffering for which we should feel only awe. I want you to sense her anguish as your own.'

'Mine?'

'Surely even a cardinal—?'

'Oh, the afflictions are many, you're quite right. Meetings and paperwork, requests for this and that, builders who don't keep to the construction schedule for my palace. There are criminals who want to be pardoned and supporters of this or that holy buffoon who absolutely must be granted sainthood to secure the faith of the people in some freezing Bavarian town.' Scipione shared a look of resignation with del Monte. 'But is it merely your superb technique that makes the saint's face so compelling to me, Maestro? I feel there's something else. Perhaps I might be acquainted with the lady.'

'Her? The model?'

Out of Scipione's sight, del Monte lifted a hand in warning.

'Quite so, her,' the Cardinal-Nephew said.

'I doubt it, Most Illustrious and Reverend Sire.'

'Do you? Why?'

'She's a whore.'

Del Monte dropped his hand and moaned.

'Your Illustriousness would never take his pleasures with a woman.' Caravaggio rolled his tongue through his cheek. 'A woman such as this, I mean.'

Scipione escaped the gaze of St Catherine for long enough to turn upon Caravaggio. His sybaritic features stiffened and Caravaggio saw something vindictive and inexorable in his weepy, little eyes. *Look out, Romans*, he thought. *This one has only as long as his uncle stays alive to tax you and rob you. He'll waste no time about it.*

The cardinal examined the painter. His focus rested on each of the small tears and worn patches in the black velvet of Caravaggio's jacket. Scorn burned through the scanty material to the artist's skin.

Caravaggio scratched the back of his neck. *Be nice, Michele. At least, try harder.* He considered mentioning that Fillide was no cheap street whore, though she was undoubtedly too inexpensive a companion for Scipione. The illustrious cardinal would need a more accomplished musician and singer, a girl or a boy who could improvise a rhyme when they weren't servicing him. In the six years since he had painted her as St Catherine, Fillide had coupled with half the priests and minor nobility of Rome, but she had added no skills to her repertoire beyond those of a purely carnal nature.

'I like this work, Maestro Caravaggio.' Scipione's voice was quiet and sharp. 'But I don't like the black frame. I'd change it. I like a gilded frame.'

Caravaggio was about to say that Scipione had better commission a painting to put in the frame first, but he caught his lip. *Silence, Michele.*

'Yes, a gilded frame would do best,' Scipione said.

'Do you think so, Your Illustriousness?'

The unforgiving eyes again. 'That's what I said. So you must assume that it's also what I think. Though I can't say that you may be *sure* of it.'

That was the trap set by the powerful for everyone around them, and for artists in particular. An undiplomatic word spoken by a courtier could be quickly corrected, but an aberrant painting hung in a church or on the wall of a palace was an undeniable testament to the artist's error and vice. Painters rehashed the work of Raphael and Michelangelo, because these departed masters protected them against accusations of dangerous, innovative thinking. But Caravaggio painted according to his heart, his reading of the Scriptures, his hope of salvation, and he painted what he saw in the world, not what Leonardo had seen a century before. Sometimes he decided to be careful and he checked his compositions against the guidelines for painters of religious subjects set out by the Council of Trent. But now Scipione decided if a work was orthodox or impious, to be praised or condemned. Paint a canvas that doesn't conform to the Cardinal-Nephew's idea of the order of the world and an artist might forfeit more than his commission. It would be the fire for him.

Del Monte crooked his hand around Scipione's elbow and laid an insistent palm on Caravaggio's shoulder. He manoeuvred both men to the high window overlooking the simple façade of the Church of San Luigi. 'His Illustriousness the Cardinal-Nephew was most admiring of *The Calling of St Matthew* when I showed it to him this afternoon.'

Goaded by a pressure from del Monte's hand, Caravaggio made great show of bowing, his head low over his extended leg.

His knee appeared through his stocking. *Where did that tear come from?* he thought. He had an indistinct recollection of a tumble in the street the night before. *By the tennis courts near the*

Piazza Navona. Someone shoved me. A lost bet which I didn't want to pay, that's right. To whom do I owe the money? The gamblers at the courts aren't inclined to forgive a debt. He swallowed hard, an ominous queasiness in his stomach.

Scipione was talking about *St Matthew*. It was nothing Caravaggio hadn't heard again and again in the five years since he painted it. The sensation around his style in *Matthew* had yet to subside. He had endured many expositions from connoisseurs on the originality with which he shrouded Our Saviour in the gloom of a basement and, in doing so, illuminated him more lustrously than all the expensive ultramarine blue on a conventional painter's palette could have done. He had suffered just as many curses and as much haughty derision, too.

But none saw it as Caravaggio did. They all thought the light fell on the grey-bearded figure at the table, that this was Matthew the tax collector, turning his finger towards himself as if to ask whether Christ called to him.

They had the wrong man. The finger pointed beyond the bearded fellow to a youth with his head lowered over the dark tabletop. He shuffled his coins, sullen and dissatisfied with his career. Most of those who saw the painting looked upon this young man as a symbol of the miserable life Matthew was about to leave behind him. But all the other figures on the canvas were content that there should be nothing more in their world than a melancholy counting-house. That despondent young man at the end of the table saw the world through a veil of unfulfilment. He was the one waiting to be called.

Caravaggio had painted the saint in the moment before he raised his head to see the darkness lift. *It had been so for me*, he thought. These paintings were the extended hand of Christ to his art, calling him on to his vocation. He was still following it, wondering where it would lead – just as Matthew wasn't saved when Christ called him; the saint had to wait years, work hard at his faith and keep the light in his sight. *Until his martyrdom.*

'The darkness, Maestro Caravaggio. Yes, the darkness.'

He felt Scipione close, the cardinal's breath on his cheek. It was sweet, like a woman's.

'We're accustomed to biblical scenes with a delightful Tuscan landscape in the background,' Scipione went on. 'Yet when I saw your *Matthew*, enclosed in a basement room, I was unable to escape from the spiritual intensity of the moment. My eye had no opportunity to wander away from it into the accompanying scenery.'

Caravaggio inclined his head to show himself gratified. The slash in his hose caught his eye again. *To whom do I owe?*

'May one find spiritual intensity in any subject?' Scipione said.

'It depends on one's spirit, Your Illustriousness.'

'Quite. Well, I'm sure you'll find whatever there is to be uncovered in his face.'

To whom do I owe? Caravaggio looked up at Scipione. 'His face? I beg your pardon, Your Illustriousness?'

'I'm commissioning you to do something to fill the nice gilded frame that, I notice, made you frown even at mention of it.'

His face? 'A portrait?' Caravaggio cocked his head as though framing the cardinal's features.

Scipione declined his chin. 'Not me, Maestro Caravaggio. Since my uncle was elected to wear the Fisherman's Ring and called me to Rome, I've had too much other business to which I must attend.'

'Naturally.'

'One such matter is to record the Holy Father's features at the moment of his elevation.'

'You want me to paint—?'

'Do it at the Quirinale Palace. You may bring your materials when you wish, but you shall begin the sittings on Sunday afternoon.'

Caravaggio went onto his knee and took Scipione's hand. With his face pressed to the man's knuckles, he directed a speculative glance at del Monte. His old patron pursed his lips. He would know how much this meant. After years in which Caravaggio was shut out of papal commissions by more conventional artists, he had arrived at the peak of prestige and of financial reward. He had impressed the chief connoisseur of a new administration at the Vatican. He would paint Camillo Borghese, Pope Paul V, and it would be a signal to every church and cardinal, every charitable fraternity and nobleman, that Caravaggio was the greatest of all artists in the Christian world.

In the corridor, the servant girl's wax brush rasped on the terracotta.

■

Caravaggio went along the Corso through the crowds of servant girls and gentlemen on their early evening promenade. The thrill of his meeting with the Cardinal-Nephew remained with him. He was to be face to face with the Pope. Could his work still be true? Would he be tempted to disguise some flaw in the skin, to make a grasping, avaricious eye seem benign and beatific? He stepped out of the path of a carriage that rattled close to his foot and stumbled against a pig in the gutter.

Work would take his mind off success and its possible corruption. He headed for the Tavern of the Moor to hire a model. He required a sister for the Magdalene he had painted back at his studio. The whores might be fortifying themselves with wine before the night's carnal undertakings. He would find the face of the saint among them.

A single lamp dangled from a beam by the bar of the tavern. Ill-shaven, hostile, silent faces flickered out of the gloom. He had the impression of entering the sickroom of a much disliked relative. At each table hands withdrew beneath the board, ready to reach for weapons, everyone gauging the newcomer. By the door, a man snored with his head beside a flagon of wine, hair dusted white from a day in some stonemason's workshop. The waiter passed with a plate of fried artichokes. 'All's well, Signore?'

'Is Menica here, Pietro?'

The waiter set down the plate. A man in a broad-brimmed hat reached his thick, dirty hands for the artichokes, pulled away the ears, and rubbed them in the olive oil on the plate. He curled an arm around his dish, as though he expected someone to grab it from him.

'Menica? Horny so early, Signore?' the waiter said. 'Wouldn't you like to dine first? We've some nice ricotta and some boiled meat. It'll set you up for your evening's sport.'

A contemptuous snicker rolled from the artichoke eater. Pleased with himself, the waiter smirked into the dark where the man sat.

Caravaggio stepped close to him.

Pietro met his eye and the smugness was gone. 'Just a joke, Signore. I know you well and I wouldn't take you lightly.'

The door opened. It slammed into the table where the mason slept. He raised his head in shock, disturbing the dust on his scalp into a thin white cloud. Two men entered, supporting each other as though they were already drunk. The taller one wore a black doublet with sleeves striped scarlet and turquoise. He held a clay bottle and fed it to his companion. 'Michele, where've you been, *cazzo*?'

Onorio Longhi wrapped his arm around Caravaggio's neck. He was pale and freckled with a red-blond strip of beard in the centre of his chin. His hair lapped over his brows into deep, shadowed eye sockets. Even when he was cheerful, Onorio's glance was a threat, and he knew it too. He took pleasure in the anxiety he created. He pulled Caravaggio close and kissed him on top of his head. 'Mario whipped that big dickhead Ranuccio at the tennis court. Didn't you, Maestro Minniti, my little Sicilian bugger?'

The man beneath Onorio's other arm embraced Caravaggio, laughing. Small and slight, he retained the confident air and the wry lip Caravaggio had painted onto his likeness six years ago when he portrayed him as the dupe of a gypsy fortune-teller. He wore the same doublet of mustard velvet in which he had posed, though it was now patched at the elbows, stained with oil paint and wine sauce. Caravaggio rubbed Mario's black hair.

'I had Ranuccio running around like a greased pig with its bowels full of beans,' Mario said.

Ah, Ranuccio. It came to him now. The money he had lost at tennis the previous day. *A bad man for a debt.*

The waiter went into the dark. Caravaggio knew there would be no work tonight, now that he had run into Onorio. He called after the waiter. 'Pietro, bring me that ricotta, after all.'

They went to a table near the kitchen. Caravaggio would have taken the bench against the wall, but Onorio slid in there with his eye on the door, wary even in his wild state.

Caravaggio settled for the stool most in shadow. 'I was looking for Menica,' he said.

'Saw her just now,' Onorio said. 'With Gaspare, the little poet. Your biggest fan.'

'I have new admirers who make Gaspare look like a small fish.'

'Do I smell a commission?'

The waiter laid the plate of ricotta on the table with a loaf of dark bread. Onorio unwrapped the cheese from the oily reeds in which it had matured. He sniffed it, called for wine, and pulled the bread apart.

'Yes, a commission. But my new admirer will be just as inclined to steal my *old* works from their current owners,' Caravaggio said.

'By Jesu, you met the Holy Father himself?'

Caravaggio smiled. 'Close enough. The Cardinal-Nephew.'

Onorio split the bread, passed a piece to Mario and to Caravaggio. 'Be careful, Michele. That man's dangerous. Even worse, he's an art lover.'

Mario giggled. The wine found its way up his nose and choked him. Onorio slapped his back. Mario blew his nose onto the floor and picked up his bread.

'I'm serious,' Onorio said. 'Cardinal Borghese has already told the Cavaliere D'Arpino he owes a ridiculous amount in back-taxes. It's just to get him to hand over his art collection, in lieu of payment. Pure robbery.'

'Lucky I don't own a thing.'

'Pietro, a candle, for God's sake. I can't see to pick the weevils out of the bread.' Onorio spat into the corner. 'You *do* have something of which he still might rob you.'

'My genius? My freedom? Don't be so dramatic.'

'Your life, Michele. He holds it in that grasping little bureaucrat's fist of his. Those well-scrubbed fingers will reach out for something they want and, when they do, you might slip between them and shatter in pieces on the floor.'

'I can wreck my own life. I don't need papal assistance.'

'Is that why you insulted Ranuccio yesterday?'

'Did I?'

The waiter brought a candle and another jug of Chianti.

'You had one of your blackouts?' Onorio said. 'Yes, you lost a few points at tennis. Hardly surprising, because you were so drunk you could barely stand. Then you told Ranuccio that if he wanted the money he had won he'd have to sniff for it up your—'

Caravaggio laughed. 'Did I?'

'Sniff for your money right up here,' you said. 'Come and get it.' You tried to bend over and show him your ass, but you fell and tore your clothes. I had to carry you away from there.'

Mario swallowed a bite of soft cheese. 'And I had to hold Ranuccio back or he'd have killed you.'

'You?' Caravaggio slapped Mario's shoulder. 'He's twice your size.'

'I'm a Sicilian. I strike below the belt. The taller he is, the easier for me to deal the fatal blow.'

'Cut off his rotten *cazzo* and toss it to the pigs for their lunch, my little southern neckbreaker,' Onorio said.

They toasted Mario's deadly blade. Mario wiped his sticky fingers on the bread and took up his goblet. '*Cent'anni*. A hundred years of health,' he said. 'Ranuccio's *cazzo* to the pigs.'

A woman entered the tavern, unveiled. She was small and pretty and her dress was expensive, but it was torn at the shoulder and her gaze was ragged and frenzied.

'Better still, toss his *cazzo* to her.' Onorio waved to the woman. She passed between the tables, ignoring the men who seized at her breasts from out of the shadows.

'Have you seen him?' she said.

'I assume you're looking for your pimp?' Onorio said. 'We left Signor Ranuccio at the French tennis courts not long ago. But I believe he was on his way elsewhere.'

'Where? I have to find him.'

Onorio pulled her into the seat beside him. 'Prudenza, he's probably with some strumpet. Stay here with us.'

Caravaggio reached out for the girl's hair. A strand was plastered across her cheek. It stuck to the corner of her mouth when he pulled it away. She recoiled and lifted her hand to the spot. Her wrist was wrapped in a soggy strip of cloth. He held the hair in the light of the candle. A brittle, drying substance encrusted it, the same earthy shade as the ochre and umber pigments ingrained on his palm.

'You're bleeding, girl,' he said.

'Fillide came at me with a knife.' Prudenza's hair slipped loose from the braid that ran ear to ear. It dropped in long, russet arabesques among the breadcrumbs.

Onorio squeezed her shoulder. 'You're lucky to have come away with your life, if that bitch was in earnest.'

'I *am* lucky.' The girl's breath was fast, as though she felt the threat still. 'She came at me with a knife and I tried to fend her off, but she cut me here on the wrist.'

'Was anyone with you when she attacked you?' Caravaggio lifted the bloody hair to tuck it into her braid.

'I was in my own house. She burst in and attacked me. She cut the corner of my mouth and when she saw that I was bleeding, she cursed me and ran off.'

He noted that she had answered a different question. He turned his cup of wine on the tabletop. 'Why are you looking for Ranuccio?'

'I need his protection.'

The girl was seventeen years old and had come from Tuscany just a few months earlier. Each man looked at the others in silence. They had been in Rome long enough to know that a whore needed more wits than this to survive.

Caravaggio spoke low, 'I don't think you—'

'He'll look after me, Ranuccio will. He loves me.'

The look, shared again by the men. It was as though an Inquisitor had called out a sentence on the girl. When a whore believed she was loved by her pimp, she was as lost as a heretic with his tongue in a clamp riding the tumbrel. They were both on their way to the flames.

'I'll talk to Fillide, my dear.' Caravaggio knew better than to ask what had come between the two women. Ranuccio's name was all the explanation he needed. The man was a procurer and a fornicator. Something about the girl disturbed him. At first he thought it was her fatal naiveté. He moved the candle in front of the girl's face. *No,* he told himself. *It's that she wants love, and unlike other whores she sees no impediment to receiving it.*

Prudenza wrinkled her nose. 'What're you doing with that candle?'

'Will you come to my home?'

'I've got to find Ranuccio.'

'Not now. Tomorrow.'

The urgent surge of her breasts slowed. *She's going into professional mode.* 'I need a model,' he said. 'I'm going to paint you.'

A thought dawned in her eyes and she smiled with triumph. 'You're *him*, aren't you? The one that painted Fillide. Onorio, why didn't you tell me this was the famous one?'

'Did you say "infamous"? You're quite right, *puttanella.*' Onorio pushed himself to his feet, ready to depart. He pinched her cheek.

'I live on the San Biagio alley behind the Palace of Florence. Ask for Michele who rents from Signora Bruni.' Caravaggio put a few coins on the table for the waiter. He opened Prudenza's hand and rubbed her palm with his thumb. *Here's a girl most would say is unworthy of love*, he thought. *Just as I am.* Those who chose a low path in life were denied its highest aspirations. But Prudenza dared to expect love, as if whoring hadn't robbed her of innocence. She was still pure, without knowing how. He smiled. *What about you, Michele? Can you find a last sliver of your unsullied core?* With a shock that made him frown, he wondered if he would know how to recognize it, were he to come across it. He folded her fingers around a thin gold *scudi.* 'Don't show that coin to Ranuccio.'

2

Martha and Mary Magdalene

A trio of skinny harlots gyrated their hips at the corner of the Corso. They called out their crude welcome until Onorio emerged into the lamplight. Recognizing him as an unloved customer, one of the whores bent her backside towards him and suggested he kiss it.

'I'll bite it, you nasty little strumpet.' He spoke with some humour, but the girl backed away, all her effrontery crushed and quailing. Onorio's features went dead, like a painting in which the artist forgot to dab a spot of light on the eyeball.

Mario took the whore's elbow. She flicked the tips of her fingers off her chin in Onorio's direction. Mario squeezed her backside and took her into the alley, laughing.

Onorio lifted his head, swivelled and sneezed. He brushed a trace of mucus off Caravaggio's shoulder. 'Never mind. You already have the same diseases I have.'

Caravaggio gestured after Mario and the whore. 'I hope I don't have whatever she's carrying.'

'You will. Soon enough.' Onorio wiped his nose on his cuff.

'Mario and me? Not since he married.'

'He has two wives. One cancels out the other, thus making him single and available.'

'I hope that isn't the kind of mathematics you use when you design your buildings.'

'Don't worry. My job is to make the façades look good. I rely on the stonemasons to keep them from falling down.'

Along the Corso, the Arch of Portugal glimmered in the torchlight. It marked the southern edge of the Evil Garden, where the whores lived by order of the Pope and where artists came to be among their own low type. Caravaggio halted beneath its pillars. He felt some force preventing him from crossing that border, as though he were unworthy of walking among the decent classes, away from the harlots and pimps and slumlords. Anyone who saw him outside the purlieu of the Evil Garden would shrink from him as if a wild beast had come down from the hills.

'What're you going to do about Ranuccio?' Like a villain, Onorio measured his pitch to reach no further than his conspirator's ears. 'The money – the bet.'

Some shred of recollection told Caravaggio that Ranuccio had cheated. Or had he created that memory, moulding it from his rage? 'It was a bad call. The ball was in. He didn't beat me. The game's void. I'm not giving a single, dirty *baioccho* to that bastard.' His adrenaline pounded, that familiar sensation of abandon, always accompanied by an absolute conviction that he was right, no matter how his anger shocked those around him.

Onorio held Caravaggio's hand. 'Ranuccio's family is tight with the Pope, Michele.' The pulse in Onorio's thumb was syncopated and uneven against Caravaggio's palm. Nothing about him was regular or natural. 'His brothers fought in the papal armies. His father's head of the guard at Castel Sant'Angelo. You hear me? The Pope's own fortress. They keep order for the Holy Father in this neighbourhood.'

'Doing a great job, aren't they? You can't walk down the street without some thug taking a swipe at you.'

'The Pope doesn't care about crime. He cares about riots against the government. The Tomassoni family prevents such trouble. So what if Ranuccio plays the tough guy. So what if he cuts up his whores. When the Pope wants a sword to fight his corner, Ranuccio will lift his blade and say, "Hail, Holy Father, those who're about to stab someone in the back salute you." If the Tomassonis run this quarter like a bunch of gangsters, that isn't the Vatican's problem.' Onorio leaned in close. 'But if you don't stay on Ranuccio's good side, it's *your* problem.'

Caravaggio withdrew his hand. 'I can handle him.'

'It isn't just *him*. It's his brothers and his father and everyone in this neighbourhood who ever got a job from them or who ever asked them to take an enemy into a dark alley and leave him there with his guts around his ankles.'

Caravaggio moaned and puffed out his cheeks.

'People say *I'm* crazy, Michele, and I admit there are times when everything goes red, you know what I mean.' Onorio leered. 'But you're taking a big risk. You're my friend. I can't let you do it.'

'Be there with me when I fight him.'

Onorio stepped back. Caravaggio's neck shivered, trepidation and passion and wild disturbance streaming through every muscle. His whole frame was in motion, even as he held himself still. He felt as though he had risen above his own body and watched it, all his actions under the control of some other power.

'Dear friend, I've seen you throw rocks at men from only a couple of paces and club them on the head with the flat side of your sword.' Onorio pursed his lips and blew. 'But fighting Ranuccio?

You shouldn't even joke about it.'

Caravaggio quivered in the lightless doorway. Night had come in full to the Evil Garden. He merged with it until he was unsure if he had stepped into a dream where he took on powers beyond those of a human.

'You can't just paint over a killing, Michele. *Pentimenti*, repentances you call them, the changes you make to the angle of an arm or the line of a neck on the canvas. A fight with a man like Ranuccio can't be repented. It'll end in blood.'

Caravaggio's breath trembled. He was coming back from the phantom unreality, descending back into his body, displacing the blackness of night from his limbs.

'I'll stand with you, if it comes to violence,' Onorio said. 'But do me a favour and don't do it. I've a wife and five children to consider.'

'All right,' Caravaggio whispered. The night was around him, but no longer in him.

'Leave Ranuccio to his whores.' Onorio laughed. 'Syphilis will take care of that dickhead. Pay him the money.'

'You're right. I'll pay him.' They embraced, laughing.

Two men passed beyond the doorway, moving with purpose down the Corso. 'It's little Prospero and that bugger Gaspare.' Onorio called out, 'Hey, Prosperino.'

The men turned. They were short and brightly clothed. Prospero was a Lombard like Caravaggio, a decade older and thick in the hips. He wore a full beard that ran grey along the jaw.

'Michele, I'm pleased to see you out and about.' Prospero's bulging eyes were set almost in the sides of his narrow head. His mouth looped from ear to ear beneath a long upper lip, like one of the ancient grotesques he copied into his paintings from the walls of Rome's catacombs, a face ready to laugh at the filthiest of jokes. He reached up to slap both hands onto Caravaggio's shoulders. 'If you're strolling on the Corso, it means you're not in jail and I won't have to bail you out again.'

'The night is young. Give him a chance to get some trouble started.' Onorio took the end of Gaspare's moustache in his fingers and pulled upwards. 'Did that hurt, little *finocchio*?'

Gaspare smoothed his moustache back into the horn shape he liked. 'Just a bit.'

'Write me a poem about it, then. Your poetry is painful to hear, so its subject should be pain.'

Gaspare smiled, blinking as though at some deep, private pleasure. The skin beneath his eyes and at the sides of his nose was red and flaking. 'Here's a rhyme: If Onorio tries to touch my mous*tache*, I'll take his fat ass and give it a th*rash*.'

They applauded and Onorio shoved the poet playfully.

'Bravo, the bullshit Boccaccio of the ribald remark.' Prospero invited Gaspare to give a bow. 'Now, come on, lads, Fillide's entertaining a few discerning gentlemen at her place on the Via Frattina. Who's up for whores, gambling, song and dance?'

Fillide twisted side to side in counterpoint to her skirt. She held the scarlet taffeta before her and let it rustle in accompaniment to her laughter. At the neckline, white lace ruched in two concave descents to meet in a point between her breasts. She had arranged it so that the upper third of her dark areola showed through. 'What do you think, *ragazzi*?'

Onorio went for a bottle of wine on the table. 'All that red cloth. You look like a cardinal with big tits.'

'Maybe it was a cardinal who bought it for her?' Prospero reached up to give the courtesan a light kiss on the cheek. With a dip of his neck, he scratched his beard over her cleavage. 'One of her gentleman clients?'

She clipped her knuckles against the crown of his head.

Caravaggio entered with Gaspare. *Scipione recognized Fillide's portrait. Did he buy her these rich clothes?* he wondered. He surveyed the room, apprehensive, as though the hedonistic Cardinal-Nephew might be reclining voluptuously on a divan.

A silver candelabra dripped wax onto the Oriental carpet spread across the table. The paintings and wall hangings floated in darkness. In the far corner, a heavy white curtain shrouded the side of the bed. A convex mirror at the foot of the mattress disclosed the elongated form of a reclining man. He wore a loose white shirt and red hose and he rested on one elbow, attentive to the newcomers. He caught Caravaggio's stare in the mirror. At first, his face was like a dangerous animal at bay, then a scornful recognition leeched out of it.

'The one who gave you that dress –' Caravaggio spoke directly towards the mirror '– is no gentleman.'

The man on the bed flicked his index finger against his earlobe twice. *You faggot.*

A black-haired woman came from the kitchen. Her skin was so pale the candle painted it like red cadmium on a new canvas. She carried a tureen of boiled mutton.

Gaspare helped her set it on the table. 'Allow me, *mia cara* Menica,' he said.

'Are you going to write a poem about how you'd like to stick your boiled meat in her soup dish?' Fillide took Gaspare's chin in her left hand. Her ring finger hooked upwards, its unnatural angle a memento of a dislocation by a rough client. 'Spare us, eh, Gaspare.'

Fillide's round face had the slight fatness of a girl. Curling at the temples, her amber hair glowed against her skin. A fresh rose pink bloomed along the flesh of her collarbone and in the hollow at the bottom of her neck. Her underlip was so full that it alone would have made the fortune of any other courtesan. She had been Caravaggio's Judith and his St Catherine. She was the Magdalene he was working on now. As she doubled over in harsh laughter, he thought her more human than the paint he had spilled for her. But only just.

Menica came to Caravaggio and stood on his feet with her arms around his neck. Stretching up on her toes, she brought her mouth close to his ear. 'Ranuccio's on the bed, Michele. He was talking about a fight – with you.'

He stroked Menica's cheek. Her skin was growing rough after her six years as a whore. Kissing her forehead, he called across the room: 'Prudenza was looking for you at the inn, Ranuccio.'

Onorio stiffened and reached for his dagger. Fillide glared at Menica. A taut laugh came from the bed as the curtain drew back.

Ranuccio swung his feet to the floor. He scratched inside his hose and found something that he flicked away with long slim fingers. His beard and hair were brown with yellow highlights, like straw rotted to damp silage. He reached for the bottle in Onorio's hand. 'Give it up, Longhi,' he said. He gave another tug before Onorio let the bottle go.

'It's funny, see.' Ranuccio held Fillide from behind, smelling her hair. 'This one tried to cut Prudenza up.'

'What do you expect?' the girl said. 'I found you naked in the strumpet's bed.'

' "Whore, I'm going to scar you everywhere," ' Ranuccio bellowed in a mocking falsetto. 'You should've heard her, *ragazzi*. She was a fury. "You dirty whore, I want to cut you. I want to cut you." '

Caravaggio interrupted their embrace. 'You'll leave her be.'

Ranuccio slipped his hand slowly out of Fillide's dress and moved her aside. 'You owe me, painter. Remember your debt?'

'He'll pay you.' Onorio slapped Fillide's backside. 'But now let's have some music and a dance.' He picked up a Spanish guitar from the corner and tossed it to Caravaggio.

As Caravaggio tuned up, Ranuccio peed loudly in a bucket beside the door. With the first notes of '*Ti parti, cor mio caro*', he hauled up his hose and moved over to Fillide. He kicked into the *villanella* with a showy step and took her with him. Gaspare rounded Menica, courtly and stiff. Onorio pulled Prospero laughing to his feet and they spun across the boards.

Caravaggio picked at the strings and sang the old Bolognese song in a clear, deep voice:

> To part from you, my dear heart
> Leaves me with bitter tears
> And my soul without you
> Cannot be healed.

Ranuccio whistled and nuzzled Fillide's neck. *That buffoon would reel about like this to a funeral dirge,* Caravaggio thought.

> Do not leave me,
> Oh my dear heart,
> For your faith.

Ranuccio slowed his step and drew Fillide to him.

> If you want to leave me
> Remember to return.
> I cannot remain alive
> One hour without you.
> Do not leave me.

Ranuccio and Fillide went to the bed. She pushed him onto the mattress and climbed on top of him, pulling the curtain shut.

Onorio stamped and clapped. 'Play louder, Michele.' Caravaggio lifted his voice above the grunts and cackles from the bed.

Their love-making was soon done and the curtain drawn back. Ranuccio drowsed contentedly. Fillide arranged her breasts and her neckline. Menica spooned out bowls of meat for Gaspare and Caravaggio. The stew steamed with the aroma of nutmeg and cloves and cinnamon.

'I have a mind for some poetry now,' Fillide said.

Gaspare bowed. 'Your heart lies on the bed, but your soul deserts it, following love and poetry to me, my Lady Fillide.'

'I meant some of *your* poetry. Not a codswallop rehash of Petrarch. I hate that weepy old milksop.'

'Hear, hear.' Ranuccio slapped his hand against the wall.

Discomfited that a mere courtesan had noticed his plagiarizing, Gaspare cleared his throat. 'You recall the painting our friend Michele did a few years ago? *Love Victorious?*'

'The little Cupid smiling like he was game for anything?' Onorio twisted the cork from a new bottle and set it to his lips.

Gaspare took up the pose of an actor declaiming, and recited his madrigal. It warned that Caravaggio's representation of love was so true that it was like the real thing – in its most extreme form.

'Don't look, don't look on Love,' he concluded. 'He'll set your heart on fire.'

'Not bad.' Onorio belched. 'You ought to publish it.'

'It was published in Venice two years ago.' Gaspare put a hand on his hip, affronted. 'I presented you with a copy of the book.'

'I don't recall it.'

Prospero nudged him. 'It's the one you put on the table in your bedchamber to make your pisspot just the right height.'

Gaspare raised his hand, but Menica caught at it.

Onorio's pout quivered with vicious humour. 'Michele, does love turn *your* heart to ashes, as in the words of our companion, the great poet of the Most Serene Republic of Genoa?'

Caravaggio put the guitar on the floor. His eyes were wide and staring, as though he observed the phantom of something dead approach him. 'Love?' He reached for the wine and took a pull. 'Do you really think that's what sets me on fire?'

■

The morning light found its way deep into his brain, as if it were the stiletto of the stealthiest assassin. Caravaggio groaned.

'Time we were going, Michele.'

He opened his eyes. Vermilion slivers of the dawn shimmered through the motes of dust. Rubbing his face, he stood, caught at his head, and gasped.

Onorio slapped his cheek lightly. 'A good night, wasn't it, *cazzo*?'

The curtain on the bed was only half drawn. Fillide's pale breast bore a livid scratch, no doubt from her companion's attentions during the night. Ranuccio snored beyond her. Prospero rose from his couch, picking at his scalp and wiping the lice against his hose.

'Come on.' Onorio gestured for haste. 'Let's be off.'

The air of the early morning was clear, free of the foul odours that would rise from the littered ground in the day's heat. Prospero blew a kiss at an old woman hauling a basket of figs towards the market in the Campo de'Fiori. 'Who can be unhappy in Rome?' The little man was missing a few teeth from tavern brawls. Those that remained shone through his ginger beard. 'Well, late sleepers don't catch any fish. I'm off, *ragazzi*.' He shambled towards the Corso.

Onorio picked up a fig that had dropped from the old woman's basket and rubbed it against his doublet to clean it. As he chewed, he put his arm across Caravaggio's shoulder. 'You didn't pay him.'

Caravaggio took the remainder of the fig and ate it. 'Once I started on the wine, it slipped my mind. Anyway, maybe he forgot.'

'Michele, this isn't you. You get carried away by your anger sometimes. God knows I wouldn't crucify a man for that. But don't pretend that you want a fight with this thug.'

Caravaggio's smile was reluctant. 'If I'm to take advice on my comportment from you of all people, *cumpà*, I must be way off track.'

'Stay at home and work.' Onorio slipped his hand under Caravaggio's arm. 'Is it money you need? I can lend you the ten *scudi* for Ranuccio. To get him off your back.'

'I'm not short.' Caravaggio pulled a leather purse from his doublet and shook it. 'Plenty in here.'

'Then in the name of the Blessed Virgin, pay the bastard.'

Caravaggio's lips tightened, as though he felt a familiar pain. He gripped Onorio's forearm and his grin opened up. 'You're right. I'll find him at the tennis courts this afternoon and give him the money.'

'I'll see you there.' Onorio wagged a finger and shook his head with relief. 'You know I wouldn't have stood by and let you fight the Tomassonis alone, *bello*.'

'I know it.'

'I'm going to Santa Maria della Consolazione. The masons are coming in to replace some of the stonework. I'd better be there to oversee it, or they'll be dropping marble down the hill as if it were the criminals who used to be tossed off the Tarpeian Rock there. Come and see the work.'

'No, I have a model coming to my place. *Ciao, cazzo*.'

Caravaggio's mouth was dry and his belly grizzled at him for food. Below the Trinità dei Monti, he stopped in the Tavern of the Turk. He drank off a mug of thin beer and took a hunk of dark bread and half an onion. He came out onto the piazza at the foot of the slope under the Trinità, rubbing the cut surface of the onion on the bread to flavour it. He chewed hard as he went up Via del Babuino.

Rome roused itself around him. A heavy-set old carpenter who had modelled for his St Peter crossed the street, on his way to his workshop in the Via Margutta. He hefted his toolbox against his thigh and waved to Caravaggio. 'Michele, what're you painting now?'

'*Salve*, Robbè. I'm doing a Magdalene with her sister Martha.'

'You don't need an old bald fellow with a white beard and a big strong chest to model for you again?'

Caravaggio pointed beyond the piazza to Santa Maria del Popolo, which housed his *Martyrdom of St Peter*. 'Everyone knows I already crucified you.'

His appetite was satisfied and he wanted to get home to prepare his pigments for Prudenza's arrival. On the right of the canvas, he had painted Fillide as the Magdalene in the moment of her conversion. He wanted to balance his composition with Prudenza as Martha, inquiring and cajoling her immoral sister. He looked forward to telling Fillide that she would be displayed in the gallery of the great Aldobrandini family alongside the woman whose face she had tried to scar. He would paint until the afternoon, then take the money he owed to Ranuccio – at the tennis courts or at Fillide's rooms. *I'll throw the money at him,* he thought, *so he knows I don't believe he won it fairly. He'll understand that it's beneath me to fight a man such as him. That alone will be worth ten* scudi *to me.*

At the burnt sienna towers of the Church of Sant'Atanasio, he cut onto the Via dei Greci, into the Evil Garden. The low morning sun struggled to drive the night from the narrow street. A pair of beggars knelt at the rough grey step of a small house, their fingers steepled, beseeching charity. The young woman in the doorway held a three-year-old boy on her hip. The boy was naked, half wrapped in a towel, as though the beggars' call had interrupted his bathtime.

Caravaggio approached, watching the girl. The house was dark behind her. Daylight seemed to penetrate the street just for her, illuminating the eggshell clarity of her neck and chest. She crossed her bare feet and lifted onto her toes, pivoting from her hip to swing the boy as she listened to the old woman's story. She let her head drop to her left so that her chin touched her collarbone, as she looked down upon the kneeling woman with compassion and reassurance.

He recognized her. It was the maid who had been cleaning the floor at del Monte's palace. *She's turning her hips the opposite way to her shoulders*, he noted, *as though she knows about the* contrapposto *pose. She has found the grace of classical form without anyone having to teach her an academic term for it.*

Caravaggio leaned against the wall by the threshold. The plaster had come away beside the chipped travertine of the doorway, exposing the brick beneath. He smiled and was surprised by how little calculation there was in his open look.

The girl seemed confused, recognizing him from the palace and wondering no doubt how he came to be at her door. The boy in her arms reached out for her sleeve. She kissed his brow and whispered to him.

Concentration replaced the smile on Caravaggio's face. Maestro Leonardo had written that a fleeting moment reflects the inner spirit and impulse of man. A painter must capture such things, more than the mere details of physical form. Memorize them right away, the great Florentine had said. As surely as if he held a sketchbook, Caravaggio traced the line of the girl's neck, etched the set of her foot with its ankle turned out, and shaded the soothing quiet of her eyes.

He took out his purse and counted his coins. Ten *scudi. The exact amount I'm supposed to pay Ranuccio.* He fed the coins, thin as shavings of Parmesan, into his chamois purse and tied the top. He put the money bag into the old beggarman's palm. *It's a ridiculous sum to give in charity. One* scudi *buys two dozen chickens. Ten* scudi

45

is three months' rent. Still, I'll tell Ranuccio that I gave the money to a homeless peasant, rather than let him have it.

The girl in the doorway regarded Caravaggio with astonishment and suspicion. He smiled at her wariness. *She's a Roman for certain.*

The beggars kissed Caravaggio's hands and hobbled away. The girl turned to go back into the dark room to finish the boy's bath.

Caravaggio caught her wrist with a light touch. He felt as though he had reached up into an altarpiece and caressed the Holy Mother. Yet he had never seen Maria painted with such force and verity, not even the sweet Virgins of Raphael or the ambiguous maidens of Leonardo. 'What's your name?' he said.

She stroked the child's chin with her forefinger. 'What's my name, little one?'

'Auntie Lena.' The boy clapped his hands, delighted to have answered correctly. She kissed his forehead.

Caravaggio sensed the touch of her lips as if her kiss had been bestowed upon him. 'I'll come back, Lena.' He went down the street, singing to himself the song he had played at Fillide's party:

> You are the star that shines
> More than any other lady.
> Do not leave me.

'Keep looking up there. Don't turn towards me.' Caravaggio came through the black curtain and lifted Prudenza's chin.

'There's nothing there, though, nothing to look at. Just a hole in your ceiling.' She shook her hands. 'All the blood's gone out of them, holding them like this. What're you doing behind that curtain, anyway? How long is this going to take?'

'A while. You're accustomed to business that's concluded in about ten minutes?' He repositioned her, feeling her shoulders through her thin white shift.

'Don't be cheeky, Michele. I know how to make them finish in less than two minutes.' She crooked and poked her finger. The whore's trick of jabbing into the rectum to hasten a client's ejaculation.

He laughed as he arranged the earth-brown cloth across her back, folding it over her extended arm and spreading it across the table. 'Now, see here? Where my hand is, focus there.'

She held her neck still, angled upwards. He went through the curtain, tying it behind him to leave only a small, round gap at head height.

Through that space, the bright light falling on Prudenza showed clearly in the mirror set behind Caravaggio. The mirror projected an image of the girl onto the canvas, a technique he had learned from the men of science at del Monte's palace. He marked in the key points of her features quickly, tracing them from the projection, so that he could set her precisely in place at the next sitting. He turned his brush around, holding it with the bristles towards him, and carved through the underpaint with the end of the handle. In single strokes, he cut into the ground layer the outline of her ear, her forehead, her jaw and her hands. He would fill in the details later, knowing that the shape and the perspective would be natural, just as seen in a looking glass.

'Why do you need a mirror in there?' she called.

'It makes my job simpler. It allows me to concentrate on what's really important.'

The mirror couldn't account for the genius with which he animated a face in pain or devotion, but it set those emotions on a replica of reality so exact that viewers marvelled at his virtuosity. Few asked how he did it – except for del Monte's scientists, who already knew. Others assumed it was pure mystery, like a Virgin standing on a cloud at the top of an altarpiece.

Prudenza opened her mouth to ask another question, but he hissed for her to be quiet. The mirror was a secret he didn't wish to share, and not only because he wanted to preserve his technical advantage over other artists. He was wary of the Inquisition. Projecting images was heretical magic.

The bark of a dog came from the loggia.

'Cecco,' he called. 'I want the lamp higher.'

His assistant came in from the loggia and hauled at a rope. The pulley squealed and the lamp rose towards the broken boards of the ceiling. The contrast between shadow and highlight sharpened on Prudenza's face.

'Just there,' Caravaggio said.

'All right, Maestro?' The boy was twelve years old, but he gave Prudenza a saucy smile and winked at her. '*Ciao, amore.*'

She puffed out her cheeks and giggled. *Both of them, only children*, Caravaggio thought. He felt a moment of good-humoured condescension towards them, then he found he had to suppress a sob. He wondered at this strange vulnerability in him. *Children, yes, but they don't live as children.*

'You want anything else, Maestro? If not, I'd like to play with Crow. I took him to the inn yesterday and had him walk on his hind legs. Everyone asked me how you taught him to do it.'

'What'd you say?'

'That you're a master of illusion who can make a poodle dance, just as you can make the Lord Jesus Christ himself appear before you on the canvas.'

'You'll get me burned at the stake. Find us some lunch.'

Cecco went down the stairs for bread and cheese.

Caravaggio mixed ochre, white and a little crimson on his palette to match Prudenza's skin tone. He loaded the bristles of a medium brush and stroked the rounds of her ear onto the canvas.

Though she kept her head still, the girl's eyes took in the room beyond the immediate radiance of the lamp. 'You haven't got much stuff here, have you, Michele?'

'I told you to look ahead, as if the Magdalene stood before you. You're talking to her, not me.'

She's right, though. Other painters of Caravaggio's age and with lesser reputations took small palaces with the earnings from their altarpieces. A mere storekeeper might live in a house like this one, which Caravaggio had rented only a month earlier. A single, long room downstairs and one above. Behind the house, a garden with its own well, and upstairs a loggia that ran the width of the house, though that was barely five paces.

The studio was almost empty of anything but props for his work, apart from a bed for him and a folding cot for Cecco. Rags for preparing canvases and cleaning his brushes brimmed out of an old chest. A halberd and a breastplate with which he gave atmosphere to his history paintings leaned against the wall beside his sword and dagger. A messy, medium-sized canvas lay across a trunk. He ate his meals from it, because he had never bothered to purchase a tablecloth.

'Who am I supposed to be?' she said.

He paused to take in the canvas. On the right, a soft-faced, smooth-shouldered young woman – Fillide. She turned her unrefined features in a melancholy gaze upon the figure Caravaggio painted now. 'You're Martha, the sister of Mary Magdalene.'

'Yeah.' She sounded doubtful. 'Who?'

'The Magdalene was a loose woman. Her sister convinced her of the wrongs she had done. I've already painted Fillide as the Magdalene. What I'm painting now is the moment when your insistence gets through to her. She starts to repent.'

'I could tell you all sorts of things Fillide's done wrong. I'd like to give her a piece of my mind about it.'

'Perhaps that's why I want you in particular to be chastising her,' he said. 'In the picture, at least.'

He pulled the easel closer to the mirror to change the focus. He wanted a clear image of the details in the braid at the crown of her head. He worked at them. Then he laid down his brush on a trolley beside his pigments.

'Can I have a look?' she asked.

'Come on.' He ran the curtain back along its rail.

As she studied the canvas, her weight rested against his chest. '*Dio mio*, I wouldn't have thought it possible. That's really me, Michele. I don't even mind that you painted me next to that bitch.'

'It's a good likeness, that's true.'

'So many shadows. You can only see part of my face.'

'It may be even darker once it's finished.'

'It doesn't matter. *I* know it's me. You painted me just as I am.' She smiled. 'Your eyes are dark, and your face and hair too, Michele. And so are your paintings.'

'It's lucky I'm not blond or my work would be bright and ridiculous like the rubbish Baglione produces.'

'Who?'

'No one important.'

'Are you really going to make me darker still? You won't be able to see me. You'll just see Fillide.'

'The shadow makes you more prominent. People will see Fillide's face right away, but they'll have to look hard to see you. They'll wonder who you were.' He caught himself. '*Are*, I mean, who you are.'

She made a puzzled face, wondering at his stumble. Her neck craned long and pale towards the painting, a few auburn strands of hair tickling across it.

He wished he had the words that would help her survive longer than he surmised she would. *I could protect her*, he thought, *but that would end with me loving her.* He shivered with fear. Love was the preliminary to abandonment. He painted the love of the martyrs for the Lord. *Look what they get in return.* 'It's obvious that you're the most beautiful thing in the painting.'

She responded lightly, unaware of the intensity with which he had spoken. 'Am I, Michele? Thanks, *amore*.'

At the Mausoleum of the Emperor Augustus, the Pope's bailiffs were whipping a whore. She was tied to the back of a donkey, her hands bound behind her, her dress ragged and fallen around her hips to expose her torso. A crowd surrounded her, exulting in the woman's humiliation. Lena stepped into a doorway to let them pass. Growing up in the Evil Garden, she had often seen such punishment. Familiarity made it no less oppressive. It was as though a cloud of hatred passed before her, noisome and crackling with viciousness.

The whore lurched forward as the bailiff gave another stroke of the cane across her shoulders. Lena winced. The donkey jumped through the crowd. *Someone must've stuck it with a knife to make it buck*, she thought. The whore arched her back and swayed, exhausted, silent, eyes vacant. Her breasts were striped with dung and offal thrown from the crowd.

These same men gambolling beside the donkey were the ones who harassed Lena when she stood in the Piazza Navona to sell her vegetables. A woman couldn't be alone in the streets of the Evil Garden without hearing shameful words directed at her. Lena knew how to give it back to them, how to mortify them before others so that they rushed away. Even in those small exchanges, she understood that men's lives were dictated by their honour, by the figure they cut before others, by their mastery over women.

Another knife went into the donkey and it galloped out of the piazza with the swaying whore. It towed the crowd towards the water mills moored in the Tiber.

Lena headed across the Evil Garden for her mother's home. Most of the whores were girls from far away, not like her. They came from Siena, where a plague a century ago had devastated the city and forced its young people to seek a living elsewhere, even now. Others were from the poor south of the Italian lands, or from Greece. They had grown up thinking that Rome was a better place, with opportunities for a good and prosperous life. Lena had always known this was not so. As a girl she had played in the streets where the whores worked, seen them beaten and scorned. She had watched their corpses swirl under the bridges with the city's refuse. She had recognized the desperation and fear in their raucous laughter before she had even been old enough to understand what it was they did.

She was twenty-three and had she lived elsewhere in Rome she would have been married by now. But the Evil Garden disturbed all the order of life. The son of a rich family had seduced her before she was twenty. He thought himself unbound in honour towards her, because she was from the Evil Garden. To those who didn't live there, the roughest part of Rome contained nothing but whores and criminals. It was a place for dangerous games, but not for marriage. Later Lena had tried to warn her sister of this, but Amabilia also was taken in by a gentleman and ended dead on the birthing bed. Death was the one rite of natural life not barred to the people of the Evil Garden.

When Amabilia died, Lena had taken her sister's baby as her own. Domenico was the single illumination in all the hatred and sadness and death around her. She sighed as she waited for a gap in the carriage traffic so that she might cross the Corso. She felt herself withdrawing from the world. The pressure of the relentless ugliness weakened her. Sometimes a strange melancholy brought her to tears while she cleaned the floors of del Monte's palace. She found herself staring at Domenico as he slept and suddenly she would weep, or she would lie in bed like a hibernating animal while her mother berated her for laziness.

She went quickly across the Corso and up towards the Via dei Greci. She thought of the artist who had spoken to her at the palace. He had approached her at first like any other lowlife gallant in the Evil Garden, though she had detected an instant of hesitation that made her wonder if it was his true character. She had rebuffed him with a good humour, because to do otherwise might cost her job. But when he appeared at her door beside the two old beggars, he had looked into her with a gaze that invited her to look back, to see what was within him. It hadn't been the proud face of a man of honour. He had signalled to her somehow that she might discover who he really was.

As she stepped through the doorway into her home, she touched the crumbling travertine of the column. *He noted this blemish in the stone*, she thought, *and it gave him some kind of pleasure.* She gazed at the spot where he had stood. Maestro Caravaggio, the footman at the palace had called him. She wondered what his first name was.

Prospero slouched on a red velvet chair in the papal robes. Caravaggio rearranged the folds of the crimson cape and spread the white lace gown. Returning to his easel, he checked the image in his mirror. With his first sittings he had outlined the pose and worked on the Holy Father's face. He had built the subtly hostile expression, the contemptuous, acquisitive eyes. Now he had no need of the impatient pontiff's presence.

'Hold yourself as if you were about to get up,' he told Prospero. 'Press your hands on the arms of the chair. You've no time for anyone.'

Prospero glanced behind Caravaggio and murmured.

'That's it,' Caravaggio said. 'Now I see more of the tension I got from him when he was in that chair.'

Without moving his lips, Prospero whispered, 'I'll bet you do. I'm tighter than a Turkish bowstring.'

'Relax. Perhaps they'll make you an Archbishop for posing in the Holy Father's robes. You've all the qualifications: a criminal inclination and an ugly face. You might even develop an appropriate taste for altar boys.' Caravaggio set himself once more to work, bent close to the canvas, filling in the projection from the mirror. He thought of the way Lena had watched him as he had left her home with the beggars. He smiled privately behind his curtain.

'I can think of certain other benefits to the status of an Archbishop.'

'I'm sure you can, Your Ridiculousness. Now shut up.' Caravaggio laid in a few more strokes with his brush before he realized that it hadn't been Prospero who had spoken. He adjusted the angle of his mirror and saw his friend's face, grimacing for him to be silent. He stepped out from behind his curtain.

Cardinal Scipione stood a few paces away, his chin between his thumb and forefinger. He leaned through the curtain to see the portrait of his uncle. His eyes glittered. 'You've captured the wariness in his expression, Maestro Caravaggio.'

It was I who was wary, the whole time I stood here with him, Caravaggio thought. He had felt as though the Holy Father were judging each stroke of his brush with those sharp, umber eyes. He went down on his knee and kissed Scipione's hand. 'Most Reverend

Sire,' he murmured. 'My apologies. I thought—'

Scipione clicked his tongue. 'Don't interrupt me. His lips,' he went on, 'they're pursed, as though his temper drew close to the boil. One gets the impression that he'll soon deliver some withering reproach.'

'Your Illustriousness wishes me to request another sitting with His Holiness? To change the expression?'

'All my life, twenty-six years, I've been trying to understand what was in his face. But you've got it in a matter of hours.'

'I don't pretend to understand it. I just looked at it.'

Scipione brushed his moustache with his thumb. 'The papal vestments become you most fittingly, Signore.'

Prospero jolted to his feet. He came towards Scipione, his skirts rustling. He went onto his knee and bowed his head.

Scipione laid his hand on the papal beret and licked his lips. Caravaggio saw that it amused him to have the pope genuflect before him.

The Cardinal-Nephew gestured towards a divan. Caravaggio pushed it over the floor tiles to the place Scipione indicated.

'Do carry on.' Scipione reclined on the long chair.

Caravaggio sensed the essence of power in the room. Prospero responded to it too. His face revealed a quiet strain.

'I've come from the Colonna Palace,' Scipione said. 'You're well liked in that household.'

'The Marchesa of Caravaggio is of the Colonna family, Your Illustriousness. My grandfather was in her service. As I grew up, she was most magnanimous towards me. I'm always in her debt.'

'She's here in Rome now.'

'Is she, sire?' Caravaggio felt a cold touch on his cheek. Mention of the Marchesa brought so many memories. Yet he needed his emotions to be clear, so that they wouldn't disturb his painting. He breathed deeply and went on. The bristles of his brush shivered rhythmically over the canvas. He worked at the scarlet highlights on the cape swooping across the pope's chest.

'When I entered, you were behind the curtain, Maestro. Now you've drawn it back.' Scipione's tone was relaxed and confiding.

'With many of the details, I prefer to employ only my eye, Your Illustriousness.'

'The curtain is a camera obscura?'

'I use a curtain and a concave mirror, and sometimes a lens suspended in the gap in the curtain. Nothing more, Your Illustriousness. Some call it a camera obscura. Others call it items kept in any lady's bedchamber.'

'People make of it more than it is?'

'An aid to seeing, that's all.' His brush filled the silence once more.

'In the gallery of this palace,' Scipione said, 'you may observe all the previous popes, painted like gods. They might've had the power of gods, but they weren't immortal. We ought to be able to read the life they led in their faces. But artists always make the pope into a saint. Some of them may have been; others certainly weren't.'

Scipione closed his eyes and quivered when he uttered the word 'saint'. *As if he were whispering to a lover*, Caravaggio thought, *some role he wanted to be played to arouse him.* He loaded his brush with a pinkish white to edge the highlights of the cape. Prospero winked at him.

'It's only right that my uncle's portrait ought to promote a different view of the Pope.' Scipione spread his fingers wide and examined his nails. 'We Borghese aren't like the old Roman families who usually take the Throne of St Peter. Look at the Colonna. Their line runs from Julius Caesar, they say, which means they claim descent from the goddess Venus herself, as Caesar did. My uncle, the Holy Father, is the son of a clerk from Siena. Does that make him a less appropriate choice to wield the holiness of his office?'

'Heaven forbid.'

'Or its power?' Scipione dropped his voice. He got up and went towards the door. He was in shadow when he turned again. 'Maestro Raphael would've painted the face and had one of his assistants complete the robes.'

'He would, Your Illustriousness.'

'Raphael is treated as a god – infallible, perfect.'

'So he is.'

'But you're no god. You're a painter. So you do all the work yourself.'

'A piece of cloth or a bowl of fruit takes just as much skill as a face, Most Reverend Lord.'

'Do you see why I chose you to paint the son of the Sienese clerk?' The Cardinal-Nephew didn't wait for a reply. Silhouetted in the light from the corridor, he withdrew from the chamber.

The door swung shut. Caravaggio dropped his palette onto his pigment trolley. It was exciting to hear from Scipione's lips why he had favoured him. *But I've never had a compliment that left me feeling so manhandled*, he thought. *I'm shaking like a girl who knows that fine words about her figure are the prelude to a rape.* 'Divest yourself, Your Holiness,' he said to Prospero. 'I can't work any more.'

Prospero removed his scarlet beret and the crucifix from around his neck. He gestured towards the door by which Scipione had left. 'Princes always fill me with fear. But there's something even more terrifying about that one.'

'It's because he told you he's not a saint, and you know exactly how people behave when they forget the holiness in them.'

'I do. For one thing there's wrestling this evening. We won't find any saints there, but it'll be fun. I'm in the mood for a good fight.'

'Where?'

'The piazza in front of the Colonna Palace.'

The Colonna. Caravaggio shivered as if at the touch of a

forgotten dream. He picked up the papal crucifix and kissed it. 'Let's go. Surely tonight I'll pick the winner.'

■

Costanza Colonna pulled at the red lace cuff of her black dress and bit her lip. As she entered the reception room, her body was tight and her breath short. She always felt this constriction when she returned to Rome, to the palace where she had grown up and to the company of her relatives. They were descended from Aeneas, the Trojan who founded this Eternal City, and they still seemed essential to its power as they circulated with their jewelled goblets and their marten furs. In Milan, Florence or Naples, she was a respected woman of fifty-five, widow of a Sforza, inheritor of great estates, mother of six noble boys, Marchesa of the town of Caravaggio. Before the cold faces of these masterful Colonnas, she was once more a thirteen-year-old flouncing through the corridors because her father was sending her to marry a surly youth in a distant, misty province.

Her brother, Cardinal Ascanio, clapped his hands and the Colonnas made for the balcony. He beckoned for Costanza to join him. She took his arm and went out above the Piazza of the Sainted Apostles.

The square was packed with men who had come to see the wrestling. In the first darkness, the torches around the ring glimmered over the jostling crowd like the lanterns of a ship at anchor illuminating the lapping tide. Costanza scanned the heads below. *Perhaps Michele will come*, she thought.

Ascanio's fingers were firm in the crook of her elbow. She recognized the same calm and calculation in him that she had known in her father. She experienced a spasm of resentment, as if this had been the man who had arranged her marriage without consulting her, and a tremor of love and loss for the great prince now almost thirty years dead. She moved closer to her brother.

'Your painter has a new commission,' Ascanio said. 'He's doing a portrait of the Holy Father.'

The crowd cheered the arrival of the fighters. The men lifted their arms. Oiled muscles flashed in the lantern light.

'His commission could be important for us.' Ascanio pursed his lips in disdain. 'For the sake of Fabrizio.'

'Fabrizio.' Costanza whispered the name of her youngest son, though it seemed to her that she screamed it, so much tension did it awaken in her now. Her husband had shown little interest in his family once he had an heir. But her children had grown more special for Costanza with each birth and with her passing years. She had been a girl when most of her babies were born. By the time Fabrizio came, she had outgrown her childish tantrums, the longing for her birthplace, the frustration with her boorish husband. Though she had been still only nineteen, she had seen herself as a woman. Fabrizio's delivery didn't terrify her with new responsibility as her other births had done. Finally she had ceased to be a child; she had become a mother. It was as a companion for Fabrizio that she had brought Michele Merisi into the household.

The cardinal's hand pressed harder on her arm. She blinked, puzzled. He sighed, as if her inability to grasp the significance of what he told her was all that could be expected of a woman.

'Your painter will be in proximity to the Holy Father himself,' he hissed, 'and to the Cardinal-Nephew.'

'Yes.' She shook her head. 'Yes?'

'Surely you see it? Your painter may beg the things that would be beneath our dignity to request. He may petition the Holy Father to compensate the Farnese with gold and land, instead of a life.

He may ask for clemency – for Fabrizio.'

Costanza took in a sharp breath. Michele might help free Fabrizio from jail. *He'll be sure to do it*, she thought. *Even after so many years apart, their childhood forged a bond Michele wouldn't forget.*

Her older boys had been preoccupied with courting the favour of their father while he attended on dignitaries in Milan. Abandoned, like her, to the quiet, provincial life of Caravaggio, Fabrizio and Michele had grown close and conspiratorial, but they had allowed her to enter their play. They came to her chamber every morning and clambered inside the curtains of her bed, blowing raspberries on her neck to wake her. She had joined in eagerly, as if to recover the childhood cut short by her father's order of marriage. The peace she had felt with them was disturbed only by her other sons. They teased Michele, called him an orphan, though he was not, and a commoner, which, because it was true, provoked him to attack them.

'See to it, Costanza,' Ascanio said. 'Our family can't afford a quarrel with the Farnese.'

'Of course.'

'The Farnese will demand revenge for what Fabrizio did to one of their number.'

Costanza's tongue bristled with bitterness. She couldn't bear to consider the actions of her son. *It doesn't seem possible that he . . .*

'If you can't get your painter to secure Fabrizio's release,' Ascanio said, 'we shan't be able to help him. To do so would mean a war with the Farnese, a Roman civil war. We need the Holy Father to call off the Farnese.'

'I see.'

'Do you? Because if your painter can't help, we must let them have Fabrizio.'

One of the wrestlers dumped his opponent onto the floor of the ring. Costanza squealed in shock at the sound of his bulk hammering onto the canvas. She watched the pinned man struggle.

■

Caravaggio came down the hill from the Pope's palace and pushed to the front of the crowd in the Piazza of the Sainted Apostles. Prospero bought wine from a stall and guzzled a long draught. He wiped his beard on his sleeve, hitched up the thin belt which drew his doublet in below his heavy belly, and handed the flagon to Caravaggio.

The wrestling ring was on a platform set at head height before the Colonna Palace. Craning his neck to watch the bout, Caravaggio saw her on the balcony of the palace with the family grandees. Costanza Colonna inclined her head to him. Some constraint froze her features. He bowed to her. When he looked up her eyes were elsewhere, but he sensed she was thinking about him. Not about his work or the life he lived now. *She'll be thinking about the old days*, he thought. *When I was her boy.* His distraught mother had collapsed after his father had died of the plague. Costanza had brought the poor woman's eldest child to her house out of love for his grandfather, who had served her as a surveyor. Michele had grown up chasing through the palace in Caravaggio with Fabrizio. *Until she sent me away.*

A groan and a cheer from the crowd. He turned to the ring. A wrestler had dropped his opponent onto the canvas and now grappled with the wriggling man beneath him. The two fighters were thickly muscled, broad across the back, peasants bred for labour and combat. The pinned man hammered the floor with his hand. A herald wearing a scarlet surcoat with the golden column of the Colonnas' crest lifted the arm of the victor.

The winner doused his shoulders in water from a ringside pail to cool himself for the next bout. It was a pleasant May evening, but the exertion and the torches in each corner of the ring made the fighters hot. The wrestler took a wineskin and slung his head back to drink. He wore his hair long. His beard was thick and black. He held the wineskin at a half-arm's length from his mouth as he poured so that it wouldn't touch his lips, like one accustomed to drinking from a shared vessel.

'Look at the size of his arms,' Prospero said. 'If that was the jawbone of an ass instead of a wineskin, we'd be looking at Samson himself.'

The torchlight caught the wine, so that the man seemed to be sucking fire. When he lowered the wineskin, the wrestler shook his head and his sweat sprayed into the crowd. His next opponent climbed into the ring and flexed his chest, swinging his arms and loosening his neck. Wagers circulated in the crowd.

'I'll put my money on the new fellow. He's fresh,' Prospero said.

A short man in a green doublet took him by the hand. 'You're crazy. You'd bet against that monster there?'

'Who the hell is he, anyway?'

'He works in the stables of Cardinal Odoardo Farnese. The new fighter's a Colonna water-carrier. Two *scudi* on the Farnese man.'

Prospero still had the man's hand, though his enthusiasm appeared to have diminished now that he knew the families for which the men fought. 'We have a bet.'

The fighters circled each other.

'Why can't people just have a good old scrap?' Prospero muttered. 'Why does this have to be Colonna against Farnese?'

'Better this than a real war,' Caravaggio said.

'The loser will start a war on the streets tonight. If the Farnese man wins, right here in front of the Colonna palace, your friends up on that balcony will have to strike back. There'll be pride and politics at stake. It isn't just two sweaty bruisers in that ring.'

Caravaggio watched the nobles above them. 'They're not my friends.'

Costanza's glance caught him. Shame seemed to overcome an attempt at shrewdness in her face, like a wealthy market shopper forced to haggle over a few *baiocchi*. He felt an unease he had known before. She had looked at him that way long ago. When he was fourteen, he had been watching artisans repair a fresco in her hall. The foreman had shown him how to trace over the cartoon, pushing pinholes into the wet plaster to make a stencil. Michele had coloured a leaf with such pleasure that Costanza had asked him if he would like to be apprenticed to a painter. When he went to study in Milan, her expression had displayed a motherly sorrow at his departure. But he had also detected the calculation of a woman whose plan was accomplished. *She wanted me gone. For the sake of peace in her house.*

The Farnese man found a hold on his opponent's waistband and lifted him. He dropped the flailing fighter on his back and drove his shoulder into his ribs. The Colonna man retched. The crowd sucked in a breath, as though it felt the impact of that blow, then all set to calling for their favourite once more.

The Colonna man's body was dark and hairless. He reached for the other's beard, gripped it, held it secure as a target. With a powerful contraction of his stomach muscles, he butted the Farnese fighter on the nose. Blood sprayed into the crowd as the Farnese groom shook his beard free. There was rage in his eyes. He flattened his palm over the Colonna man's face.

'He's gouging him,' Prospero shouted. 'Stop him.'

'It's no holds barred, *cazzo*.' The man who had bet against him laughed.

The Colonna fighter squirmed. He might have conceded, but his hands were pinned; he could make no signal. When his eyeball came free, he screamed, and the herald grabbed at his tormentor to end the bout. The winner raised his fist. Blood ran down his forearm, tracking the protruding veins as though his lust for the fight had opened him up and laid bare the inner workings of his murderous physique. The herald knelt beside the losing Colonna man. He covered his mouth with his hand. His face turned a pale green. Even the torches glowed less richly, as though blanching in horror. The winner faced the Colonnas on their balcony and bellowed over the roar of the crowd. 'Farnese, Farnese.'

The faces of the aristocrats on the balcony soured in fury that a brutish groom should exult in his victory on behalf of an enemy as eternal as the stones across the way in the Imperial Forum. They hurried inside, until Costanza was the only one left.

The tips of her fingers tapped the balustrade as she waited for Caravaggio's eye. She jerked her neck, signalling to him to join her in the palace.

Prospero disputed the legality of the Farnese victory with the man in green, refusing to make good his wager. Caravaggio laid his hand on the winning better's face and lightly shoved at his eyes with his fingertips. So soon after witnessing a blinding, the man forgot his bet. In a panic, he dropped onto his backside, groping for a way to rise amid the press of the crowd. Prospero punched Caravaggio's arm and made his escape.

A groom led Caravaggio across the courtyard of the Colonna Palace and into the summer apartments. The ground-floor rooms faced the mandarin grove in the secret garden. A fountain shot pale blue splashes of moonlight through the fruit trees.

Costanza entered the chamber. To Caravaggio, it was as though a familiar portrait had come to life. She stepped out of his memories.

Her hair remained so black that it took her skin beyond white into a realm of pallor that Caravaggio thought he might not be able to mix on his palette. Perhaps if he ground up pearls and dove's feathers, he could match it, though that seemed more appropriate to a sorcerer than a painter. The texture of her skin was the work of a magician too, barely lined. When she came towards him across the terracotta floor, her eyes were a purple brown in the light of the double-branched candelabra.

'Michele.' She reached her hands towards him. They were scented with jasmine and he lingered over them as he kissed them. He had grown accustomed to women whose fingers savoured of filth and toil.

'My lady, I'm delighted to see you back in Rome. It's been a long while.'

'My visit was not planned.' Her voice was uneasy. 'Since my last time here, I see that you're no longer Signor Merisi. They have started to call you after your home town.'

'I'm known as Caravaggio now, it's true. Though that title really belongs to you.'

'It does me honour, as Marchesa of Caravaggio, that your art should place the name of my town on the lips of everyone in Rome.'

You mightn't think so, if you heard what they said about me, he thought. 'Your estates prosper?'

'They do. And your sister Caterina has another child, a girl. Named Lucia, after your mother, God rest her soul.'

'You were more of a mother to me.'

She cleared her throat, like someone trying to cover another's faux pas. Her breath shivered and the flames on the candelabra stuttered, as if her indecision sucked the oxygen from the room. 'When you were a child, you were like my child. Now you're a man, I love you still.'

He squeezed her hand and rubbed the pad of his thumb on her

knuckle. 'I think of your generosity whenever Rome gets – oh, I don't know – too wild.'

She lowered her eyes. 'I need your help.' The candles glimmered on the gauze that covered her breast.

'At your command, my lady.'

'Fabrizio's in trouble, Michele.'

Caravaggio's tension seemed to reach into his throat and cut off his air. He croaked out his words, 'Is he in Rome?'

'He is.'

'What happened?'

'A fight.'

'Don't you have people to take care of these things? A purse for the injured man. A bribe for the arresting officer.' Even as he spoke, he understood. *This is too serious for the usual remedies. There's a great danger here. But for whom?*

'It's a Farnese,' she whispered.

Fabrizio, what have you done? He made a quick calculation of his connections, of men who might help Costanza's son. Her urgency communicated itself to him; he felt it pulse in his neck.

The two wrestlers in the piazza had represented the battle between these great families, each with their monumental palaces on either side of Rome and their armies of retainers ready to take up cudgels and daggers and to shed their blood. He thought of Fabrizio and some hot-headed young Farnese duke. The same violence, but with nobler weapons. *And consequences for you too, Michele, if you get involved.*

He looked into Costanza's pleading eyes. She had helped him so much in his life, but now that she wished for his aid, her demands could disturb the position he had worked so hard to establish. He knew she saw his reluctance and that it pained her.

This isn't your gaming debt to Ranuccio. This is a woman to whom you owe more than you could ever repay. 'I'm at your service, my lady. Always.'

Her fingers reached to Caravaggio's shoulder. They were tentative. He wondered that in all these years she hadn't touched him except to allow his kiss on her knuckles. He shuddered. It seemed as though the force of generations of her family's nobility, of princes and generals and even a pope, coursed from this tiny hand into his body. It was the power that might demand a man go to his death, and it numbed him.

'Michele, you're painting the Pope's portrait,' she said.

They wait years for their moment, these nobles, and then in an instant they see their opportunity, he thought. *Loyalty is an elegant word for blackmail.*

Her hand was still, but her touch seemed to circle his neck and travel down his arms and back. He regretted his reluctance. She came to him because she knew what Fabrizio had meant to him. But he couldn't suppress his bitterness. *If you hadn't sent me away, perhaps this would never have happened. Fabrizio would be a different man. And so would I.* 'What expression would you have me paint on the Holy Father's portrait, my lady?'

'Forgiveness.'

He recalled the shrewd little eyes on the canvas he had left at the Quirinale. Mercy on that face? *That'll be a work of imagination no less than a ceiling frescoed with the god of the sea and all his nymphs.*

'I can try, my lady. I can try.'

◼

Prudenza came in the middle of the night. She climbed the stairs and twisted Cecco's nose to wake him.

'Get yourself below, little fellow,' she whispered. 'I need a place to hide tonight.'

Cecco wrapped himself in his blanket and stumbled down the stairs, grumbling. Prudenza lay on Caravaggio's bed. She pushed her hand under his sleeping cap. Her fingers moved in his hair.

In the darkness, he ran his palm over her face. He was careful to avoid the wound Fillide had cut beside the girl's mouth, but she flinched when he touched a new bruise around her eye. 'Fillide threw a stone,' she said. 'I can't go home. You don't mind, do you?'

She was playful in the face of an implacable hatred. He had a vision of her dead, dropped into the Tiber with the refuse from the street. He looked across his studio to his easel and the unfinished *Martha and Mary Magdalene*. He used to think his work would outlast time, but when he touched Prudenza he knew that anyone could walk up to his canvas and take a dagger to it. Once it was dry, porters would carry the painting to the Lady Olimpia Aldobrandini's palace and she would display it in her gallery for the respectable public to view. Everyone would feel justified in criticizing it, free to mock it. He had heard them do so with his other works. Why shouldn't one of them decide it ought to be destroyed?

His work hadn't immortalized this girl. Canvas was no more resilient to violence than flesh. It rotted more slowly and people gave it a higher value, but it was as fragile as bone and skin. He found her hand and held it. Soon he felt the warm looseness of sleep in her fingers, and he shivered for her.

■

'What a jumble of rotten shit.' Caravaggio went into the side chapel towards the painting. Eight yards high, five yards across, *The Resurrection*. A lithe Christ struck an effeminate pose holding a flag at the upper centre of the canvas. Languidly strumming lutes and puffing flutes, the angels surrounded him. Tiny cherubs reclined under the angels' buttocks like cushions in a courtesan's boudoir.

Prospero followed Caravaggio through the Easter crowd in the Church of the Gesù. 'I'm trying to get a commission out of the Jesuits who run this place,' he said. 'Let's just get our communion cards stamped and be off. Don't make trouble.'

'Look at these silly buggers. The damned, they're supposed to be.' Caravaggio's voice was loud enough to draw the attention of the worshippers awaiting the Eucharist. He heard Prospero's warning, but the canvas goaded him with its incompetence and pomposity.

In the lower reaches of the painting, turning their faces from Christ, the sinners rested. They were guarded by a swordsman. 'He's a caricature of the assassin in your *Martyrdom of St Matthew*,' Prospero said. 'But all the turbulence of *your* work is so fey and banal here.'

'The condemned don't exactly look like they're suffering the torments of hell.' Caravaggio laughed. 'It's as though Christ just told them he didn't like what they're wearing.'

A sharp voice, nasal and imperious, cut through the babble of the congregation. 'Your sacrilege doesn't surprise me, Merisi.'

Giovanni Baglione held his plumed hat at his hip. His chest puffed out under an expensive padded doublet studded with knotted lengths of silk. His chin was high, pugilistic and triumphant, like one of the nudes in his *Resurrection*.

Prospero nudged his friend. 'Be nice.'

Caravaggio felt a glimmer of compassion for the man. *Why can't he just paint? Why this competition with me? His technique isn't so bad. He could make something of himself. But he'll never match my work.* 'Baglione, let's not get into anything here.'

Baglione's eyes flickered around him, as though he believed the entire congregation waited for his response. His slender fingers, gloved by soft skin farmed from an unborn calf, flicked at a lapis lazuli rosary. 'If you don't stop your slander, I'll have you called before the Inquisition.'

A crowd gathered about them and Caravaggio felt the onset of a rage trembling through his chest, growing with each breath. 'You think I'm scared of the Inquisition?'

Prospero lifted his palms in resignation. 'Here we go.'

'I care for art.' Caravaggio tugged at a silk rosette sewn over Baglione's breast. 'If that leads to insults, it's only because I care for art more than I worry about your feelings.'

'Paint as you wish,' Baglione said. 'But I say you're here to destroy art. Your technique—'

'My technique is good enough for you to make a hash of copying it in this clumsy piece of dung on the wall behind us. It's the worst thing you've painted. I've never heard anyone say anything good about it.'

Caravaggio was so emphatic that the Jesuit at the altar raised his head from the Host. It wasn't unknown for a fight to start in the crowded quarters of a church and the priest tensed in alarm. Caravaggio shut his mouth, and the Mass went on.

Baglione headed for the door. 'Maybe the Inquisition would like to hear about you and Cecco, your little butt-boy.' He dodged between the worshippers ascending to the church. 'You wished for the commission of this *Resurrection* yourself. It's clear that you're envious of my status.'

'I eat dickheads like you for breakfast.' Caravaggio leaped down the steps to pursue Baglione. In his haste, he collided with a heavy gentleman. He found himself dazed and pressed to the steps by the fallen man's weight, his feet higher than his head. Upside down, he watched Baglione rush across the piazza, his cape flowing behind him.

Prospero took Caravaggio under his arms and sat him upright. 'Let's go back into the church,' he said. 'We have to get the Holy Host inside you before the Devil takes you.'

Caravaggio rubbed at a trickle of blood from his eyebrow.

In the piazza outside the Pope's palace, the bailiffs hauled a criminal into the air by the *strappado*. Lifted at the wrists with his hands bound behind his back, his shoulders dislocated before he had risen a dozen feet. He screamed that he was innocent of whatever small crime had incurred this punishment. The market-goers gathered to jeer. At the foot of the pole, another offender was bent double in the stocks. His tongue had been pulled forward and caught in a clamp, a penalty for speaking ill of the government. Caravaggio crossed the square to the palace gates.

Scipione Borghese was at the window when Caravaggio entered to work on his portrait of the Pope. The cardinal held the edge of the curtain between a finger and thumb, as though he were peeling back an undergarment to look on the very sex of his lover. He gazed with a quivering intensity at the man writhing on the *strappado*. 'You've been called to the courts many times, Maestro Caravaggio. Have you ever—?'

'Been tortured for evidence? No, Your Illustriousness.' His voice was louder than he intended. *Still nervous around Scipione, aren't you, Michele*, he told himself. *Or are you anticipating some torture?*

Scipione frowned as though he was sorry not to hear how torture felt. 'I saw you cross the piazza. You didn't stop to watch the punishment.'

'The view is better from up here.'

A nasty shadow clouded Scipione's eye. 'You're bleeding.' He prodded the spot where Caravaggio had cut his brow in his fall outside the Church of the Gesù. A scarlet bulb of blood ran down his finger. 'Could you use this to paint?'

'Blood? As a pigment, you mean?'

Scipione wiped his finger on Caravaggio's doublet. 'Yes.'

'It rots and gives off a foul smell, Your Illustriousness.'

'You've tried it?'

'No. But I know what happens to blood.'

'I'll wager you do.'

The man on the *strappado* bellowed as he came down. The crowd in the piazza thinned and the bailiffs untied the prisoner. His arms dangled from shoulders strangely squared by the dislocation. He dropped to the cobbles.

Caravaggio went onto one knee. He imagined Fabrizio undergoing his punishment like the criminal outside. As if he held his friend's tortured body in his arms, he felt a pang of wounded love. The skirt of the cardinal's red cassock rocked before him. 'I beg of you a favour, my lord.'

'Ask.' It was as though Scipione's voice came from some other organ than his throat, so strangled and tense did it seem.

'My beloved mistress the Marchesa Costanza Colonna has a son.'

'Several sons.'

'I speak of Signor Fabrizio. He's held for some offence. Might Your Illustriousness grant him a pardon?' The painter kept his head down. He should have flattered Scipione, spoken of his famous capacity for mercy and other qualities churchmen liked to think they possessed by the grace of God. But he reckoned Scipione would have felt mocked, and he anyway doubted he could bring himself to speak such words. His mind was overcome with the pain awaiting Fabrizio.

'For a crime of this nature, the Holy Father himself must grant a pardon,' Scipione said.

Heat crept around Caravaggio's throat. *A crime of this nature.* He had neglected to ask Costanza of what her son stood accused. *What has she asked of me?*

'If he had merely killed a peasant or even a gentleman . . .'

There it was. He recalled Fabrizio's handsome, playful face. Caravaggio had known men who had done others to death. He never knew how to detect the wickedness in their eyes until it had been made plain. In the Evil Garden, all men's features flickered with butchery.

'. . . then I'm sure something could've been arranged. But he killed a Farnese, a member of a powerful family, whose support the Holy Father needs as much as the Colonnas. You understand the politics? We can't simply overlook this killing.'

There was no way back. 'I beg of you, Your Illustriousness. I owe a debt of gratitude and loyalty to the Marchesa which I would pay at any cost.'

'Would you, now?' Scipione laid a hand on Caravaggio's shoulder. 'Finish the picture.'

Once Caravaggio's voice started to slur, Onorio found it hard to follow his friend's surly dialogue. Something about a brother – or someone who was like a brother – and the Colonna family and Cardinal Scipione. Onorio assumed there had been a complaint to the cardinal as a result of the fracas with Baglione at the Church of the Gesù. That hardly merited this morose mood. Scipione wouldn't be too upset. His painter had been in far worse rumbles.

When the food came, Onorio pointed at the platter the waiter had laid before them. 'Is this goat's cheese, Pietro?'

'It's from a cow,' the waiter said.

'Which cow? Your mother?' Caravaggio growled.

'Leave the poor little slob alone, Michele.' Onorio grinned as the sullen waiter made for the bar. Others recoiled from Caravaggio when he was in this mood, but Onorio enjoyed it. This was when he felt the greatest bond with him. They alone were fearless and not to be toyed with. A night at the inns and whorehouses with Michele gave him a feeling of camaraderie that was bone-deep, as he imagined soldiers must feel when they fight a battle side by side.

Caravaggio cut a slice of cheese and ripped away some bread. 'More like a brother to me than my own damned brother ever was . . .'

'I didn't know you had any family left, *cazzo*. Remember my brother Decio? If he wasn't in holy orders, he'd be chained to the oars of a galley.'

'Decio's trouble,' Caravaggio lifted an unsteady finger before Onorio's face, 'like you.'

'My record is much the same as yours, Michele.'

'I'm poison.'

'It's in our blood.'

'Fabrizio . . .' Caravaggio shook his head. 'Blood? That's not why I do these things.'

Why, then? Onorio wondered. *Does Rome do this to us? Or is it that we're men who know we're talented enough to be needed even by people who detest our behaviour?*

The door of the tavern opened fast. Onorio tensed, peering into the dim light to see who entered. Mario Minniti walked in between the tables. He was breathless. 'Fillide killed the poor bitch.'

Caravaggio stopped chewing. 'Who?'

'That girl Prudenza, she's dead.'

Caravaggio let his head drop back against the wall, his eyes shut. Onorio frowned at him. Something in his friend's stillness reverberated like the tremors he had experienced when he

74

was in Naples once and the earth had jolted the walls of the buildings.

'Fillide found her in bed with Ranuccio,' Mario said. 'Before he could stop her, she slashed Prudenza and the girl bled to death. Ranuccio put her body in the street so that Fillide won't have to go to trial. He doesn't want to lose two of his whores in one day.'

Onorio held up his hand to silence Mario. The little Sicilian was always heedless of the emotions of those around him. He watched the candle's trembling touch over Caravaggio's immobile features. *His compassion endures even after a decade and a half in the Evil Garden*, he thought. *Michele can't hide it from me, though the rest of Rome thinks he's the Devil himself.*

Caravaggio rubbed his face and moaned like a man waking from sleep. Then he looked with disgust around the inn.

Onorio watched his friend close himself up. Still, the girl's death had broken him open for just a moment and some softness had leaked out. *She meant that much to him. But he'll have to block it out now. If you can't do that, you have to get out of the Evil Garden.* 'This quarter is crawling with whores who'll pose for you,' he said. 'Find another one, Michele. One with more sense, this time.'

'May God bless her. He has taken her to His care.'

'It's only in stories that whores are redeemed, Michele.'

'What about me? How am *I* to be redeemed?'

Mario giggled, but Onorio's response was quick and wondering. 'Your painting, Michele. Your painting is from God, and *it* will redeem you.'

Caravaggio's eyes fixed on him. Onorio wondered at what he had said. *Can painting save a soul? Can the churches I design bring salvation? When an artist draws, does he create something holy in his own mind?* Caravaggio returned the smile. *He's pondering the same thing.*

'If some day I make just one painting that's true,' Caravaggio said, 'maybe then God will take my soul and it'll be clean. But how will I know when I paint that picture?'

Onorio had an answer, and he was puzzled that it had come to him. 'You'll know. You'll *feel* clean. Like you've been washed.'

Caravaggio rose. He put his hand on Onorio's head. Then he went to the door.

■

He took some raw sienna and thinned it with linseed oil. Cecco grumbled at the light. 'It's the middle of the night, Maestro.' The boy turned onto his side and pulled the blanket over his pale back. With delicate strokes, Caravaggio laid a new shadow over Prudenza's face. *They'll wonder who you were*, he had said to her, when she'd asked why he had obscured her features. *But I'll know. I see through all this paint. I see what's underneath. I see you.*

He laid down his brush.

3

The Madonna of Loreto

In the weeks after Prudenza's murder, Caravaggio withdrew from the whores in the taverns, even from his friends.

Impatient with this rupture, Onorio came to his house. 'You need to get out. You need a woman,' he said. 'Much as it might go against the grain for me to say this, perhaps you ought to try a girl who doesn't sell it.'

'You mean a . . .'

'An honest woman.' Onorio laughed. 'I'll concede that without my good wife's influence, I'd be out of control.'

Caravaggio recalled Onorio's brawls, his couplings with street whores, the insults he yelled at the bravos in the piazzas. 'I'd hate to see you *without* your wife's restraining influence.'

He went to the Corso and bought a pair of gloves to fit a woman. They were red silk. He thought red would look well on her. He stared north to the gates beyond the Piazza del Popolo. Prudenza was interred there among the whores and heathens.

He could barely bring himself to admit that he sought love. *A girl who isn't a whore,* he mused. Each stroke of his brush linked him eternally to the women he painted. He suffered for them, even after they were gone. *Because I come to love them, I can't deny it. When they're taken from me, it's as though my work were destroyed, too.*

Lena's door was open. She held the boy under his arms. He stood on her feet and she walked him around the room, giggling. An old woman in the corner applauded. Lena peered down at the boy's feet to see that they didn't slip from hers. Caravaggio wondered when he had last seen such calm and unaffected goodness as he beheld in Lena. His chest expanded and his breath deepened.

The boy saw him and flattened himself shyly against Lena's skirt. *I should've brought something for the child*, Caravaggio thought. *When I come again.* It surprised him that he should wish so fervently for a next time. He stepped through the door and held out the gloves.

Lena took them. 'Are they special gloves for scrubbing floors?' She showed Caravaggio her hands. The dirt was grained in her knuckles and thick under her nails like a clumsily outlined sketch in charcoal.

'Perhaps I bought the wrong thing?'

She smiled at his embarrassment. 'They're lovely.'

The girl's mother drew him into the room by his elbow. 'Come, Signore. Will you have some wine?'

'Thank you, Signora . . . ?'

'Antognetti, Anna Antognetti.' She poured wine into a thick wooden cup.

The boy grizzled. Lena put her hand to his forehead. 'You're hot, little one. Still sick?' She fed the boy a sop of bread soaked in water and wine.

Caravaggio drank. 'Your sister's boy?'

'What makes you think he's not mine?' she said.

78

'He called you Auntie Lena, remember? When I was at your door with the old beggars.'

Lena's mother reached for Caravaggio's hand and whispered, 'The Lord took my Amabilia as she gave birth to this little one.'

'His father?'

Lena concentrated on the bowl of diluted wine before the child. Her mother worried her lip with a few grey teeth. 'In this quarter of the city, Signore, the father could be anyone.'

'Mama.' Lena clicked her tongue. 'Take another sip, Domenico.'

Anna shrugged. 'I brought eight babes into the world, Signore, but Our Lord carried them all away through sickness and bad childbirths. Except for my Lena. I fed them all myself, after my husband Paolo passed on. I used to buy vegetables from peasants and resell them in the Piazza Navona. It's not a good trade and men treated me as if I wished to sell myself. My legs and my back allow me to do it no longer. Lena has taken over, when her work at the cardinal's palace allows it.'

So Lena was a *treccola*, calling out her wares in the piazza, as well as a maid. Such work was often a cover for a whore, an excuse for her to be out in public when decent women were kept at home. He wondered if that was Lena's game. *Another whore? Even when I think I've found an honest woman.*

'What's your trade, Signore?' the old woman asked. 'The gloves you gave her are expensive. Your own clothing was once fine, too, though now they look like you'd been beaten and robbed.'

He grinned at her frankness. 'More than once, my lady. I'm an artist.'

The friendliness receded from Anna's face. An artist presented no way out of the whore's quarter for her daughter. 'She has another suitor.'

Lena dropped the bread into the bowl and glared at her mother.

'A notary. He works with the Holy Office. He carries out commissions directly from the Holy Father.'

'Perhaps I'll run into him,' Caravaggio said.

'Around here? He lives in a nicer part of the city.'

He reached out to squeeze the boy's chin. 'If he works for the Holy Father, it's possible I might see him at the Quirinale.'

'The Pope's palace?'

'I'm there every day. I'm painting the Holy Father's portrait.'

The old woman scrutinized him with the shrewdness of the street. *The same expression I painted on the Pope*, Caravaggio thought.

'I'll have other commissions soon. When I do, I'd like to paint your daughter.'

'Me?'

The old woman touched her daughter's leg. 'When by the hands of God and Blessed Maria I should be removed from this life to a better one, you'll need something more than a housegirl's wage, Lena.'

The girl popped another piece of dripping bread into the boy's mouth. 'I'm not as reluctant as you think, Mama. I like this gentleman.'

Caravaggio inclined his head in mock courtliness.

'What'll you paint me as?' she asked.

He rocked his head side to side. 'Oh, probably the Madonna.'

She caught her lip in her teeth. 'Me?'

'Don't laugh, girl,' the mother said. 'You're pretty. You'll look as good as those Madonnas in the churches.'

'Oh, Mama.'

'And the Maestro'll clean you up.' She reached for the girl's soiled fingers. 'So you'll look like the Madonna, not a skivvy.'

'The priests will think they've seen the Madonna for the very first time,' Caravaggio said. 'Just as if she had come up and touched them.'

Lena lifted the boy onto her lap and fed him the last of the bread.

Anna showed Caravaggio to the door. 'There're plenty of priests who'd like to be touched by my Lena. But if the Virgin appeared to them, they'd die of guilt.'

He heard her giggling as he went towards the Corso.

■

In the time of imperial Rome, Emperor Domitian's stadium was used for foot races, while chariots ran at the bigger Circus Maximus. When a fire damaged the Colosseum, the stadium hosted the blood sports of the gladiators, too. Its marble cladding was pillaged to build churches and palaces for the popes, for the Pamphilij family, the Orsini and the Colonna. But the brick and concrete of the lower arcades, where the ancients had visited prostitutes after the day's competition, were incorporated into the ground floor of the buildings on what became one of Rome's central public spaces. Because the stadium had been modelled on a Hellenic design, the Romans referred to it by a Latin corruption of the Greek words meaning 'the place of competition' – *in agones*. In the later dialect of the city, the phrase contracted and mutated, so that the piazza was called 'Navona'.

It was still a site of competition, as intense as the confrontations between the gladiators and almost as vicious. The games of football played across its cobbles were for money. There were few rules. The results were disputed with as little finesse as the ancient games.

Caravaggio came down to Navona from the French tennis courts with Onorio. A heavy football arced through the air beyond a crowd of cheering spectators. It dropped at the feet of a tall figure in a loose white shirt.

Caravaggio peered into the twilight. 'Is that Ranuccio?'

Another player charged, lunging for the leather ball. The tall man put his foot on top of the ball and rolled it to the side. At the same time he reached down and swung a fist straight into his opponent's nose.

'Definitely Ranuccio.' Onorio laughed.

A bookmaker in a heavy cloak stood at the edge of the play. Onorio called out to him. 'I'll lay a *scudo* against Ranuccio's team.'

Caravaggio hesitated. He didn't want to revive the old antagonism with Ranuccio.

The bookmaker turned. 'Onorio, I'll take that bet. Hey, you've been at the tennis courts?'

'For some fencing. A Spanish gentleman and a soldier from Urbino.'

Ranuccio came out of the game to drink from a flagon of wine. He seemed to have taken a blow, because his right leg gave way a little with each step.

'The Spanish swordsman was good,' Onorio shouted. 'He'd have you tied up in knots, Ranuccio.'

'That's what you say.' Ranuccio swilled the wine. When he saw Caravaggio, he spat onto the cobbles.

'I'd have put ten *scudi* on him to beat you,' Onorio said.

'The ten *scudi* your friend still owes me?' Ranuccio waved the flagon towards Caravaggio. 'I know the swordsman you mean. Contreras, right?'

'That's him.'

'I've seen him fight. I'd take your money and shove it up his ass, before he'd score a hit on me.'

Onorio moved forward. 'No chance. Dickheads like you are worth a penny each. Right, Michele?'

Caravaggio held up his hands. *I know where this is going. Neither of them can stop now.* He couldn't fail to back his friend. Even

Ranuccio would have been right to disdain him, had he done so.

Ranuccio threw the flagon at Onorio. He grabbed a sword from one of the spectators to the football game. A crowd closed around the two fighters. Caravaggio pulled one of the football players off Onorio's back and put his knee into the man's ribs.

He waited for more swords to be drawn, but as far as he could tell the fighting was with fists, bottles and stools from the nearest tavern. Then he saw steel flash between the bodies of the men before him. Onorio came to his side with a broad smile and his teeth outlined in blood.

'Ranuccio gave me a good one right in the mouth.' Onorio was as exhilarated as a child wrestling with his father. 'But I cut him up a bit.' He raised his dagger. They left the mêlée and rested against the massive bowl of the Fountain of Triton. Onorio dabbed at his mouth with a white handkerchief and spat blood into the pool.

'You must be cut inside your cheek,' Caravaggio said.

Within a few minutes, the fight broke up. Ranuccio's brothers led him away from the brawl. He was bleeding from his hand, his wound wrapped in the tail of his shirt. He grinned at the blood on Onorio's handkerchief. Ranuccio pointed his injured hand at Caravaggio and made some joke to his companions. They smirked and trotted past the Church of San Giacomo. Caravaggio thought that if Ranuccio had seen his dead body propped against the fountain, he would only have laughed harder.

◼

An usher showed Caravaggio along the broad, high corridor of the Quirinale Palace towards Scipione's chambers. The scent of damp plaster was on the air.

'That smell . . .'

They came to an open double door. 'Maestro Reni from Bologna has been frescoing the Chapel of the Annunciation. That's what you can smell.'

The fresco was almost complete. A couple of fat cherubs swung a censer. The Virgin lay on her bed, pregnant. Joseph was holding off some bearded fellows at the door. Everything was done in pastel shades like a washed-out Raphael. Caravaggio grimaced. He was sure everyone would love it.

The usher went to the first pew. Scipione was on his knees in prayer. He rose and came towards Caravaggio swinging his rosary. The artist bowed low. Scipione tugged his hand away almost before the kiss. His cheeks were flushed with wine.

The Cardinal-Nephew led Caravaggio out of the chapel, his hand on his shoulder. It was the barest of touches and yet it seemed to reach deep beneath the skin, like an unwelcome caress. 'Keep away from the Tomassonis, Maestro Caravaggio.'

'Most Reverend Lord?'

'They're powerful in their part of town. That makes them very useful to me. There's some dispute, I gather, between Signor Ranuccio Tomassoni and you.'

'Sire, it's of no importance. A matter of—'

'Ten *scudi*. I know. But blood has been drawn now too – at the Piazza Navona.'

Caravaggio was about to say that it had not been him who cut Ranuccio, but he was reluctant either to make excuses or to admit that he had been present at the brawl in the piazza.

'It seems unlikely that you and Ranuccio will conclude such a conflict with a polite apology. I wish for you to cease this dispute.'

'Will Ranuccio . . . ?'

'This shall be communicated to Signor Ranuccio too.' Scipione crossed to the window overlooking the courtyard of the papal palace. 'You'll have to go into hiding. The police must make a show of arresting those involved in the fight. But only when you finish the portrait of the Holy Father. After that, I wish for some frescos in my new palace, Maestro – for the loggia outside.'

A fresco? He might as well ask me to sew him a nice scarf or give him a haircut. 'Why don't you ask Maestro Reni to do it?' he said, imparting as much scorn as he might to the artist's title.

'I might ask him, of course. He didn't do badly with this chapel. And I haven't asked *you* to do it yet. But why not?'

'I work in oils.'

'Fresco is the greatest test of an artist's skills. You have to complete the painting before the plaster dries on the walls. There's no time for corrections or touch-ups. Isn't that true?'

'In a fresco, one can't control the light.' As he talked about his work, Caravaggio's resentment of the banal daubings in the chapel left him and he became expansive. 'No doubt your loggia is beautiful, Your Illustriousness. The sunlight streams over it all day.'

'It does.'

'That's why it's so pleasurable for you to be there.'

'Quite so.'

'My paintings are made with a single source of light. To create shadows that bring out the features of my models. In so doing I illustrate their emotions.' He held his hands in front of Scipione's face as though they carried the beam of a lantern. The cardinal's eyes followed his fingers. 'If the light came from here, I would see a different Cardinal-Nephew than if I were to put the source of light down here.'

Scipione nodded, understanding. *He doesn't bother to argue that it would only be a trick of the light*, Caravaggio thought. *He knows that he wears many faces, and they'd all be worth a portrait.*

Caravaggio gestured at the sunny courtyard. 'In the loggia, all faces are flat and dull, because the light is uniform. If I look at you this way, you're just the same as if I stand over here. What am I to search for as an artist when every perspective is identical? How can I show that what *I* see is different, when it isn't? The sun gives life to everything, but not to painting.'

He caught himself and frowned. *What is it that* does *give life to painting? Is it only the light?* Lena's face came to him and he smiled.

Scipione patted at Caravaggio's wrist. 'That's how you capture the character of a man?'

Caravaggio shrugged. 'When a painter looks at a man, the man thinks, "How will he make me look? Will I recognize myself? What if he sees me as I really am?" The painter's eye draws out every man's guilt. That's why it's hard to paint a saint from life.'

'Very hard, indeed. But what if the guilt is the painter's?'

Caravaggio's easy feeling left him. He shuddered and looked at his hands. 'Then the painting would show what even the artist didn't know.'

◼

Lena saw him as she left the Thursday meat market behind the Madama. He kept to the shadows under the wall of the palace as if he wished not to be noticed. She came to his side and caught his arm.

'I'm waiting to model for you, Maestro Caravaggio.' Her voice was light and playful. She set her basket against her hip. The tripes packed inside it slopped towards her.

'I'm still painting the Holy Father,' Caravaggio said. 'I'll come to you as soon as I need a—'

She wondered that he stuttered before her. He didn't seem like the kind. *Is he having second thoughts about revealing himself to me?* she thought.

'As soon as I need a—' he repeated.

'A Virgin,' she said.

He smiled with an embarassed shrug.

'I'm going the same way as you, it seems,' she said. 'Will you accompany me?' She started to walk and he caught up beside her.

She looked at him sidelong and pursed her lips, pretending to be affronted. 'Is it that you don't wish to paint me anymore?'

He shook his head, reached for her basket. 'Let me take that.'

'It's not heavy.'

'Really, give it to me.'

His hand on her wrist, he took the basket. He examined her fingers. She wondered if he was thinking about the gloves he had bought her. 'I don't wear them when I'm working.'

He didn't register that she had spoken. He rubbed his thumb against her knuckles.

'My hands *do* get dirty, don't they? Look at them now. They're an awful state,' she said. 'This morning I was cleaning the grooms' waiting rooms at the palace. A big mess those gentlemen make.'

His touch was very hot. He let her go.

They went into the Via della Scrofa. She took longer strides as the market crowd thinned, holding her hands before her belly and swinging her shoulders. *A man who spends his days with the Pope himself*, she thought, *walking beside me.* She glanced at his features. They seemed feverish, as if he actually did see her already as the Virgin and were wrestling with the presence of God. *Perhaps you have to be a bit odd to do what he does. The Pope might even expect it. If a man arrived to paint him wearing stockings without holes in them and a jacket that wasn't spattered with oil paint, the Holy Father might throw him out as an impostor.*

'You have some pigment on your chin.' She pinched a lock of his black beard between her index finger and thumb. She ran her fingers to the end of the beard, but only yellowed the entire strand with the oils. 'It hasn't come out.'

'It won't. If you get oils in your hair or on your skin, you might as well leave it there. You can try to clean it, but you'll just spread it around and rub it in.'

'I bet I could get you clean.' Her daring made him laugh. *With relief*, she thought, *as much as with amusement*. 'You didn't change your mind? About me modelling?'

He shook his head and sucked in his lips. 'Lena, I may not be able to see you for a while. I have to hide. The police . . .' She waited for him to look at her, preparing a coquettish smile to encourage him. But he stared at the dirt where his feet fell.

'Even so, I've already seen you in the pose in which I'll paint you, as soon as I'm free again.' He closed his eyes. 'I've seen you as the Virgin. Standing at your door with Domenico. And then also when you were playing with him, walking his feet on yours.'

'That sounds like me, not the Virgin.'

He whispered, 'You'll see. There's no difference.'

He's not like the others in the Evil Garden. He's not just after my honour. Understanding and amazement suffused her chest like warmth from a brazier. *He really does see the Madonna in me.*

'I have to wait for the right commission, of course.' He looked up, noticing the awe in her face. 'What?'

She blushed. 'Nothing. Go on.'

'That's how I work, you see. Someone, a cardinal like del Monte, pays me to do a canvas for him, and only then I get my models together for the painting.'

She rocked on her heels, as they waited for a gap in the flow of carriages so that they might cross the Corso. *If he sees the Madonna in me, what do I see in him?* He carried a sword and lived in the roughest neighbourhood of Rome. No doubt he mixed with bad sorts – all artists did. But he was gentle; she felt it. *That's why he's come to me. I've never been like the other girls round here, either. We're different, him and me.*

She lost herself, as if she were dreaming. He took her arm to go across the street, and she jumped as though she had been woken from a sleep. 'You can call on me in the meantime,' she said, 'while you're waiting for a commission.'

'What will your suitor, the notary, say about that?'

Her gaze drifted to the other side of the street. She hadn't expected him to remember the papal notary who came every week to press her to marry him. She would have liked to explain that the man was two decades older than her, that she hated his arrogance, his assumption that she would want him simply because of his position and wealth. It was hard to find the words now. It was difficult enough for *her* to understand her resentment. She ought to have welcomed the man's attention. She was a menial at a palace, who supplemented her income selling vegetables in the Piazza Navona, and he was an employee of the Holy Father. The notary could have tried to buy her honour for a night. Perhaps it was the fact that he hadn't done so that made her dislike him. It would have been more honest than the pomposity with which he declared that he would have her only on the terms decreed by the Church. She felt disdain in his declarations. By making a show of his refusal to buy her, he indicated that he believed her to be for sale. Like most men, he saw a poor girl as a whore who had yet to find a pimp.

'He's just someone my mother knows.' She flicked her hand in dismissal. 'When you paint, how long does a model have to stand in the same pose?'

'Three or four hours at most. In one day, that is. You'd have to come back again and again.' He held her glance. She felt their faces drawing closer, the slow, bewitching course to a kiss. She moved towards him. The tripes slopped to the side and the basket tipped. Caravaggio took a step to rebalance, so the innards wouldn't fall to the floor. He laughed, shyly, with her.

Anna was laying out anchovies to dry for a *puntarelle* salad when they reached Lena's house. 'Did you get the sprouts, my girl?'

'No, I forgot, Mama. I'll go back out for them.'

'Better clean those tripes first.' The old woman saw Caravaggio and wiped her hands on her apron. 'Maestro, how good of you to pay a call.' She curtsied. He glanced at Lena. They smiled at her mother's formality.

Lena unwrapped the grey tripes and slapped them onto the table. 'I have to get to work,' she said. 'Unlike you, I never have to wait long for a commission.'

'I didn't say I *have* to wait a long time. I wait only for the *right* one.'

He was on his way through the door into the street. She rolled up her sleeves. 'Maybe I should've been an artist.'

He lifted his chin, questioning.

'It's my inclination, too,' she said, 'to wait for the right one.'

■

Costanza Colonna determined to hide Caravaggio until the papal police had finished their sweep of the brawlers from the Piazza Navona. She called him to her rooms at the Colonna Palace and told him he would find refuge at her son Muzio's lodgings nearby.

Caravaggio shuffled before her and scratched at his beard.

'What's wrong, Michele?' she asked.

His head dipped, side to side. 'My lady . . .' He shrugged. 'Don Muzio?'

'It's a matter of convenience and urgency, Michele. The fight was in one of the most important public places in Rome. Blood was spilled. The police want to make some arrests. They left you at large until you had made the final touches to the Holy Father's portrait. But now you have to hide.'

'But Don Muzio . . .'

Costanza recalled the tension between her eldest son and Michele. It had been years since the older boy had teased Michele for his low birth. They were grown men now. Surely their duty to her would outweigh those old disputes.

'I'd prefer to take my chances,' Caravaggio said.

Costanza brought her hand down on the white leather cover of the armchair where she sat. *Why do men take nothing seriously, except their honour?* Men were trapped forever in their boyhood relations. Michele would be wound tight by her son's taunts, just as he had been when they were boys at her palace. *Plague orphan, that's what Muzio used to call him.* Taking over the Marquisate since her husband's passing hadn't reduced her eldest son's eagerness to show his superiority to others. He goaded Fabrizio every time they met. Michele was even more vulnerable.

Caravaggio glanced about the room as though he didn't trust its silence. *Is he so hunted?* she wondered. *I see now that he has been helpless all this time.* An outsider in her home, he had been reminded of it by her husband, by Muzio, even by the servants. *Only Fabrizio and I welcomed him. But the love we offered failed to mute the rage in him.*

'Don Muzio and I, my lady, have unfinished business,' Caravaggio said.

'What can you mean?'

'You remember, in the Oratory . . . ?'

'But that was twenty-two years ago.'

He shrugged. *Muzio wouldn't have forgiven it, either,* she thought. The last time they had been together, her son had taunted Michele while they played in the Oratory of the palace chapel in

Caravaggio. Fabrizio had defended him, but Muzio had accused them of dreadful sins against nature. Her husband had overheard from the cloister. He had struck Fabrizio a fearful blow across the head and given him a kick to the very buttocks he believed to have been defiled by Michele. Fabrizio told her later that her husband had looked at Michele the way the priests glared at heretics who refused to repent in the fire. After her husband had left the Oratory, Michele had beaten Muzio with a candlestick until Fabrizio had restrained him.

She shivered as she had when her husband came to her chamber to order that Michele be sent away. She had resisted, until she saw Michele with the painters making the fresco some weeks later. It had seemed an opportunity to restore peace to her household and to give the boy a chance at a career in which he wouldn't be tormented by his past.

Did I send him away because of my own revulsion at what he did with Fabrizio? She had always thought it a good deed she had done for her ward. Now she doubted herself. She rubbed her fingers against her thumb, as if she counted the beads on a rosary.

She watched him shifting awkwardly on the flagstones before her, like the boy she had sent away. She saw it now. There had been love between him and Fabrizio, though she had never experienced such feelings herself. Some part of her had failed to mature beyond the age at which she had been dispatched to be a bride. *I made him leave because their love exposed me as a child still. I felt a mother's love, but never a lover's emotions.* She had put Michele on the mail coach and sent him to Milan, hoping never again to think of the love she had been denied.

'Very well,' she murmured. 'I'll hide you here at the Colonna Palace for a few days. I'm only a guest and I risk the displeasure of my brother, but I'll see that it's done.'

'Your Ladyship has always shown herself most gracious towards me.' He bowed with a formality that seemed to mock her.

As he went towards the door, she whispered to him, 'I'm sorry, Michele.'

He reached for the door handle. 'The fault is mine, my lady. It always has been.' Without turning, he left the room.

■

That summer of 1605, the conflict between the supporters of the French and Spanish monarchs escalated on the streets of Rome. Caravaggio had witnessed its spark, the defeat of the Colonna wrestler by the groom from the Farnese palace. The bout in the Piazza of the Sainted Apostles had led to a night of brawling in the neighbourhoods each family controlled. In turn, every animosity in the city ignited. It was as though someone had set fire to a tree at its trunk and now the flames reached out along the branches to the smallest twigs and to the buds of the fruit that would be. The Farnese and the Colonna. The men who lived on the Quirinale hillside against those whose homes were near the Campo de'Fiori. Frenchmen versus Spaniards. And among the many contentions coming into leaf that summer: Caravaggio against Ranuccio Tomassoni.

One afternoon, Costanza Colonna came with a message from del Monte: the police were no longer interested in the fight at the Piazza Navona; Caravaggio could come out of hiding. He went straight to Lena. She was just home from work at the Madama Palace, removing her headscarf, when she saw him in the door and smiled. It thrilled him that the brightness moving in her features was for him. He was accustomed to admiration, but he recognized something else in her face. She drew him away from the door, reached up and kissed him.

This would have been the moment to take her to the back of the room, to lead her behind the curtain to the padded board that served as her bed. But he found himself untroubled by lust and even wishing to prolong this period of – of what? *Of innocence,* he thought. It was an unaccustomed sensation and it filled him with a curious energy. *Could it be this is what those who've done no wrong feel?*

'Let's go for a walk.' He caught her around the waist.

She slipped away from him. 'Is it really a walk you want?'

He looked down at her breasts, bit at his lip playfully, and nodded.

'Take me somewhere you really like,' she said. 'I want to know more about you.'

'That won't take long. I'm a very simple man.'

'That's not what people say.'

'What do they say?'

She spun her finger at the side of her head and they laughed.

He took her to the Piazza Farnese. In each corner of the square, bravos loitered, waiting for a fight. They flexed their fingers in their gloves, and they touched the hilts of their swords as though they might, without noticing, have mislaid these blades of more than four feet in length.

For once, Caravaggio allowed himself to believe that the tension around him wasn't his concern. He led Lena under the barrel entryway of the Farnese palace. She glanced up at the family's fleur-de-lis carved into the ceiling coffers and touched the rose-marble columns at the side, plundered from the Baths of Emperor Caracalla. 'Why're you bringing me here? Do they need a cleaning woman?'

'I want to show you that I have my reasons for being a little crazy.' He turned his finger beside his head as she had done.

'You don't need an excuse for that, but I'm willing to listen.'

They went towards a broad, enclosed staircase. Across the

courtyard, another platoon of edgy swordsmen affected to lounge against the massive pillars. At the landing, a fountain splattered its stream into an ancient sarcophagus. Lena splashed water over Caravaggio. She giggled at her own mischief. *She's not accustomed to the freedom to be herself in a palace*, he thought. He chased her up the steps, laughing.

At the head of the stairs was a gallery hung with the paintings of the greatest masters of the last century. When Caravaggio had been there before, there were always a few gentlemen and their ladies admiring the art. Now the long hallway was empty. The swordsmen in the piazza had dispelled the art lovers. A chill of apprehension edged his happiness.

'Who's this cold fish?' Lena smiled.

A portrait of a cardinal, distant and withdrawn, craning his thin neck.

'Alessandro Farnese, painted by Maestro Raphael. See how his face appears to come out of the picture? This was something new in that time. It makes you feel as though you're in conversation with the painting, with the man himself.'

'I don't think I'd like what he'd have to say.'

'Here he is again.' He moved to the next canvas. A hunched pontiff on a throne, his nephews paying him homage. 'Now he's older. He's become Pope Paul III. This is by Maestro Titian. See how he painted everything in red tones?'

'The Holy Father looks like an animal, frightened and ready to pounce at the same time.'

'Everyone looks like that, if you examine them closely enough.'

'That isn't how you look.'

'You barely know me.'

She touched her finger to the tip of his nose, stepped ahead and pointed. A Virgin and Child with St Anne and the Baptist, and at their feet a rotund cat. 'I like this.'

'It's by Giulio Romano, a pupil of Maestro Raphael. He took his composition from Maestro Leonardo. At this time, every artist began simply to copy the finest elements of those who'd been before. The Madonna is very well done, but a little empty, no?'

'The best part is the cat.'

'Let's call it the *Madonna of the Cat*.'

She purred.

He spread his arm along the gallery. 'All these works are full of symbols. They don't just tell a story. You have to know the meaning of the bunch of grapes in the Baptist's hands to understand the *Madonna of the Cat*. You can't just look and see it for itself.'

'How am I supposed to know what those things mean?'

'The artists and the men who buy paintings don't care about *you*. Come, I'll show you one man who wants to make it easier for everyone.'

They went along the loggia. He glanced into the courtyard and noticed that more swordsmen were moving in from the garden at the back of the palace.

He led her into a gallery facing the Tiber. It was narrow and only twenty-five paces long. The gods of myth wooed and battled each other across the ceiling.

'There at the centre, see? Bacchus and Ariadne.' He watched her eyes move slowly over the luxuriant colours. 'You might not know the stories or even the names of the gods. But you know what's happening. They're marrying. They're experiencing the joy of love. It's right there. You don't need to know anything else. No need to read the symbols.'

Pensive, she let her fingers rest delicately on her bust. 'That's why you like this room?'

'That, and the way he uses space. Don't you feel as though they're all going to fall out of the ceiling and land on top of you?

They have real bulk, even though they're actually painted on a flat surface.'

'Do you know how to do that?'

'Yes, but once in a while I get it wrong. Annibale made no mistakes on this ceiling.'

'Annibale?'

'Carracci. The Maestro from Bologna who painted this work.'

'Do you know him? What's he like?'

It pleased him that she asked about the character of the painter. *She sees the humanity of what he's done. For her, this work isn't just decoration.* Then he looked down into the garden. The remaining swordsmen funnelled towards the courtyard. He had the first intimation of having mistaken the situation. 'We'd better go.'

They returned to the loggia. The bravos gathered around a massive statue of Hercules, the height of two men, in the arcade across the court.

He pulled at her arm, but she held still. 'You said you'd tell me your reasons for being a bit crazy.'

He stared across the courtyard. 'Annibale finished that fresco three years ago. It was the marvel of all Rome. All the painters thought it was the best thing ever done. He worked on it for four years for Cardinal Farnese. The cardinal didn't even thank him. He sent a servant to Annibale's rooms with two hundred *scudi.*'

'So much.'

To you, girl, yes. 'You don't understand. I get paid that much for a painting that takes only three months.'

'He was cheated, then.'

'Whatever a cardinal offers, it's the deal you get. You can't claim to be cheated by a prince of the Church. Annibale went crazy. Four years of intense work for almost nothing. He sits alone in the dark now, doesn't accept visitors to his home. He'll be dead soon enough.'

'What'd you do if one of these cardinals tried that with you?'

'I keep waiting to find out. *That's* what makes me crazy.'

■

The swordsmen strode towards the gate. Caravaggio recognized their faces from the tennis courts and the football game on the Piazza Navona. He hurried to leave the palace. He wanted to be away before these men dispersed into the streets.

'Painter,' Ranuccio jogged out of the mass of men towards Caravaggio. 'Is this your new slut?'

Caravaggio pulled Lena away. 'I've no quarrel with you, Tomassoni.'

'I beg to differ.' Ranuccio's brothers came to his shoulder. He squared up to his full height, a head above Caravaggio. 'I don't think I've seen this whore before.'

'Watch your mouth.'

Ranuccio waved his gloves as though Caravaggio had made a poor joke. He scrutinized Lena. 'Nice big tits. Girl, did he tell you what happened to Prudenza, his last tart?' He drew his finger across his throat.

'You're no gentleman.' Lena spoke with defiance, but Caravaggio heard the tremor underlying her words. He had to get her away from Ranuccio.

'Your boyfriend certainly isn't a gentleman. But surely you already know that.'

Caravaggio took Lena's arm and hustled her to the entrance. Rounding the corner, he thought at first his way was barred, then he saw Onorio among the swordsmen crowding through the gateway.

'Michele, what the hell are you doing in there?'

'He's been educating me,' Lena said.

Caravaggio laughed in relief now that the girl was away

from Ranuccio. 'Go home, Lena.'

She reached for him. 'Michele, don't —'

'Quickly, before this fight takes off. I can't leave, not after what Ranuccio said to me.'

She hesitated, as if considering what she might say to dissuade him. He shook his head and touched her chin with the point of his index finger. She kissed his cheek as she went.

'She's a nice little piece, *cazzo*.' Onorio tapped Caravaggio's behind. 'So Ranuccio's in the palace?'

They went into the courtyard, a dozen yards from the rank of Farnese men.

Caravaggio wondered at himself. An hour ago he had been as perfectly happy as he could have imagined, alone in the galleries of this palace with a woman who beguiled him. Now, one thrust could be the end of everything. *Is that how your life will pass? Is that how it'll be?*

Ranuccio stepped out from among the Farnese men. 'Where's your strumpet gone, painter? I want to put my horn up her so that you'll have the horns of a cuckold on your head.'

Caravaggio lifted his hand to his mouth and bit at the knuckle of his middle finger, baring his teeth.

'You bite your finger at me? You insult me.' Ranuccio drew his blade and advanced.

Caravaggio withdrew his own rapier from its scabbard. A shimmering, glistening rasp vibrated from its edge up his arm and through his torso.

The first impact, a parry, as Ranuccio leapt forward and thrust. His blade was a half-dozen inches longer than Caravaggio's and his reach was bigger, too. Caravaggio feinted at Ranuccio's sword, then he lunged and stabbed for the man's bicep. His tip ripped the fabric of Ranuccio's doublet. He felt flesh under the point of his sword.

Ranuccio spun away from him and stood apart, probing inside his shirt with his left hand, his eyes on Caravaggio, wary and angry.

Around them, the duel became general, thirty men on each side. The friction of steel edge against edge was like the pealing of ill-tuned bells in all the church towers of Rome at once.

Ranuccio took up his guard, and lunged. Caravaggio parried with a turn of his wrist, leaning forwards over his right knee to deliver his riposte. Ranuccio barely pulled his head out of the path of the thrust and came at him again.

His attacker's blade seemed to Caravaggio to be a claw, a snake, a tendril of some tropical grasping plant. His throat was dry and his feet willed him backwards out of danger. But the sword in his hand pulled him closer. The urge to wound his man was irresistible.

The hilts of their swords locked together. Caravaggio stepped in low and punched Ranuccio in the throat. He lifted his foot and kicked down on Ranuccio's kneecap.

He felt the big man sink. Grabbing Ranuccio's sword hand, he pulled back his own blade for the coup. *Is it to be now? Am I to prove as murderous as they say I am?*

A blow caught his temple with the force of a kicking horse. He fell and rolled. On his knees, he slashed blind so that his attacker might not approach until he had regained his senses.

Someone dragged him by his collar. Onorio spoke in his ear, 'I have you, Michele.'

He blinked hard. A man he knew for Ranuccio's elder brother, the soldier Giovan Francesco, was before him. *It must've been him who prevented the* coup de coeur, *the final thrust home*. He felt reprieved, like a man freed on the gallows. He hadn't killed.

Caravaggio was on his feet now, but he saw double and his head was heavy. Onorio steered him to the gate.

Ranuccio leaned against his brother's shoulder. 'It's not over, painter.' His voice was drawling, slurred.

'We'll fry your balls, you scum.' Onorio gestured for the other Colonna men to withdraw. A few came to the gate, sucking at cuts or binding wounds. Most were laughing and swapping insults with the Farnese men in the courtyard.

They crossed the piazza. 'Quick, before the patrols arrive.' Onorio called to a slim swordsman whose refined hauteur appeared undisturbed by the duel. 'Ruffetti, our friend needs a doctor.'

As he approached, the swordsman frowned with not a little horror. 'Bring him to my house,' he said.

Caravaggio lifted his hand to his temple. It came away red with blood.

The investigators from the criminal court found Caravaggio in bed at Ruffetti's house with wounds in his neck and the left side of his head.

One of the officers pulled a chair up to the bed. 'A Farnese man died of his injuries after the fight at the palace.'

'What fight?' Caravaggio touched the bandage on his throat and coughed.

The two investigators shared a glance. The seated one, small and spare and grey-skinned, raised his eyes. The other stroked his thick black beard. They were familiar with the direction this was going to take.

'A brawl, a swordfight at the Farnese Palace this week. Colonna men entered the courtyard. About two hundred took part.'

Caravaggio almost said there had been no more than sixty. He saw the thin investigator edge forward in his chair, waiting to be corrected. 'That's a lot of men. Was anyone hurt?'

'I told you, one of the Farnese men died.'

'May God have mercy upon his soul.'

'People said they saw you there.'

'No chance. I've too much work to do. Who said I was there?'

'Reliable witnesses.'

'No one I know, then. Anyway, I'm too busy for such things. I'm painting a portrait of the Holy Father.'

The man in the chair hesitated, but his colleague craned towards Caravaggio, holding onto the bed post. 'We heard you'd finished that portrait.'

'The Cardinal-Nephew and I have been consulting over the frame for the portrait. You can ask him.'

'We might do that.' The bearded investigator jabbed a finger at Caravaggio, but the one in the chair clicked his tongue.

'What happened to you?' the little investigator said. He took a tablet from his pocket and scribbled a note with a stylus.

'I hurt myself with my own sword.' Caravaggio tried to conjure up a laugh of self-deprecation. 'I fell down the stairs somewhere near here.'

The stylus scratched across the tablet. 'Where?'

'I can't remember where exactly. I was a bit, you know – I was drunk.'

'Boozing with the Cardinal-Nephew?' the bigger man said.

'By Jesu, Cosimo,' his companion hissed. 'Did anyone see you? Or come to your aid when you fell?'

'There was nobody about at the time.'

'Why did you come here?'

'Luckily I realized I was close to the house of my friend Signor Ruffetti, the advocate.'

Another glance between the investigators. *That's right, gentlemen*, Caravaggio thought. *I have friends who know the law.* 'There's nothing more I can say.'

He listened to their gloomy descent on the stairs. When he swallowed, his throat felt as though it would blow out in every direction right through his neck.

In the afternoon, Onorio brought him a flask of wine. He sat on the edge of the bed, as Caravaggio drank.

'One of the Farnese men died.' Caravaggio rested the bottle against his thigh.

Onorio's skin was flushed with excitement and his eyes were bright. 'He was no one important.'

'What would they say if I had died?'

'They'd say you should've killed Ranuccio when you had the chance.' Onorio slapped his leg. 'There's nothing wrong with a little blood on your hands. It makes a man of you.'

Caravaggio blinked. '*You* killed the Farnese man?'

'Give me the bottle, *cazzo*.' Onorio's voice twinkled with enthusiasm. He tipped the wine into his throat.

Caravaggio shivered. Onorio had taken a life. He seemed to have become unknowable to Caravaggio, to have passed into a world where his only companions were the dead. 'I've been lying here, thinking about how close I came to death,' he said. 'I could've been finished.'

'You're right. Dying is very easy.' Onorio shoved open the shutters. The sun swept into the room as though the darkness had accrued like a layer of dust.

'My father and grandfather died in a single day from the plague,' Caravaggio murmured.

'Everyone dies. You'd think that we died more than once, so much does dying abound. There hardly seem to be enough people living to satisfy all the dying that must be done.'

'Now I've died my first and second times,' Caravaggio pointed to his throat and head, 'I've fewer deaths to fear.'

When Onorio went whistling down the stairs, Caravaggio

drifted into sleep. He dreamed that he fought Ranuccio again at the palace. This time, he was driven to his knees and Ranuccio thrust his rapier through his chest. He fell, his head on the cobbles of the courtyard, watching the statue of Hercules as if it lay on its side. Ranuccio ran past, chasing Lena, laughing. He caught her. Caravaggio awoke, screaming.

Footsteps on the stairs. He sat up, shaking, sweating, his throat rebelling against his cry.

Scipione entered, his moustache twitching with delight, like a thespian responding to his cue.

'Quite a cry of horror. I often evoke that reaction, Maestro Caravaggio. But do calm down,' he said.

Caravaggio swung his legs off the bed.

'Stay as you are.' Scipione gave his hand for a kiss. He wrinkled his nose and pulled his arm back after the briefest of touches. 'My dear, you are a mess.'

'I fell down some stairs. I hurt myself on my own sword . . .'

Scipione sucked in his breath. 'I'm not investigating you, Caravaggio.'

'Yes, Your Illustriousness.'

Scipione sat carefully, as though he didn't trust the chairs in a commoner's house. 'It wasn't many days ago that I told you not to make trouble with the Tomassoni boys.'

'Yes, Your Illustriousness.'

'I remind you that the head of the Tomassoni family is the chief of the guards at Castel Sant'Angelo. In times of trouble, that castle is the refuge of the Holy Father. That means Tomassoni is someone on whom the Holy Father himself must depend.'

Caravaggio winced, lifted a hand to his throat.

'If the Holy Father were to go to Castel Sant'Angelo and find the doors barred or the guard –' Scipione brushed his moustache with his thumb '– unwelcoming, it would be a catastrophe for all Christians.'

'I'm always deeply indebted to the Holy Father and to Your Illustrious Lordship.'

The cardinal steepled his plump fingers. 'I dined at Cardinal del Monte's palace last night. I conversed with a man of science who informed me that humans are the only species that carries on vendettas. I thought of you.'

Naturally.

'Vendetta, it seems, is the thing that distinguishes us from the animals,' Scipione went on.

'And belief in the true God, My Lord.'

'There're many who don't share that belief, and of course they shall die like animals. But you're making fun of me. Don't. Your conflict with Ranuccio is human. I ask you to be a little divine – to rise above it.'

'Are you never vengeful, Your Illustriousness?'

'Don't compare yourself to me. In my case, vengeance *is* divine. It has the sanction of the Holy Father.' Scipione stretched to touch Caravaggio's arm. 'I'm trying to help you with the issue of Don Fabrizio Sforza Colonna. I wish to show you my regard, as your patron. I wish to secure the happiness of the Marchesa Costanza Colonna.'

Caravaggio would have taken the cardinal's hand and kissed it, but Scipione restrained him with surprisingly easy force. He was stronger than he looked.

'I have to buy off the Farnese to get them to overlook the killing of their cousin by Don Fabrizio. It doesn't help me to have you brawling in their courtyard.'

'There were a lot of men there. Not just me.'

'I have no dealings with those other fools. Whereas from you I have commissioned a picture – of the Holy Father. And I wish to have more.'

'But Tomassoni impugns my honour and—'

Scipione's tone went in one moment from his customary languid smoothness into the high-pitched frenzy of a thwarted child. 'You're my man, damn it. Behave like one on whom I can rely.'

He rose from the chair, listened to its joints creaking back into place. He went to the door. 'When you've recovered, go and see the family of Cavalletti the merchant, may his soul rest in peace. They've bought a chapel in his memory at Sant'Agostino.'

Scipione went down the stairs. He was out of sight when he added, 'They want a Madonna.'

'From me?'

'From Scipione's man.'

◼

The house where the Virgin had heard she would bear the son of God arrived from Nazareth in the time of the Crusades. Angels bore it away from the threat of destruction at the hands of the Mohammedans. They set it down in Loreto, a town in the Marches overlooking the Adriatic. Many great artists painted the transport of the Holy House through the skies, always showing Maria alongside her old home, flying with the seraphim. In his will, the merchant Cavalletti left a bequest for an altarpiece, an image of the Madonna of Loreto.

The merchant's brother-in-law, Girolamo de'Rossi, held the contract towards Caravaggio.

'I won't paint the Madonna flying like a bird, you know,' the artist said.

De'Rossi rubbed the sheet of paper between his thumb and forefinger. 'I could ask Maestro Baglione to do it.'

'Baglione will certainly give you a Virgin no one can believe in.'

'Do you mean you don't take the miracle of the Holy House seriously?'

'I take everything seriously. But I'm not like any other artist. That's why I've gained such a reputation.'

De'Rossi tried to smile.

'Don't worry, Signore.' Caravaggio took the contract. 'I believe in the Madonna. When I paint her, I'll be in her very presence.'

He leaned over the table, took the quill, and signed.

◼

Lena stood on a box with her sister's boy on her hip. Caravaggio brought in a pair of old beggars he had hired on the street outside the Tavern of the Moor and had them kneel in supplication.

'You're bathing the boy and someone calls you to the door, Lena. You want to get back to the bath, but you also feel compassion for these simple pilgrims before you. Look into their faces.'

'That's how it was when you came along to my house the first time,' she said. 'But aren't I supposed to be the Virgin?'

'Don't try to imagine how the Virgin would behave.' He knelt behind the beggars. 'Look at them, Lena. I want to know what *you* feel when you see them.'

'They seem like good, old people.'

'They walked all the way from their home to see you, endured robbery and hunger – just to look into your face. Would you turn away?'

'No. Except I remember that Domenico started to feel a bit cold.'

'Right, the Virgin wouldn't forget the child either. So swing a little on your toes just as you are, because you're thinking of the boy and that you need to get away. But look into their faces too.'

She let her chin rest almost on her shoulder, shy of the responsibility he gave her to be a channel for the Virgin, yet filled with pity for the beggars.

He stepped back to his booth, slipped inside the black curtain, and saw the projection of his models on the canvas. He dragged the easel forward to make the image sharper. When he had them in focus, the figures were vivid before him. A flurry of joy made him clench his fists and bite at his lip. The painting wouldn't be done for months, but here he had already seen it.

In the reddish brown ground he had laid over the canvas, he took the handle of a brush and carved the positions of his models. The old man's dirty feet pushing out towards the viewer; the beggar woman's cheekbone, sharp from age and hunger; the child's hand gripping the crimson velvet of the dress Caravaggio had bought for his Madonna; Lena's foot, arched on her toes, and the line of the collarbone where her chin reached down.

A few more cuts into the underpaint to mark the models' positions, and he left the booth. He chalked around Lena's feet so he would know where she was to stand for his next session, and did the same each side of the old people's knees. Then he let the child go to the courtyard to play with the beggars, while he built the skin tone of Lena's face and shadowed her nose and eyes. After a while he heard a small groan. 'Your neck aches?'

She smiled. 'Yes. Can I have a look?'

'There's nothing much to see yet.'

She swayed at her hips. 'What does the Holy House of Loreto look like?'

'It looks like your house.'

She turned her head to the side, smiling and wary, expecting some trick. He watched her image where it was projected onto his canvas. He wanted to bring her inside the curtain. *Where no one would see us. Except my Madonna.*

'You're the Virgin. You live exactly where you live. Right down to the plaster falling away from the wall and the chips in the doorframe,' he said. 'It's the place where Christ grew up. Do you think he lived in a palace? Or a church? Was he a prince?'

'He was a carpenter.'

'Where do carpenters live? In the Quirinale Palace?'

'There's one on our street.'

He put down his brush and his palette and came to her. He took her hands. She rubbed at the oils in his palm with her fingertips. He caught his breath. *This is how it'd feel to receive a message from Heaven. It wouldn't be in Italian or Latin. It'd come as a sensation and you'd comprehend it instantly. The same way I feel before a great work of art. I* sense *everything, before I* know *it.*

He folded back the curtain so that the basic elements of the composition were visible to her on the canvas. 'I'm not doing this painting the way others have done the Madonna of Loreto. I don't want people to say, "Ah, the Virgin can fly and, oh, what a nice house she had." I want them to know all the purity of the Madonna's soul and to be filled with the love she gave the world through her son.' He came closer to her. There was expectation on her face. *She knows what I'm going to say. She feels the same thing. She's* with *me.* 'To paint such a thing, I must feel those emotions. And I do feel them. Because I love you.'

Lena's eyes flickered between the image of herself on the canvas, incomplete and still, and the animated face of the man beside her.

'If I ever paint anything worth looking at again, it'll be because I'm thinking of you.'

She lowered her glance and let her shoulder touch his. 'But I'm not, you know . . . There've been one or two gentlemen . . .'

'I didn't say that you *are* the Virgin.' He raised her chin with one finger. 'I see the idea of her in you, and you make that idea real. Without you, she doesn't exist.'

He touched her mouth with his lips.

Del Monte watched him highlight the edge of the dirty step on which the Virgin twirled with her child. The cardinal lifted his beret and scratched his scalp.

'Baglione and the Academy won't like it,' he said.

'I'd cut it to shreds with my dagger if they did.' Caravaggio leaned close to the canvas.

Del Monte took in the whole painting, as tall as two men. 'It's magnificent,' he murmured.

'But?'

'The Church has guidelines for the portrayal of religious subjects.'

'Since when did *you* care about such things?'

'Don't misunderstand me. Some say I may one day be Pope – but I prize art as the greatest reflection of God's light on earth.'

Caravaggio put his brush crosswise between his teeth so that he could take another from a pot at the foot of his easel. 'So?'

'Your Madonna has dirty toenails, Michele. Her skin has some flaws around the eyes. The Holy House, on which successive popes have expended enormous sums, is portrayed here as a slum dwelling.'

'Christ was a poor man.'

'But the Holy Father is not.'

Caravaggio stretched his back. He kept his eyes on his last few strokes of paint, assessing them.

'If Our Virgin Lady lives in poverty, Michele, why should anyone venerate a rich man who wears expensive robes and pads around his palace in red slippers?' Del Monte examined the painting, his face aglow with an admiration no doctrinal quibbles could suppress. 'Will you at least give her a halo?'

From beneath his tray of pigments, Caravaggio produced a pair of compasses. 'I thought you'd never ask.'

When his Madonna was finished, Caravaggio sat before her in the quiet of the late afternoon. The winter sun went down. Its beam through the edge of the shutter crossed her body like a heavenly caress. *Nothing else should touch her*, he thought.

The house was silent. He had sent everyone to the Tavern of the Moor, telling them he would follow for dinner. He wanted to be alone with her, before he gave her to the Church of Sant'Agostino.

The wound on his neck ran like a thick seam gathering him together. *If the scar weren't there, I'd slip to the floor, a suit of clothes with the stitching unpicked.* His hair had grown back over the cut on his temple, but he sensed something at work beneath the skin. His body was struggling to repair whatever damage he had suffered there. *Perhaps the impact of the sword knocked something free in my brain, to let me know there's no 'next time'.* At any moment he might cease to exist – with no opportunity to explain, to say farewell, to apologize. *The last thing I said to Lena might simply be the last thing I ever say to her.*

He saw this in the way he had painted his Madonna. *I'm not playing games*, he thought. *Here she is. Anyone who sees her will know exactly who I am too, even if I'm gone, taken in a brawl or by disease.*

In his first years in Rome, his canvases had been whimsical and satirical. He painted cardsharps, for the amusement of cardinals who liked to imagine the forbidden darkness of the inns and the lowlifes within; nubile boys bitten by lizards, as if nature wished to warn of the dangers of love; youths peeling fruit, unaware that someone crept close to watch their pale necks, their delicate fingers. His works were clammy and foetid and disreputable like the bars and bedchambers where he passed his time.

When had he changed? What had started him on the path that led to this Madonna?

The Rest on the Flight into Egypt. He barely knew what he had done at the time, a few years after arriving in Rome. A scene of the Holy Family succoured by the music of an angel as they fled the vengeful Herod, painted with the dreamy clarity of the Venetian school. But later, in the gallery of the Lady Olimpia Aldobrandini, he had recognized that his heart was imprinted on the canvas.

In that painting, exhausted by the journey, the Holy Mother rested her cheek on her baby's head. The little Jesus, also half-asleep, picked at her mantle, as though he dreamed of feeding at her breast. Menica's friend Anna had modelled for the Virgin. She had understood that her life as a cheap whore wouldn't be a long one. Still she had faith that there might be an escape. Caravaggio had illustrated her hope and fear and acceptance in the drained, loving Virgin. The love of a mother who knew her son would be a sacrifice and was yet willing to undergo the hardships of the desert to preserve him for it. *I saw all that in the face of a whore.*

Anna had been dead a year now, at twenty-five, her skin wasted and scarred, her red hair dry and lustreless. He was with her at the end, and she had reminisced about the sixteen-year-old beauty he had painted as the Virgin. When she expired, he had dropped his head to her breast and shocked himself with his weeping. He had known many whores who had disappeared from the streets with little more than a shrug from him. Yet he had cried for Anna as though she had invented death, a malignant novelty displayed in a gallery which only he might view.

He touched his fingertips to his new Madonna's toes and traced the arch of her foot. He had to let her go. He kissed his fingers and went down the stairs to the street.

He reached the Tavern of the Moor. In the darkness of the

inn, he squinted to adjust his eyes. Something fluttered near the lantern by the bar. It was a hand. Lena was waving to him.

■

They drank rich wine from the volcanic island of Ischia. Lena pressed against Caravaggio's shoulder. With his cup in his hand and his friends around the table, he felt a rush of enthusiasm that made him boisterous and extravagant. He loved everyone. Across the table, Gaspare nuzzled Menica. Mario Minniti stabbed his dagger into the board between Onorio's fingers until he cut the skin. Onorio flattened his hand against Mario's nose and laughed when it bled. Prospero licked at the wound in Onorio's thumb and moaned like a dog.

Onorio pushed Prospero away and drew Caravaggio to him. 'Come gambling with me.'

Caravaggio waved him off and drank some more wine.

'You finished your Madonna. You need to cut loose, like you always do when you complete a painting.'

'I can't. Scipione has arranged a new commission. I need to start right away. Tonight I'm celebrating, but tomorrow I'm back in the studio.'

The architect slugged down the rest of his wine. 'What's this new commission?'

'*The Death of the Virgin*. For the Barefoot Carmelite Fathers at Santa Maria della Scala.'

'It's not really your style. The Virgin floating up towards heaven while all the disciples raise their arms and eyes in wonder.'

Caravaggio battered at his friend's arm. 'Do you take me for Baglione, *stronzo*? I won't paint her the traditional way. I'll paint her dead.'

Onorio was quiet and intent.

'I've painted Christ dead,' Caravaggio said. 'Why not his mother?'

'You can show Jesus dead, because we know he's coming back. No artist ever showed the Virgin's death as anything but a glorious ascension to heaven. As if she simply didn't die.'

'Still, dead she shall be.'

Onorio's sullen eyes peered from beneath the fringe of his hair with such malevolence that Caravaggio held his breath. 'So your model for the dead Virgin would have to be dead – to be truly lifelike.'

Though Onorio spoke in a murmur, it stilled Prospero and Mario. They watched him, knowing what was on his mind and fearing it. Caravaggio thought of the man who died in the sword fight at the Farnese Palace and Onorio's unscrupulous boast that he had killed him.

'Let's go and get you a Virgin. Let's go and kill a whore.' Onorio's teeth glimmered in the candlelight.

In a single breath Caravaggio was sober. His lips quivered as he tried to form the words that would end this.

With a sudden burst, Onorio threw up his arms and bellowed. 'I had you, you bastard. I had you.' He grabbed Caravaggio and kissed his head. 'I really had you going.'

The laughter around the table was relieved and horrified. Onorio punched Caravaggio lightly in the stomach. His guts chilled, as if the playful jab had disembowelled him.

'By Jesu, I nearly died there,' Mario said.

Onorio reached over the table, half-rising, and bestowed a kiss on Mario's cheek.

Lena held Caravaggio's hand in hers. 'I'd do it, Michele. I'd be the dead Virgin.'

His pulse was quick from Onorio's joke. It picked up still more as she spoke. *I couldn't watch her even* pretend *to be dead.*

'I enjoyed being a model,' she said. 'I liked that you told me what the Virgin might think. That I could imagine the Madonna's thoughts and show them on my face. It won't be difficult, after all, to be the dead Virgin. I'll just have to lie there.'

'Then you should get Menica to do it,' Mario said. 'That's how she makes her living.'

Menica flipped her finger off her ear.

Lena knitted her fingers into Caravaggio's hand. 'You haven't let me see the finished *Madonna of Loreto*. When can I have a look?'

He stared into his cup. For now, it was still his. *She* was his, on the easel of his studio.

'I, too, should like to see your Madonna,' Gaspare said. 'So that I can write a poem about it.'

Lena's not like those other dead girls. I'll protect her. Caravaggio made himself jolly. 'Allow me to give you some of my own verses. They're not as fine as the sentiments of our true poet Signor Gaspare, but perhaps they're more appropriate to these surroundings.'

He lifted his cup and took a long draught. Then he said,

> I'd like to put my penis
> In Botticelli's *Birth of Venus*.

His friends guffawed.

> But Michelangelo's Sacra Famiglia
> Doesn't make me want to feel ye.

Onorio hammered the table with his palms. 'True poetry.'
Caravaggio went on, 'Giovanni Baglione —'
'Here it comes,' Prospero said.

> Giovanni Baglione's *Resurrection*
> Gave me no erection.
> But Caravaggio's *St Catherine*
> Invited me to thrust in.

Mario mimed the act of love against Prospero's shoulder. Caravaggio grinned.

> Maestro Reni painted Moses with his stone tablets.
> Michele's Madonna'd make me break the commandments.

Lena laughed in good-humoured shock. Caravaggio squeezed her hand.

Gaspare raised his arms. 'The true work of art is womankind. May I? Lady Menica Calvi —'

'— one *scudo* to suck me.' Mario giggled.

Gaspare tried again. 'Lady Menica Calvi —'

'— two *scudi* to fuck me.'

Lena's nose touched Caravaggio's beard. 'Why don't you write a poem about me?'

He rose so fast that his hips jogged the table. His friends reached out to catch their drinks. He pulled at Lena's arm. She stumbled after him to the door of the tavern. Prospero hooted and made a bawdy gesture with his forearm.

Caravaggio went so quickly down the Corso that Lena had to run to keep up. His silence was sudden and violent, but her features were composed, unworried. He took her to his studio.

In front of the *Madonna of Loreto*, Lena stood more motionless than her image in the picture itself. In the quiet, Caravaggio thought he could hear the Madonna's skirts as she swung her hips.

'Maestro Raphael frescoed the Prophet Isaiah on one of the pillars in Sant'Agostino. When they hang this Madonna in that church, do you think anyone will ever so much as glance at Raphael's work? It's you they'll come to see. You still want me to pen some doggerel for you?'

She shook her head and moved backwards until she dropped onto his bed.

When they had made love, she wrapped herself in his blanket and stood before the *Madonna of Loreto*. 'They're praying to her, these two old beggars. But she's not granting them a blessing.'

He rose from the bed. 'The Madonna knows she ought to take the baby back inside. With the strength of their devotion, they must persuade her to stay and bless them. I want people to see this in the church and realize that *they* must draw the grace out of religion. *They* have to bring the Virgin to life. *They* have to make her real.'

'Lucky for you I'm not the Virgin then. You don't have to try so hard.'

'Lucky for me.'

'Yeah, you've got it easy.' She took his naked body into the folds of the blanket with her. 'The old people in the picture remind me of my grandparents.' She rested her cheek against his shoulder. Her chestnut hair dropped over her chest and to her nipples of that same dark redness. He ran his fingers through it. It was the first time he had touched her hair this way.

'Are *your* grandparents still with us?' she asked.

He remembered his grandfather's eyes when his father had closed them in death. His years at the Marchesa's palace, the fights with Costanza's sons, the chill of his family home when he visited his melancholic mother. The hand with which he caressed Lena's hair was the same one that had wrenched at Fabrizio's hose and clasped his buttocks. *Everything is different*, he told himself. *I'm not bound by the life I've led any more than my art is in thrall to works painted long ago.* He shook his head. 'There's no one.'

'No parents? No brothers or sisters?'

'No one.'

He felt an extra pressure from her cheek on his breast.

'Poor baby,' she said. 'Everyone you loved had to die.'

4

he Death of the Virgin

The bald heads of the apostles caught the light from a high window. For a joke, Caravaggio made Onorio model as St John, who was noted for his gentleness. In the foreground Menica bent double as the tearful Magdalene. A red canopy was the only sign of richness in the poor dwelling where Caravaggio set the scene of his new painting.

He had worked for months on the canvas, but still he had only an outline cut into the underpaint with the handle of his brush where he intended the Mother of God to lie. He couldn't bring himself to paint Lena as a corpse laid out on a simple bed board. When he saw her, he was reminded always of life, not death.

As *The Death of the Virgin* progressed, so Lena's pregnancy showed. He went to the market on the Piazza Navona to find her. She was wrapped against the winter damp in a heavy cape, calling the price of the onions piled in the basket at her feet. The chill caught her throat and she hacked out a cough, her hands on her belly. A young trader pushed an empty cart past her. He spoke a few words, leering at her pregnant stomach and thrusting his hips. She flicked the tips of her fingers off her chin to return the insult.

When Caravaggio reached her, the pallor of her skin alarmed him. *I waited all this time for love*, he thought. *Now I can barely feel it because I fear losing it. Perhaps that would be just.* It was as if his feelings for Lena had to be weighed against all the bitter lusts of his past.

'My feet are swelling up,' she said. 'Mama says it happens to women later in their term. You'd better hurry up and put me in your painting, or you'll have to change it to a Madonna and Child.'

He blew out a hot breath like smoke. He pictured her reclining dead in the void in his painting, her sufferings at an end. How could he depict her death? He had always painted from life. He remembered Onorio's macabre joke at the inn. He gasped and closed his eyes.

'Michele? What's wrong?'

He lifted her basket. He was frightened because the thought of her death terrified and satisfied him. *It would destroy me, but it's what I've got coming to me for the life I've lived.* 'I shouldn't let you do this during the winter. You're carrying my child. The market's no place for a woman in your condition.'

'Has something happened between you and Ranuccio?' she said.

'No, it's nothing.' *I'm the only person who terrorizes me.* He hefted the basket out of the piazza.

When he left her at the house on the Via dei Greci, her mother gave him a spiteful look before she shut the door. *That's what I deserve. She knows I'll never marry her daughter. I'm like all the other scum in the Evil Garden.* But as he hunched away through the cold, he imagined Lena rising from the deathbed he had painted for her. She illuminated his unworthy canvas. He went to the Tavern of the Moor and kissed Menica with such enthusiasm that she giggled and blushed. 'I'm going to be a father,' he said.

He came back to the piazza the next day, determined to take Lena away from the market. He wanted to bring her to his studio, to light a fire to warm her, to paint her again. A mountebank bellowed from a wooden platform, brandishing a pot of powder he claimed cured worms. The quack's daughter stamped and played violin at his side. She was shivering and her skin was grey. *Lena looks as unhealthy*, Caravaggio thought. *Have I let her continue to sell her vegetables in this piazza just so she'll appear sick enough to play the corpse of the Virgin in my painting?* The conman raised his voice still more to be heard over the women arguing nearby. 'I have here a radish whose magic cures toothache,' he bellowed.

Caravaggio followed the squawking catcalls to the corner where his girl stood. Lena swayed, her hand against her brow. A trio of women, their heads covered in shawls and their faces behind veils, were berating her. One of the women struck her hard in the belly.

He barged into the back of the woman who had hit Lena. She stumbled and rounded on him. 'Ah, it's you, painter. My Ranuccio will finish you and your street whore.'

Sudden helpless rage trembled in him. He picked up a few of Lena's onions and hurled them at the Tomassoni women. Each throw found its mark and the women rushed away, yelling and cursing. Lena sat on the cobbles behind her basket, rocking, her eyes squeezed shut.

He crouched beside her. 'Let me take you away from here. This work will be the end of you, Lena.' He thought of the happy moment when he had laughed with Menica and he decided to make his proposal. '*Amore*, I want you and me to—'

'They didn't attack me because I'm selling onions, Michele.' Her face was light green and her hands were grey.

He touched her belly. In her condition, that blow from the Tomassoni woman could be dangerous. His eyes were wet and lost.

She frowned and groaned.

His hopes of fatherhood, even the possibility that he might marry Lena, were an illusion. Her connection to him brought her into danger. Ranuccio had surely sent the women of his family to attack Lena with the intention of goading Caravaggio into a duel.

'Let me take you home.' He tried to lift her.

'Pick up the onions you threw at those women first.'

'I can't do that. It's beneath my—'

'Pick them up, Michele.' She spoke sharply, winced and clutched her abdomen.

He gathered the vegetables, shame making him hot. He helped Lena up and felt her weakness as she leaned on his arm.

'You missed one, Maestro.' Baglione sat at the edge of the Triton fountain. He held up an onion, turning it in the light. 'A little soiled. But that makes it perfect for one of your works. Still life with mildewed vegetables and rotten fruit.' He rolled the onion to Caravaggio across the filthy cobbles.

◼

He ran along the Corso the next day. He barely knew it, but he was calling her name as he went. His white smock, smeared with paint, billowed behind him. A gentleman on horseback made a gesture to a friend as though he were lifting a tankard. His companion whirled his finger beside his head.

At the house on the Via dei Greci, Menica dandled Lena's nephew on her knee. Mother Antognetti muttered tearful supplications as Caravaggio went beyond the curtain where Lena lay in bed.

She slept with an exhaustion that recalled the sacrificed body of Christ on a crucifix. Her skin was the sickly Indian yellow of pasta water, her hair dry and dishevelled. One arm dangled off the bed board, the other lay on her distended stomach. Her red dress stretched across her torso. Her feet were swollen. The flesh below her neck was slack, where she had already built up a little fat for the foetus to feed from. Puffy folds gathered at her eyes, as if this was the first time she had ever slept.

He had imagined her like this when he dreamed of the birth – spent and depleted. He had pictured her propped on her elbow, cradling the baby beside her breast and resting while his friends came to admire the child. But the Lord had taken his child. *My sins merited this penalty*, he thought. The punishment was visited on Lena's body, but it was intended as an affliction for his monstrous soul.

He watched her a long time. She opened her eyes once and smiled at him as if it took all the energy she possessed, then she went back to sleep. When he realized that he was committing her image to memory so that he might paint her as his dead Virgin, he stared down at his hands and wept because he knew his art wanted him to be as alone as God did.

Lena's mother pressed his shoulder. He shrugged her off and stepped back around the curtain.

The boy reached out for Caravaggio from Menica's lap. Menica glanced up at him. 'Domenico, do you want to play with Uncle Michele?'

He went to the door. 'I'll be with Onorio,' he mumbled.

■

Menica took Lena across the Tiber to see *The Death of the Virgin* at Santa Maria della Scala. Though she rarely left the Evil Garden, she knew the way through the narrow, impoverished streets of Trastevere. The Carmelites ran a home for fallen women in their monastery adjoining the church. Menica had sneaked over here with a few battered whores, when their pimps were in the taverns, and deposited them at the Casa Pia. She never stayed. She had no need of instruction from the Barefoot Fathers. She had experienced vices even the Church had yet to damn.

Lena walked slowly. Perhaps she was still weak from the miscarriage, but Menica thought it more likely the girl feared meeting Caravaggio. This morning he would be with the carpenters at the church, installing his painting. He had spoken no more than a few words to her in a month.

At the door of the church, Lena's eyes were wet. *Michele has a couple more weeks to make this right*, Menica thought, *then the tears will stop and she'll turn hard.*

The carpenters had set the backboards for the hanging: four rough planks at the top of the space and, ten feet below, four more to support the foot of the painting. The edges tapered a little, making the two ends of an oval. The workmen lifted the canvas under Caravaggio's direction. His voice echoed through the church. *Here he's in command.* She glanced at the tottering girl beside her. *You'd think a man whose pictures are so unconventional, who seems to have so much strength and to be able to make his own path, wouldn't be like other men. But he's just as confounded as the rest of his sex by the needs of a woman.*

As they approached the canvas, Lena put her hands to her face. The Virgin's corpse was spread across the foot of the picture, lying as Lena had when she lost her baby.

Caravaggio saw the women. Menica thought he might have turned back to his workmen had Lena been alone. Instead he came reluctantly to the girl weeping behind her hands. He shifted on his heels before them, irritation twitching over his features.

Menica followed Lena's eyes. The jade-green colour of death was on the Virgin's face. *She's only seen herself as the tranquil* Madonna of Loreto *before. She won't have expected this.* 'It's the saddest thing you've ever done, Michele.'

123

Caravaggio glanced at the painting as if she had pointed out a quality he had neglected to notice.

'It shows you still care about Lena, I suppose,' Menica added.

An injured flicker in his eyes indicated that he wondered if she might doubt such a thing. 'Let me show it to you.' He reached for Lena, but she pulled away.

'I thought you were going to paint me dead.' She wiped her eyes with her sleeve.

Menica heard the rage behind her sobs. *I was wrong. She's already turned hard.*

'Instead you've shown me when I was worse than dead.'

'It's – it's the Virgin,' Caravaggio stammered. 'She's the embodiment of love. Menica, tell her. *You* see it, don't you?'

Menica ran her hand across Lena's back and shook her head. They went out of the church.

They rounded the refuge for fallen women and went down to the river. Crossing the Ponte Sisto, they shivered as they passed the freezing washerwomen scrubbing laundry on the sandbanks, and returned to the Evil Garden.

■

'He has no beautiful ideas of his own,' Baglione said, 'so he must paint everything from Nature – at least, Nature as he sees it.'

The abbot of the Carmelite monastery pushed his hands into the sleeves of his cassock. 'No beautiful ideas?'

'Caravaggio depicts only the surface appearance of things.' Baglione ran his disapproving glance over *The Death of the Virgin*. 'My dear Father Abbot, what should be shown in the death of Our Lady Maria? The corpse of a woman whose soul has left her?'

'Not at all. She should be filled with grace.'

'Because?'

'Because she's ascending to heaven. Lifted by a force beyond life and death.'

'You're right, of course. Her glorious assumption of the mantle of heaven.'

'Though one might add that the Church has yet to rule on whether the Madonna died before her ascension, or if she was transported while still living.'

Baglione looked displeased. He touched the ends of his moustache. 'Would the apostles stand around the cadaver of a bloated whore?'

The abbot swivelled towards the nave of the church. A few dozen people had come over the river to Trastevere to see Santa Maria della Scala's newest artwork. It was only a day since it had been hung. The abbot thought it a most impressive depiction, but Maestro Baglione didn't agree. Recognizing the noted painter, the onlookers edged closer to hear his opinion. The abbot thought Baglione was vain and pompous, even compared to other artists into whose company he was occasionally thrown by his duty to maintain the frescos and statues in his church. But Baglione had received commissions from the Vatican. If he condemned a painting, it might cause trouble with the monastery's patrons and endanger all the good work of his monks.

'I'm not an expert on art, Maestro Baglione.' The abbot hesitated. He couldn't simply reject the work. That might offend the Cardinal-Nephew. Scipione had engineered the commission for Caravaggio.

The artist arched his brow. 'Go on.'

'Your theological points are worthily made, too.' The abbot bit at the corner of his lip.

'Indeed.' Baglione advanced to within a few feet of the canvas. He gestured towards the dark spaces around the Virgin. 'See how Caravaggio cloaks all his mistakes in shadow?'

'Mistakes?'

'There are many, here in the details.' Baglione rose on his toes, as if he had just uncovered one more flaw in the painting. 'The model, by the way, is a girl from the Evil Garden who is his –' Baglione lowered his voice, but his hiss was loud enough to draw a shocked breath from the eavesdroppers behind the abbot '– his whore, a fallen woman to whom he is unmarried, though she recently carried his child.'

The abbot dropped down the single step beside the altar as if he had been shoved.

'One of our great theologians wrote that prostitution serves the good of the public as do sewers, did he not, dear Father Abbot? It's a conduit for wicked impulses which would otherwise pollute respectable women.'

'Yes, yes, I know the passage from Aquinas.'

Baglione acknowledged the crowd that had gathered now beneath the painting, solemnly inviting them to join him in righteous indignation. 'I never thought to find that one of our holy churches would be the cesspool into which such a sewer might deposit its filth.'

The abbot scratched his thin arms. He had brought a harlot into his church. He had befouled the house of God.

Something struck at his shoulder and clasped it. He moaned. Was divine vengeance already come down upon him? Quaking, he turned towards the altar and retribution. But it was Baglione, pinching him with his gloved hand.

The abbot stammered, 'Help me, Maestro Baglione.'

■

Del Monte scented himself with ambergris from the stomach of a sperm whale to counter the anticipated reek of the tavern on Caravaggio. He regretted what he had to tell him. He had seen the sorrowing soul of his old protégé in every inch of *The Death of the Virgin*. That Holy Mother would never rise to glory beside Her Son; she was dead, and those around her grieved like people without faith. *When will he be here?* the cardinal wondered. *How many inns can there be for my footmen to search?* He dabbed a few extra spots of the scent along his lace collar and inhaled.

Caravaggio entered the study and weaved across the floor. It was evident that it cost him some effort to stay upright. His knee-length pantaloons were dusted with the lime innkeepers spread in their privies. Olive oil and gravy smeared his doublet. His whole body pulsated with tiny, seemingly uncontrollable motions. Yet his jaw was clamped so tight that del Monte thought he might hear the man's teeth creaking like the boards of a ship in a storm. He caught a whiff of sweat as Caravaggio bent to kiss his ring. He inclined his nose to the ambergris on his collar.

'I'm sorry to tell you that the Shoeless Fathers have rejected your painting, Maestro Caravaggio,' he said.

Caravaggio grimaced and swayed. 'Fine.' He slurred even this briefest of utterances.

'Maestro Baglione . . .'

A mumbled curse.

'Maestro Baglione has been heard to say that you cover up your mistakes with shadows.'

A snort of contempt, his fist tight around the hilt of his sword. *He used to have a servant to carry that for him, like a gentleman*, del Monte thought. *Now he wears it, as if at any moment he means to use it.*

'Cardinal Scipione has requested that I find a buyer for the rejected painting.'

'Yeah?' The artist's lips barely moved.

I wonder he doesn't belch at me. 'I've some hopes of the Flemish fellow Rubens, who's acting as agent for the Duke of Mantua in certain purchases. He's an admirer of yours.'

To that, only a shrug and a queasy gulp, as if Caravaggio strove not to vomit in the cardinal's study. Del Monte pursed his lips. *At least he still has that much respect for me.*

'Michele, you understand the seriousness of what has happened?'

'You mean the pregnant whore thing?'

'Exactly.'

'She's not a whore. She's not pregnant either. Not any more.'

'The Carmelites – encouraged by certain artists – suggest that it would've been more appropriate to depict the Virgin carried heavenward by angels.'

'When I see people flying, it's usually because I've been too long in the tavern.' Caravaggio stretched out his arms, flapped them and let them fall. His smile was forlorn.

'For heaven's sake, even Maestro Carracci painted the Virgin's death as a joyful moment.'

'I expect he regrets it. Anyway, Annibale's good, but he's not me.'

He has withdrawn from me before, del Monte thought, *but never like this.* Caravaggio was shut away behind this roughhouse façade, as if he were locked up with a courtesan for the weekend. Everything he painted aroused controversy – criticism of his work couldn't be the only cause of this conduct. *It must be that girl.* 'The art in our churches is not for our amusement. It's supposed to be inspiring. If you don't paint the Virgin ascending mystically into the sky, the worshippers at the church may fail to believe that it happened.'

'The body doesn't ascend. Haven't you heard about such a thing as a soul? That's what goes to heaven.' Caravaggio closed his eyes, looking inward. He opened them suddenly, seeming to panic, scanning the room as if he feared his spirit had stolen away while he spoke. 'What's left is a bag of bones.'

Del Monte considered that Caravaggio may have deliberately

presented himself in this condition, almost like a corpse, the living example of what he wanted people to see in *The Death of the Virgin*. A body, abused and wasting, meaning nothing, and a soul that made of itself the purest art.

'I have, indeed, heard of the soul,' the cardinal said. 'I very much fear for yours.'

At the Colonna palace, Caravaggio crossed the secret garden on a path of stone chips. The early sun evaporated the night's damp in wisps of vapour from the mossy side of the pines. A grove of mandarin trees made the air fragrant and spotted the stark light with bright winter fruit. His mouth dry from the last night's wine, he craved their sweetness. But in the palace some servant would be spying. He didn't want to embarrass the Marchesa by picking the prince's produce. Her man must be well behaved. *Here, at least*, he thought.

Costanza Colonna rose from a granite table set among the mandarins. She wore a dark scarf bound across her head, arranged a fraction above her hairline so that a few delicate curls might protrude onto her brow. In front of her belly she held a flea fur, the pelt of a pine marten intended to lure vermin from her body.

She lifted her chin clear of the ruff at her neck and beckoned to Caravaggio. He kissed her hand, found it cold and, with a grin, rubbed her knuckles with his thumb to warm them. 'My lady, what news of Don Fabrizio?'

Her face floated insubstantially in the flat light. *Like the Virgin the Shoeless Fathers would've preferred me to paint.*

'I grieve as if my son were dead already, Michele,' she whispered.

'My lady, I pray you don't. I've spoken of Fabrizio to His Illustriousness, the Cardinal-Nephew.'

'Does the Cardinal-Nephew give you hope?'

'It's complicated. The fight between the Colonnas and the Farneses . . . You know.'

'He's waiting to see who wins?'

Caravaggio touched the hilt of his sword. The sweetness of the mandarins on the air made him bilious now. He wanted a drink to settle his stomach.

'I must trust that the Colonna will win, for my son's sake,' Costanza said. 'But who'll win the battle over your new work, Michele, now that the Carmelites have decided it isn't their kind of Virgin?' She wrung her hands, her features taut and troubled.

'Is it *your* kind of Virgin, my lady?'

Beneath its attempt at blitheness, his voice revealed a grim longing. Costanza frowned. He tried to reassure her with a smile, but he could only simper, his mouth bitter and crooked.

It was she who had set him on the path to art, when she observed him watching the painters fresco her hall in Caravaggio. He knew that she had recognized some light in his face that was illuminated only then. He remembered the sensation of the brush in his hand as the master of the fresco had given him a chance to lay in some burnt umber and Indian red, for the boot of a saint. The wooden brush handle had felt so natural in the crook of his thumb and index finger that it had seemed he had been cut from the same tree.

Costanza had come forward with Fabrizio and her eldest son Muzio, and the fresco master had pretended only then to notice her.

'Your son is a natural painter,' the master had said.

'He's not her son, you fool,' Muzio had snapped.

The brush had shaken in Michele's hand. The master, who had hoped to gain the lady's favour by indulging her child, had glared at him, as though he had told a lie.

'But he's a natural artist, nonetheless,' Costanza had said.

'It looks just like a real boot, Michele.' Fabrizio had crouched beside him. 'It's wonderful.'

Costanza had decided that he ought to be apprenticed to a painter in Milan. Michele had been seven years in Costanza's house and he was fourteen years old. He couldn't deny that the career of an artist was an attractive prospect or that she had been generous in paying Maestro Peterzano in Milan to oversee him. But throughout his training, he had wished to be home with her and Fabrizio. He had thought he might return as the steward of her household when he grew up. Yet that would have been to take the formal role of a servant, to confirm him in the lower status with which Muzio taunted him. There had seemed no way home – or, as he now saw it, no home at all. In Milan, he had wondered if Costanza had sent him away to be rid of a boy she no longer wanted in her house. He speculated that behind her warmth there was an inborn contempt for the low-bred, for the boy who had corrupted her darling Fabrizio. When he had drunk too much wine, Michele felt confirmed in this belief. That was when he became helpless before his anger and he brawled and fought in the Milanese taverns. Costanza had sent him to Rome to escape the trouble he had caused in Milan, but that had felt like another expulsion and he had become yet more volatile.

Painting made him feel whole, filled with joy and touched by something sacred. But his status as an artist was lowly, on a par with uneducated craftsmen. Whenever his self-control lapsed, the face of the man before him would transform into the disapproving glower of the fresco master for whom his artistic talent was less important than his low breeding, and then Caravaggio would have to smash the features that reminded him of the home he had lost.

Costanza fretted at her flea fur. 'Your portrait of the Holy Father was well received?'

131

'I remain in the favour of the Cardinal-Nephew. That outweighs one dissatisfied customer.' He touched her hand. She barely noticed. He would have told her about Lena and the baby, but he didn't wish to add to her worries. His voice shook with fear and guilt at what he kept unsaid. 'I'm still Scipione's painter. My influence over him will be greater as time passes. Be assured Fabrizio shall be in his thoughts.'

She watched him, her mouth slightly open. He sensed that she knew what he felt. She always noticed the smallest details of his feelings – as if his soul was the dew evaporating from the moss of a tree.

Costanza covered her face and whispered a prayer. When she was done, she took Caravaggio's hand. She led him to the edge of the garden and paused to admire a grotto, a collage of classical sculptures all dug out of the ancient Baths of Diocletian. 'When I was here last with Fabrizio, he liked this one best.' She prodded at the heavy folds of flesh gathering above the hips of a legless Poseidon.

'Fabrizio never knew much about art. This statue looks like the whole torso is slipping down over the groin.'

She was pleased at his familiarity. 'It's the heroic style.'

'No one ever had a body like that. At least, no one who wasn't also fat here, here and here.' He slapped the muscular stomach, chest and arms of the sculpture. 'Michelangelo exaggerated this sort of thing. Now other artists base their figures on the mistakes he made.'

'But he was a great artist, nonetheless.'

Caravaggio groaned. 'The old fool used male models for his female figures. I use women to create women.'

'Why not copy what Michelangelo did?'

Caravaggio met her eyes. She felt them grasping at her. 'I want to know what women look like, not what I wish they looked like.'

They entered the palace and went up to the winter apartments arm in arm. The ceilings were frescoed with scenes of the Battle of Lepanto. Costanza's father strode over captive Turks. She stopped beside a long red carpet captured from the Turkish commander's cabin on his flagship. It was patterned with wide, seven-pointed leaves, meandering vines and delicate buds. Caravaggio stooped to lay his hand on the carpet. He seemed lost in his own memories.

'Just when my father was claiming this carpet as the spoils of his victory in battle,' Costanza said, 'you were born, Michele. It seemed to me as if you were a gift to commemorate the honour of my family. You still are.'

Caravaggio's head was bowed. His hand spread over the sharp patterns of the carpet. He was silent.

She gestured down the gallery of rooms. 'My father received this palace in return for that victory. But I'd rather be the woman who received you into her household than have a gift of the greatest mansion in Rome.'

He looked up at her, his eyes glassy.

'If you watch us closely enough, it's love that is to be found in a woman, Michele.' She clasped his face and kissed his forehead. 'I'm glad to know that you're looking.'

As Caravaggio went out into the Piazza of the Sainted Apostles, the Colonna water-carriers were coming from the Tiber with the palace's supply for the night. Their jugs slopped cold riverwater down the flanks of their donkeys and onto the men's legs. The last one passed with his teeth chattering so loudly that Caravaggio thought at first it was the donkey's feet on the cobbles. He wore a patch over one eye. Caravaggio recognized the wrestler he had seen gouged by the Farnese groom in front of the palace. The man shambled beside his donkey, hunched and miserable. Losing that bout had robbed him of more than his sight.

The honour that was so vital to men seemed so destructive to Caravaggio. *It's love that is to be found in a woman.* Costanza's words made it suddenly clear that Lena needed him. Still he hesitated, unsure if he ought to go to her as darkness fell. They had barely spoken since she had lost the baby. All the dangers she faced – the enmity of the Tomassonis, the hazards of birth – originated with him, and so he had withdrawn to protect her. He had turned to Onorio and the taverns, when he ought to have supported her. Wouldn't it seem to her now that he had come for nothing more than a tumble in her bed?

His confidence faltered and he went to the Tavern of the Turk. He sat alone in its darkest corner. Alcohol rolled through him like a nauseating tide, sweeping his thoughts away from Lena towards all his resentments. What had del Monte said? *Baglione has been heard to remark that you cover up your mistakes with shadow.* That fool. Shadows revealed things at their clearest. A man's face in the daylight was full of detail. One might spend hours reading what it had to say to you and understand nothing. In the darkness of the tavern, you detected no more than a malevolent glimmer of an eye, or the sudden vicious baring of a tooth. The shadows distilled a man to his basic wickedness – or to the sufferings most worthy of our compassion.

Candles flickered across the faces of the inn's patrons. Some hunched over their food, dejected and tired. Others swilled wine into mouths wide with manic mirth. Sores shadowed their skin and their suppurating eyes glinted. *Baglione doesn't know what he's talking about*, Caravaggio thought. Mistakes could no more be hidden in the darkness than in the fullness of day. Men were sweating, coughing, bellowing receptacles for filth and disease, but they bore within them something eternal. An artist didn't cleanse a body of its earthly imperfections in order to show what lay beneath: he saw directly to the soul within.

Then Lena returned to him. She floated forwards into the light of the candle on his table, and then receded as though she were a corpse carried on the eddies of the tide around the piers in the Tiber. Her voice sighed like the water rippling against the banks.

'Why didn't you show her some compassion, you bastard?' he shouted, slapping his chest.

A ripple of wary silence spread outwards from him through the inn. He had painted Lena dead, because he didn't know how to live with her. *If she were dead, I'd be tragic, and I might mourn my impossible love. Instead, I must face my failure at being with a living woman.* He addressed himself again, but in a whisper this time. 'What do you know of compassion?' He went to the door. 'Can't you show some to her?'

He stumbled up the Via del Babuino. 'Lena, Lena,' he murmured. He had drunk more than he thought. He cursed himself for failing to go straight to her from the Colonna Palace. Promenading gentlemen seemed to laugh at his expense, and the carriages veered towards the side of the road to run him down. *I'll make it right, amore.*

As he approached the corner of Lena's street, the crowd thinned. He noticed an extravagant hat moving towards him beyond a group of Spanish sailors. The man in the hat paused beside a lantern. It was Baglione, and he spotted Caravaggio just then. The peacock feathers in his hatband fluttered as he looked about for an escape.

Caravaggio advanced, picking up a stone the size of an orange in each hand. A sudden pounding in his head and neck overcame him, as if he were a soldier drummed into battle. His first pitch caught the brim of Baglione's hat and the stone rattled over the steps of the Greek church. Baglione ducked into the Via dei Greci. The throw released some tension and Caravaggio hurried to the corner with a smile of quickening hatred. 'Come back here, Baglione, you turd.'

The next stone only skittered past Baglione's feet. *He's fast*, Caravaggio thought, *or I'm slowed down by booze*. He took up another rock and juggled it.

Lena watched him from her doorway, pale and fretful, a bucket of kitchen slops in her hands. She shook her head and tipped the bucket into the gutter.

At the far end of the narrow street, a few torches illuminated the ludicrous hat. Baglione was gesturing towards Caravaggio, frantic, retreating even as he urged the police patrol to arrest his rival. Caravaggio dropped the rock and kicked it away with the side of his foot.

'Lena, I want to make things right.' His voice was slurred.

The woman put her hand to her brow. From the room behind her, Domenico called her name. 'Go to sleep, little one,' she said. 'It's late.'

'Is that Michele outside in the street?' the boy said.

'I told you to go to sleep.'

'I heard him talking.'

'No, it's not him. It's someone else.' She whispered to Caravaggio, 'What do you think you're doing?'

'I came to tell you I've been wrong.'

Her head tilted towards her shoulder. The street was dark. He couldn't read her face, but he heard a wounded scorn in her voice. 'So you threw stones at some man? To show me how wrong you've been?'

'Not just some man. That's Baglione. He's—'

'You couldn't give me your attention when I was sick and you've failed again now.'

'That's not how it is.'

Her voice softened. 'I'm not ready for this, Michele, just not ready.'

He glanced towards the patrol. The constables closed in on him. 'Go inside, Lena.'

'Michele—'

'I'm sorry. Anyway, don't get involved in this.'

'May I see your permit for that sword you carry, Signore?' The corporal at the head of the patrol threw back his long black cloak and put his hands to his hips.

Lena closed the door, softly.

Caravaggio recognized the corporal. He had picked him up many times before. 'Ah, it's you, Malanno.'

'Signor Merisi, good evening. No surprise to find myself confronted with your charming face.'

Insolent bastard. Caravaggio reached inside his doublet and handed over a folded sheet of paper. 'You'll see that I'm entitled to carry the sword, as a member of the household of Cardinal del Monte.'

Malanno called forward a constable with a torch to give him light to read. He sucked at his teeth, disappointed. 'It's in order.' As he folded the paper, he glanced at Lena's door. 'May we accompany you on your way, Signor Merisi?'

'I'm not going anywhere.'

'You must be going somewhere.'

'All right, I'm going towards the Colonna Palace.'

He peered at the corporal. The torch over his shoulder shadowed Malanno's features. He held out the permit. 'Here you are.'

Caravaggio reached for the paper. The policeman withdrew his hand, teasing, so that Caravaggio snatched at the air. He grabbed the paper and smelled the corporal's dinner on his breath. Malanno grinned at his patrolmen. Before he slipped the pass into his doublet, Caravaggio ran it in front of his lips and muttered, 'Shove it up your ass.'

'What was that?'

Caravaggio clicked his tongue. *Nothing*.

The constable touched his hat. 'Good evening to you, then, Signore.'

He watched them go. The light was out behind the shutters of Lena's home. She didn't want to hear from him. He had missed the chance to make things right with her. His jaw pulsed with tension. He murmured again, 'You and everyone with you can shove it up your ass.'

This time the constables heard him clearly. The patrol halted. Malanno leered in the torchlight.

■

Scipione Borghese scribbled a note at the bottom of the letter and shoved it aside. His secretary shook sand from a silver box to dry the ink. The cardinal felt a few grains on his fingers and twitched them in irritation. He flicked the letter so that it fluttered to the floor. The secretary dropped on one knee to catch it.

His manservant draped a fur over the Cardinal-Nephew's shoulders. Scipione took another paper from his desk and read it, pacing towards the fire. He sat in a chair of curved wood. Without looking up, he gestured towards the grate. The manservant pumped at an iron bellows to feed the flames.

'Bring him in,' Scipione said.

The door opened at the far end of the room. He watched the fire and listened to the footsteps advancing across the expanse of his study. He held out his hand. Caravaggio knelt to kiss it.

Scipione dropped the paper on his chair when he arose. He regarded Caravaggio as if he were an ancient relic dug from the soil of the Forum. The artist looked worn. His clothing was dirty and in need of repair. *No*, Scipione thought, *it ought to be replaced entirely. He looks disappointed and hungry. Is that straw poking out of his hair behind the crown? If he were an antiquity, I doubt that I'd add him to my collection.* He warmed his back against the fire.

'I appreciate that at least on this occasion you didn't pick a fight with a member of the Tomassoni clan,' Scipione said. 'You have my dispensation to make rude comments to the night watch whenever you so wish.'

Caravaggio hesitated, then bowed. 'I humbly thank Your Illustrious Lordship.'

Scipione held still. Something about the painter's voice didn't sound humble at all. It was resentful, even superior. He stroked his beard and took a deep breath of the jasmine oil freed by his fingers. 'People tell me you're a killer. Or if you're not yet, you will be soon enough. They say you bugger boys, too.' He pushed down the ends of his lips and raised his chin as if to acknowledge that he viewed murder and sodomy with equanimity. 'They tell me one can find the proof in your art.'

'All paintings are full of death and naked boys,' Caravaggio said. 'It's just that no one ever noticed it before *I* painted dead men and young nudes.'

'It seems not everyone wishes to be made to look.'

'I'll do *The Death of the Virgin* over again, if Your Illustriousness wishes it.'

'I do not.'

'The Shoeless Fathers—'

'Shall remain tasteless, as well as shoeless.' Scipione inclined his head towards the paper on the chair. 'Unlike them, I'm a man of discernment.'

Caravaggio picked up the sheet and read it. He dropped to his knee before Scipione and kissed his hand, with fervour this time.

The cardinal plucked the straw from Caravaggio's hair and rolled it between his fingers. 'The Confraternity of St Anne of the Grooms will be pleased to purchase a painting from you, as you see.'

'For their church near the Vatican?'

Scipione liked to shock. *If only my position allowed me to use this power for surprises more often*, he thought. *For pleasant surprises.* He pursed his lips and made his moustache twitch. 'For the Holy Father's own basilica.'

'For St Peter's?'

Scipione watched the ambition and exultation gleam out of Caravaggio's eyes. St Peter's was the most important location for a commission. An artist might measure himself against the great masters whose work was displayed there. *To the glory of God?* Scipione mused. *Well, why not?*

'I believe the Confraternity will want some sort of repetition of Maestro Leonardo's painting of the Virgin and Child with St Anne. Needless to say, I shan't expect you to do any such thing.'

'I'm most humbly grateful to Your Illustriousness, most humbly.'

That's better, Scipione thought. *That sounds more like it.*

◼

The boy Domenico rolled a leather ball across the floor of packed earth. Caravaggio bounced it back, but his attention was not on the game. He watched Lena, uncertain, gauging her face in the half-light of her mother's home.

'I was scared when I saw you throwing stones in the street, Michele,' she said.

Resentment touched him like a cold breath. He had no way out but to beg her forgiveness for a fight in which he had been the insulted party. The ball dropped in his lap. He squeezed it. 'I'm sorry,' he muttered. The boy reached out, lifted the ball by a loose thread, and swung it towards his chin with a laugh.

'You scare me when you're angry. You shake like an old man.' Lena bit at her knuckle.

'It's a matter of honour, Lena.'

She was crying. He reached for her shoulder, a hesitant touch, but she allowed his hand to remain.

'What'd you have me do? Be a spineless peasant? I'm a gentleman. *Better* than a gentleman, because I have skills beyond the use of my sword. Yet the nobility talks down to me as if I were paid to spread whitewash by the yard. I *must* be taken seriously.'

'By men?'

'What's life without a little danger?' He tried a laugh, but it was halting and sour.

'Isn't it a dangerous enough world in which we live?'

'Dangerous, yes. But disease and accidents are like the food we eat every day. Danger that's actively sought has the savour of a dish of rare delicacy.'

Lena's hazel eyes probed him. He was sure she had heard the hollowness of his words. He felt as though he had been quoting Onorio.

'What brings honour to men always involves the suffering of others. Eventually you'll suffer for it, too. I fear for you, Michele.' Lena drew her hands down her face as though she were wiping away the dirt of the day. 'There was a shooting star last night. Its tail pointed towards the Holy Father's fortress as it fell. Everyone says it's a sign that evil times are coming.' Her eyes were full of regret. Their frankness disconcerted Caravaggio. Fillide and Menica wouldn't have allowed their heartbreak to be so visible. Lena didn't conceal hers.

It occurred to him that he was more like Lena than he had known, because he lacked the faculty of his friends in the Evil Garden to disguise what they knew. It was all there in his paintings. The deaths witnessed in street brawls and the pitiful fear in the eyes of his self-portraits. He raised his head. His mouth opened in surprise.

'What is it, Michele?' Lena said.

A curious, slow smile. Lena was dangerous, because she didn't carry her shame like the bandages on a leper's sores, concealing but not curing. Menica and Fillide or gentle dead Anna would have comprehended the honour which compelled him to attack Baglione. They might even have admired him for it. Lena saw it only as something that came between them.

'I want to paint you again,' he said.

She sniffed and wiped her nose on her wrist.

'Lena, I painted *The Death of the Virgin* that way because I felt it deeply, when you lost the baby.'

She shook her head. A woman bore her scars buried beneath the skin – not as the livid mark of a blade, but like the soft fontanelle of a child's skull before the bone bonds. An unseen vulnerability that could only be detected with gentle exploration.

'I saw you when you were almost dead,' he said. 'I felt responsible for the way those Tomassoni women attacked you. By loving me, you came close to death. People tell me I'm a troublemaker who'll end up killing someone. When I saw you, I wanted to keep all the dangers of my life away from you. Ranuccio hates me. He'll try any way he can to hurt me.'

'There're so many ways to die, Michele. Can't we expect to be loved first?'

He dropped to his knees, held her waist, and put his head in her lap. He breathed as though he had just come from under the surface of water.

Domenico laid his head beside him, smiling, and put his thin arm across his back.

5

he Madonna with the Serpent

He painted them as a family. Lena as his Madonna, her skirts hitched up for work around the house, leaning forward to support Domenico, her bare foot on the head of a serpent, demonstrating how to kill it. The naked boy represented Christ, and the viper crushed under his weight was the image of evil. Caravaggio set Lena's mother beside them as St Anne, the Saviour's approving grandmother, pausing in her housework to watch the destruction of wickedness.

When he had painted Lena as the dead Virgin, Caravaggio had done with her as he wished. *As if she were a whore*, he thought. *Perhaps I behaved towards every woman I've known that way.* The love between them seemed pure, cleansed now. She did things to please him, unbidden.

He had never been so happy. Something had been freed in him. He ascribed this to the liveliness the Antognettis brought to his studio and his love for them. The way Lena tickled the boy when Caravaggio wasn't watching, the boy's fascination with the painter's mirrors, the old woman's pride in the talent of her daughter's man. He could see his own contentment in the paint too, feel it in his brush. On the canvas, every fold in the women's skirts seemed entirely true to him. He wanted to step into the painting. He knew the Madonna would welcome him. In spite of all the wrong he had done in his life, she would draw his head to her breast, just as Lena did every night.

He seldom stopped working or even left the house. He was glad that he didn't. Onorio informed him of the tension in the streets, the crowds gathering outside the palaces to brawl or throw stones. The conflict continued between the Farnese and the Colonna, the Pope prevaricating between the two sides. Each morning dogs chewed on the corpses in the open sewers.

'I stand at the edge of these battles,' Onorio said, one day when he had come with news of another street fight.

'That doesn't sound like you.' Caravaggio glanced down from his stepladder, where he was texturing the ceiling above his Madonna, a rough green like oxidized copper.

'Once in a while, someone just asks to have his head split open and I oblige. But mostly I don't bother with it all. It's no fun without you.' The shame that racked Caravaggio after his rages was alien to Onorio. He accepted his own furies. They were in the nature of things and confirmed that life was neither more nor less immoral than him. He was in tune with the imperfect world. Those who believed in a better existence or who restrained what flowed through them were, he believed, the same blockheads who would sacrifice themselves for a lost cause. He tossed back a mouthful of wine and swirled what was left in the bottom of his cup. 'Ranuccio's always there, when the trouble starts.'

Caravaggio put his brush between his teeth and worked at the paint with his fingers. 'Is he?'

'He asked me about you.'

'Give him my regards.'

'I shall insult him with grace and tell him it's from you.'

Caravaggio bowed. 'You're too kind.'

'He hasn't forgotten the ten *scudi* you owe him.' Onorio refilled his wine. 'Or the duel you had at the Farnese palace.'

Caravaggio came down from the ladder. *I haven't forgotten either*, he thought. *But the memory makes me quake with all that I have to lose now.* He nodded towards his canvas. 'What do you think?'

He had done Lena's hair with a touch of red in it that he hadn't noticed when he painted her for the *Madonna of Loreto*. It made her look less Greek, gentler. Her face was wide and delicate, tapering to the small chin he loved to hold between his thumb and forefinger. The skin around her eyes was grey with the exhaustion of hard labour. Her jaw was tinted to a shade of charcoal too. Though she never complained about her health, he wondered how strong she was.

'A commission for St Peter's, the centre of Christendom.' Onorio paced before the canvas. 'Appropriate really, because you've been behaving like a monk since you had that run-in with Baglione and the night patrol.'

Caravaggio shrugged.

'But at the same time you've been preparing to drop your pants to the entire Church.' Onorio pointed to the Madonna's fingernails. They were ridged black with dirt. 'Your work is amazing. Truly, I can smell the stinking little hovel where these peasants live. But how do you think the cardinals will like that? With their perfumed beards and their clean linen every week?'

'I expect it to elevate them.'

Onorio laughed and shook his head. 'Come and have some fun. There's boar-baiting outside the Colonna Palace.'

'Also very elevating. But no, thanks.'

Shoving back the shutters, Caravaggio watched Onorio descend the narrow street to the Piazza of the Sainted Apostles. Beyond the end of the alley, a crowd was building. Its murmur of excitement caught him and he almost cried out for his friend to wait. In the piazza four men climbed into the ring, their heads and torsos armoured. A massive boar scuttled through a trapdoor and sized them up. One of the men dodged towards it in his bare feet and clubbed it on the side of the head. The crowd bellowed as the boar charged.

Caravaggio bound his arms across his chest. He was alone with his work, while the men below in the crowd were joined in camaraderie. He had been apart from others just like this ever since things had gone wrong with Fabrizio. He thought of the moment when Costanza's husband had heard the accusation of sodomy against Fabrizio and the young Merisi boy. He had demanded that Fabrizio deny the lust and sin in which he had engaged with Michele. But Fabrizio had been silent. Michele had seen that this would be too much for the furious man and that his friend was about to be disowned. He had been without a father and he wouldn't allow Fabrizio to share that fate, so he had spoken up. 'I made Fabrizio do it,' he had said. The Marchese had beaten Fabrizio for succumbing, but Michele had known that it was a cleansing punishment. Soon enough, the Marchese would act as if Fabrizio were unstained – and Michele would be gone.

In the piazza, the boar upended one of the armoured attackers. The others beat the beast into the corner of the ring, while the fallen man scrambled to his feet.

■

After his *Madonna with the Serpent* had hung two days in the Pope's basilica, Caravaggio received a message from Cardinal del Monte that it may be removed. He hurried across the Tiber and elbowed through the Easter pilgrims in St Peter's Piazza. Threading between the piles of building materials laid by for its final construction, he entered the greatest church in Rome.

He crossed the nave to the altar of St Anne. A sombre group of men surrounded his painting. He recognized them as the members of the Fabbrica, the committee charged with overseeing works commissioned for St Peter's – rich men and prelates, some of them his patrons and admirers. They greeted him with embarrassment, as though he were a troublesome relative arriving drunk for a funeral.

Del Monte intercepted him. Someone was addressing the others. Caravaggio went onto his toes to see who it was. 'What the fuck is Baglione doing here?' he said.

The cardinal put a scented finger to Caravaggio's mouth.

'He's talking down my work again, isn't he?'

'Michele . . .'

The men averted their eyes. *They know my work and they've told me they love it*, he thought. *What're they doing here with Baglione?*

His rival went up a step to the altar, so that he was directly in front of the painting. At the height of his head, Lena's foot crushed the snake.

'Gentlemen, what are we to make of this ugly Madonna?' Baglione saw Caravaggio and flinched.

Del Monte laid a hand on Caravaggio's sleeve, holding tight.

'She's not ugly.' Caravaggio's voice echoed through the basilica. 'Hers is the most beautiful face in all art.'

Baglione drummed on the canvas with his knuckles. 'She's a dirty little peasant woman. Her features are fine for a whore from the Evil Garden, but they lack the dignity of the Madonna.'

'Even Christ wouldn't be worthy of a mother as perfect as her,' Caravaggio shouted. 'Whoever wants to see a Virgin more beautiful must go to heaven.'

Del Monte put his hand to his forehead. He blew out a long, resigned breath and turned his sad, grey eyes on Caravaggio. The men of the Fabbrica murmured in indignation. *What're they going to do with my painting?* Caravaggio turned about him, pleading and apologetic and outraged.

'You're here to destroy painting.' Baglione declaimed like a man who had learned his lines well. 'You rob art of all its dignity and you drag it through the filth of Rome's lowest quarters. Look at St Anne, the mother of the Virgin. You portray her as an old crone, a repulsive slattern – in our holiest church. It is an insult to the tomb of St Peter, to the skull of St Andrew, and to all the other sacred relics.'

'Call yourself an artist?' Caravaggio yelled. 'You're not fit to grind my pigments.'

'And Our Lord himself, naked. Naked. What a disgusting sewer your imagination is, Merisi, that it should conjure such a disrespectful image of Our Saviour.'

Warm perfumes wafted from the rich men's clothing. From his own body, Caravaggio detected a miasma of sweat and dirt and rage. What had he brought into their church anyway? Was it the love he believed he had painted? Or had he truly perpetrated the outrage of which Baglione accused him? There was no tranquillity in his head, no way for him to think through what he had created. His brain spun and desperation pulsed through all his limbs. The silence of the wealthy connoisseurs shocked him. Couldn't they see what he had intended?

'This painting isn't from my imagination,' he said. 'Only from my eyes. I saw this woman walking with her nephew's feet resting on her own feet. A game, you see? They were laughing. They were full of love. Don't you think the Virgin loved her son?'

Del Monte spoke in a reassuring tone, measured for the benefit of the men around him. 'This composition, Maestro Caravaggio, implies a physical element to the Virgin's love.'

'Between mother and son.'

'Of course, but this isn't just a mother and son. This is the Virgin and Our Lord.'

'It's the same thing.'

Cardinal Ascanio Colonna, the head of the Fabbrica, lifted a hand for quiet. *My Marchesa's brother*, Caravaggio thought. *He'll back me. I'm a Colonna man.*

'As a senior member of the Sacred Office of the Inquisition,' Ascanio said, 'I'm charged with the maintenance of the Index of Prohibited Books, the list of immoral works whose theological errors corrupt the faithful. Works subject to destruction wherever they're found. You may count yourself lucky, Maestro Caravaggio, that the Holy Father never commissioned such an index of paintings.'

Caravaggio reached out, as if to hold del Monte's hand, but he withdrew his arm and tensed it against his thigh. *I'm alone.* He looked up at his painting. *Lena, just watch Lena. She won't forsake you the way these men have done.*

Baglione sauntered past Caravaggio. He tried to look grave, but the ragged triangle of beard beneath his bottom lip twitched with triumph. The patrons watched Baglione with impatience. *They're unimpressed with him. But I went too far*, Caravaggio thought. *I made it impossible for them to defend me and I gave my enemy the chance to disgrace me.* He had been so busy reacting to meaningless slights against his honour in the inns and on the tennis courts that he had forgotten to guard the only thing that really mattered: his art. He turned to his Madonna. Lena's face was patient and compassionate.

Cardinal Ascanio moved towards the door. Baglione and most of the Fabbrica went with him. Del Monte remained.

Caravaggio spread his arms wide over his canvas and laid his hands on the skirts of the Madonna and St Anne, as though clutching at their legs for support.

The door of the church slammed shut.

'It's my fault. I admit that I saw this coming a long time ago,' del Monte said. 'I should've warned you.'

Caravaggio pushed the heels of his hand hard against his eyes. 'What do you mean?'

'Your private commissions for me are one thing. You're granted all the freedom I may give your genius.' Del Monte raised his arms as though in supplication. 'But your public commissions have become more and more daring. Since *St Matthew*, you've needled the artists of the old style, like Baglione, until they've come to hate you. You threaten everything they've ever worked for.'

'I don't care about them.'

'But you need other artists on your side. Cardinal Ascanio knows nothing about art – any more than he understands the works he consigns to his Index of Prohibited Books. He takes his lead from well-known artists and collectors. I've spoken up for you, but all the major artists in Rome are against you.'

'Not all. Most of them steal my style – even Baglione.'

'Wouldn't they like their more talented rival removed from the scene? They won't defend you. They produce work that has elements of your style, but without the provocative ideas.' He came close to Caravaggio. 'Our friend Signor Giustiniani keeps your *Love Victorious* behind a curtain in the last room of his gallery. When he unveils it, his guests are shocked, delighted – even titillated. Do you think that's what the Fabbrica wants people to feel here as the Holy Father says mass before them? This Madonna is too forceful for the Church. You must show more respect.'

'For what? For art as Baglione sees it?'

'I'm sorry to tell you, but yes. For art.'

'Art is a whore who's being treated like a boring, old housewife,' Caravaggio said. 'Her husband always does it to her the same way. It's time someone threw her against a wall and gave her —'

Del Monte shouted, 'Michele, remember where you are.'

'— the hard fucking she deserves.'

Del Monte looked up at the Madonna. 'Of course, you're the one to do this.'

'Yes, I'm the one,' Caravaggio said. 'I've had some experience of whores.'

Del Monte stroked his moustache. His anger had been momentary. Now he was solicitous. 'If Art is such a lady, do you think this treatment will be pleasing to her?'

'That's the point. I don't care what this strumpet called Art likes or dislikes. I'm ready to pay for it, so I'll take my pleasure as I wish. Even if she goes around telling people I have no delicacy or finesse. A whore treated like a lady is unbearable.'

Del Monte blew out a low whistle. 'Believe it or not, your strange soul holds the key to other people's spirits. The followers of the heretic Luther want people to hear God speaking directly to them. The Roman Church believes people ought to experience God only in its basilicas. There, they must witness Him in your paintings. Your soul must experience God, so you can show Him to us.'

'I thought my soul was important so that I could complete commissions for Cardinal Scipione.'

'That just keeps you out of jail. Perhaps one day it'll save your head from being separated from your shoulders.' The cardinal examined the Madonna. 'She's magnificent, Michele. You've mistaken the boundaries of art within the Church. But you've done something perfect, nonetheless. Unfortunately, that isn't the point.'

'What *is* the point? Do they want me to change it?'

The cardinal gazed at the Madonna and her naked child. 'The Fabbrica has already decided. The painting is to be removed. Not fit for St Peter's. I'm to find a buyer for it.'

Caravaggio dropped to the step below his canvas. He put his

hands in his hair, squeezing his temples with frustration.

'In the meantime,' del Monte said, 'this art of yours will be out on the street. Like the other whores.'

■

The rejection of another of his paintings sent Caravaggio back to the Evil Garden and the fierce, depraved life that skulked there by night – the Tavern of the Moor, the Tavern of the Wolf, the Taverns of the Tower and of the Turk, the brothels around the crumbling Mausoleum of Augustus. Onorio glowed with a gleeful spite, exhilarated to have his friend back. Caravaggio, bitter and raucous and unrestrained, complained about the Fabbrica and the cardinals and the Pope, until even Onorio put a hand over his mouth for fear of the Inquisition.

Damn Baglione, he thought. *And del Monte, who was supposed to shelter me. And Cardinal-Nephew Scipione, what kind of a protector is he? And Costanza . . . No, she isn't asking too much. But let the rest of them be damned.*

Every night his jaw hurt from the tension shivering through it. He was constantly flushed and fuming with alcohol. Del Monte and Scipione seemed to flit before his eyes going from table to table at the inn, tossing money to Baglione who skipped across the canvas of *The Madonna of the Serpent*, dancing a villanelle with Lena.

Whenever Caravaggio stopped by the little house on the Via dei Greci, he found Lena impatient with his stumbling arrivals late at night, his rants about the Fabbrica, his drunken attempts to take her. He would awake on the bedboard at the back of the room, his hungover brain clawing to escape his skull, Domenico giggling and tickling his feet. Lena would stare at him, sour and frustrated, from the kitchen table and he would drop back on the bolster and wonder how much further he had pushed her away that night.

At the end of May, the Vatican put on a gala for the first anniversary of Pope Paul's coronation. In the afternoon, a boat race on the Tiber ended at the bank with a brawl between the crews. An oarsman took a swing at someone and was stabbed to death. By evening the streets were filled with people who had been celebrating the whole day. They were drunk and petulant. Every laugh sounded unhinged, on the edge of a snarl.

Caravaggio and Onorio left the Tavern of the Tower and crossed the Evil Garden to the tennis courts. In the street beside the Palace of Florence, a game was underway. A cord strung across the street marked the centre of the court. A dozen yards either side of it, a chalk line on the cobbles set the back of the playing area. The walls of the street were lined with spectators, wagering on the outcome. The game concluded as Caravaggio and Onorio arrived.

'It's our friend Signor Ranuccio,' Onorio said. 'Looks like he just won.'

Ranuccio picked up the ball, a leather casing around packed wool with a lead pellet at its heart. He smacked it high in the air with his long-handled racquet and lifted his arms. The crowd mingled, making good on the bets. Some of those who had wagered against Ranuccio pelted the loser with dung from the street.

Ranuccio glanced over the heads of the gamblers. 'Painter, what about double or quits on that ten *scudi* you still owe me?' His smile was open and joyful, which made Caravaggio hate him more.

Caravaggio handed his cloak to Onorio. He had suffered all the insults he could take from powerful men before whom he must suppress his anger. He didn't have to endure Ranuccio's goading. He cared nothing for the ten *scudi*. He only wanted to finish Ranuccio, to push his face into the dirt and fill his mouth with it until he choked, as if he were stifling all the snobs of the

Fabbrica and Baglione too. 'Give me a racquet.'

Ranuccio signalled his serve as required. It was one of the game's few rules that he should call out, 'Eh.'

Caravaggio returned the serve. His shot glanced off the wall of the palace. Ranuccio chased it down, but Caravaggio backhanded the ball straight down the centre of the court. A few in the crowd cheered. Most bayed their derision at Ranuccio.

He doesn't know yet, Caravaggio thought. *He thinks we're just playing tennis. He'll understand the stakes soon enough.*

After only a few points, Ranuccio was sweating hard and breathless. 'You should've had a rest before you played another game,' Onorio called to him. 'Or you should've challenged Michele to a game of cards, so you could do it sitting down.'

Ranuccio flicked his fingers off his chin.

'You waste all your energy tupping your whores.' Onorio played to the crowd. 'You've less facility at sports that're played standing up.'

Ranuccio's elder brother, Giovan Francesco, jostled Onorio. They exchanged threats under their breath.

Ranuccio served. He went for Caravaggio's return. His shot was intended to bounce off the palace wall, but it caught a window ledge. It came back towards him and the point went to Caravaggio.

The painter felt a stillness within. Excitement came before a contest, and fear in the fraction of a second when defeat was inevitable. The time between was filled with the instinctive, absolute focus of the hunt. His eyes on Ranuccio were dead.

With the next point, Caravaggio sent his ball wide and deep, almost to the chalk line. At full speed, Ranuccio stretched for it, missed, and went head first into the wall, to the amusement of the crowd. His brother dragged him from the ground. Ranuccio stared at Caravaggio, his feet apart, his racquet held with the force of a weapon.

Now he knows what we're playing for, Caravaggio thought. 'My serve.'

Ranuccio lashed the ball back to him.

The game was tight, the rallies short, each man striking with such force that his opponent could barely keep the ball alive once the initiative was lost. They were quickly to the deciding point. Ranuccio had Caravaggio on the defensive. He advanced towards the cord and volleyed deep. Caravaggio flicked the ball wide. It ricocheted off the head of an onlooker. The deflection wrong-footed Ranuccio and the ball rolled to a halt behind him.

Ranuccio picked up the ball and made to serve. Caravaggio came to the cord. 'It's my game, Tomassoni.'

Ranuccio grumbled under his breath and set himself for the serve.

'Hey, *coglione*, you lost,' Caravaggio said.

'It came off that fool's head.' Ranuccio wiped at the sweat on his bruised brow. 'It doesn't count.'

'What're you talking about? Spectators are in play.'

'No, they're not.'

'Where do you think you're playing? In the court of the French king? It's a street game. You know the rules.'

'The game's not over.' Ranuccio came towards Caravaggio. 'It didn't *bounce* off that man. He stuck out his head and nodded the ball past me. He did it deliberately. That's not in the rules.'

Tremors of unstoppable fury shuddered through Caravaggio, the aftershocks of the agitation he had been forced to repress in the presence of his wealthy patrons. 'You lie through your throat.'

At the side of the street, the onlookers argued over the call. The man whose head had been struck by the ball claimed innocence, but those who had bet on Ranuccio converged on him.

'We're not finished yet,' Ranuccio shouted.

'Shut up. It's over. You can say farewell to that ten *scudi* now.'

Caravaggio poked Ranuccio on the shoulder with the end of his racquet.

Ranuccio swatted it away. 'You dirty faggot.'

'Once you've done kissing your money goodbye, you can kiss me here.' Caravaggio turned and slapped his backside.

A swordsman's turn of the wrist and Ranuccio had struck him on the shoulderblade with the frame of his racquet. Caravaggio spun and swiped at Ranuccio's chest. They clubbed each other with their racquets, until Onorio and Ranuccio's brother came between them.

Caravaggio jabbed his finger at Ranuccio. 'I'm going home for my sword, you prick.' He threw his racquet like a spear.

'You know where to find me. I'll cut you up.'

Caravaggio rushed away to collect his weapon. His breath came in shuddering snorts. *It's now*, he thought. *It has to be now. Let him die, and I'll be free.*

At the corner, the man who had blocked Caravaggio's shot slumped against the palace wall. He was bleeding from his nose and staring with puzzlement at the blood on his palm, as though it were a text in a secret language.

Once they had their swords, they rushed past a game of *pallone* on the way to the Tomassoni house. A player drove his wooden armguard into the nose of a youth on the opposing team who had made the mistake of watching the ball loop through the air. 'Did you see that?' Onorio laughed. He spotted Caravaggio's naked, stern concentration. 'No, of course you didn't.'

Mario Minniti caught up with them on the way. 'A duel, I heard. Let's hope his seconds join in. Then Onorio and I can make it a general brawl. Michele, try a few feints, a disengage and a cut-over. Then take a long step in with your left leg and shaft him in the groin with your dagger.'

'You're obsessed with the groin, aren't you, Sicilian.' Onorio clapped his hand to Mario's shoulder. They laughed like boys on their way to see a game, excited and carefree.

Caravaggio ceased to hear anything. The evening darkness deepened. He glided down the streets, the shadows cradling him. Ranuccio wouldn't be able to spot his outline. He would rush into the light and kill his man.

At the doorway of the Tomassoni house, his breath surged in his body, all his force ready for this. He would kill his man. *Kill him.*

'Come out, if you've got the balls,' Onorio yelled. He picked up a stone and threw it at a first-floor window. The moment it connected with the shutters, heavy feet sounded from inside.

Caravaggio drew his sword, a gilded hilt from Ferrara, a Toledo blade, the bevel glistening down its length like an icy vein. He sighted along it as Ranuccio came out of the courtyard flanked by his brother and another soldier. With his left hand, he drew out a dagger as long as his forearm.

The seconds threw some insults, but Caravaggio heard only his breath and the blood in his head. His mouth was dry. He flexed his grip around the sword handle. Thumb and index finger met above the crosspiece to control the blade, protected by the sweeping guard of the quillon block. He shifted the dagger in his other hand so that his thumb lay along the spine of the blade, bracing it, the flat of the knife facing him, not the edge.

Ranuccio advanced. The two men extended their sword arms, right feet forward, the tips of their rapiers high and *en garde*. Ranuccio's pupils were long slits across his cobalt irises, like a goat's eyes. Caravaggio wondered if he were fighting some kind of evil beast, then he realized his opponent was mad with such fear and exhilaration that it distorted him.

He had practised the sword so often with Onorio and watched so many duels at the French tennis courts, his movements were instinctive, but he made himself check his position. He had to be sure not to forget his technique in the rush to kill. He set his feet apart the width of his torso, twisting his hips to keep both shoulders facing Ranuccio, his right arm leading, his left arm ready with the dagger. He engaged the muscles of his belly, to stay light on his feet.

As they circled, Caravaggio watched his opponent's body. He might parry the rapier easily enough if he saw the signs from Ranuccio's arm and torso before the attack advanced. It was the hardest thing to learn when he had first held a sword, not to be mesmerized by the killing tip as it dangled half an arm's length from his face. *Watch the arm*, he whispered to himself. *Watch this big bastard's bulky torso. It'll be as if he were shouting, 'Now I'm about to try and hit you this way.'*

Ranuccio lifted his chest a fraction. Caravaggio parried before the man extended his arm fully into his thrust. Again Ranuccio tried, perplexed and furious at Caravaggio's sharp defence. The heavy sword glanced aside with a delicate, almost feathery contact, as Caravaggio turned his wrist upwards and nudged the oncoming blade beyond his shoulder.

Caravaggio thrust, the tip of his blade making for the eyes. Ranuccio slapped it away with a hasty jerk to the left. He jumped backwards and crouched low. *The fool ought to have parried with a roll of the wrist*, Caravaggio thought. *It would've kept his point on me. He might even have counter-attacked. Either he's nervous or he's not much good.*

He tried to recall their first fight at the Farnese Palace. He couldn't remember the way Ranuccio had moved, but he knew he had beaten him. He cleared that fight from his mind. He was here and this time it was to the death. *God help me.* He whispered an *Ave*.

With a shuffle and a short spring, Ranuccio made another high thrust. Caravaggio let it come onto his blade. He took his left foot across behind his right, pulling his body out of the path of the thrust. With an upturn of his wrist, the point of his rapier rose above Ranuccio's sword. In the same movement, he went forward a quarter step with his right foot and felt his tip catch in Ranuccio's upper arm.

He backed away. Ranuccio went onto one knee and fingered the wound. Pain replaced the rage in his face.

Giovan Francesco was only a few yards from his brother, but still he yelled to him: 'Ranuccio, remember all I taught you.'

The older Tomassonis were soldiers, Caravaggio thought. *They fought for the faith and for the Farnese in Flanders and Hungary. Ranuccio's problem is that he's never had a chance to prove his manhood. All his bravado is bullshit.*

'Not much of a teacher, are you, Giovan Francesco?' Onorio laughed. 'This dickhead couldn't spear a whore with her skirts over her head. Good thrust, Michele. Keep the big idiot moving. He won't touch you.'

Ranuccio snarled, came up from the ground and forward in one motion.

'Dirt,' Onorio shouted.

From Ranuccio's dagger hand came a spray of dung and mud he had grabbed off the street. Caravaggio blinked hard and rubbed his face with his sleeve.

Ranuccio laid into him with a heavy slash. It took Caravaggio's rapier almost out of his grip, hammering it to his left. *Thank God it wasn't a thrust, or I'd be skewered now.*

His eyes still clouded, he went by instinct to his right. *Get behind your sword.* He put up his guard and felt Ranuccio slash once more. Through the grit, he could just about see. Not the blade, but the arm and the set of the body. *Here he comes again.* Another step to his right and this time Caravaggio followed his parry with a thrust that connected.

Ranuccio cursed. A cut to the head, above his ear.

'Lucky for you he couldn't see where you were, Ranuccio, or that would've been the end for you,' Mario bellowed. 'You cheating bastard.'

Caravaggio retreated a few steps and squinted hard through the remaining dirt around his eyes. A dozen bystanders had gathered, hanging back from the duellers and their seconds. They were quiet. Even in Rome, where blood was sport, they knew they were about to see a man die, and it silenced them.

His sword arm high, Caravaggio closed on Ranuccio. He pretended to hesitate, made his eyes freeze with fear. He wanted Ranuccio to sense an opportunity. Ranuccio fell for it. He bared his teeth and slashed. Caravaggio relaxed his wrist and let Ranuccio knock his blade low. The force of his own blow left Ranuccio off balance, leaning to Caravaggio's right.

Then Caravaggio made his move. A step forward with his left foot. He swung his rapier in a high arc onto Ranuccio's head. It glanced off the crown as the man dropped to the ground.

'A fine move, Michele,' Onorio said.

Ranuccio lay on his back, pushed himself up on his elbows, and spat at Caravaggio's boots.

'This is your shaming for the insult you gave me.' Caravaggio spoke loudly, so that the onlookers in the shadows of the Via della Scrofa would know that he had fought for his honour.

He took one step back. Ranuccio's features relaxed. Caravaggio saw that the ugly defiance of a moment before had been the expectation of death and that Ranuccio now believed he would be allowed to live.

As he put his hand to his wounded head Ranuccio barely moved his lips to speak, but Caravaggio heard him. 'I'll make your whore Lena screw every john in the Evil Garden.'

Caravaggio's ribs tightened. A single lunge, and his blade sank into Ranuccio, even as the man scuttled away from his thrust. He pierced him in the groin.

Ranuccio doubled up and rolled. Caravaggio felt the muscle and skin slicing on his sword, as though his hand dug inside the living flesh.

With a sudden outcry, Ranuccio's brother jumped forward. He unsheathed his sword and came at Caravaggio. Now it was no duel. It was a battle, and Giovan Francesco had been a hero in the field. Caravaggio thrust at his attacker, but Giovan Francesco gave him the simplest, most effective response. A parry and riposte in one motion, high, from inside the line of Caravaggio's sword. Caravaggio heard the scraping of the two blades, a million tiny contacts, the pitch rising as Giovan Francesco's sword slid along his own. Then the tip had him below the ear. He twitched his head away and his scalp turned cold.

Onorio shouldered Giovan Francesco off-balance and retreated with Caravaggio at his back. Mario was beside him, his sword en garde.

Ranuccio sat on the ground, doubled over. He opened his eyes, the lids coming apart slowly, weeping and red. He held his groin. Blood darkened his hands and soaked his turquoise pantaloons. His face was full of shame, like a man embarrassed by incontinence.

Onorio kicked a rotten cabbage from the gutter. The muck of the street sprayed across the wounded fighter's face. 'May you rest in peace.'

'I'm not dead,' Ranuccio said.

'You will be soon, *cazzo*.' Onorio parried another thrust from Giovan Francesco.

Ranuccio spoke through white lips. His face was earnest, as if he were a parent explaining something simple yet vital to a small child. 'I don't want to die.'

Caravaggio opened his mouth, but he wasn't sure if he wished to console Ranuccio or to apologize. Death had been a point of honour for them. Now it was something else, the seeping of blood into the street, puddling between the cobbles and soaking into the vegetables dropped by traders on their way to market.

Mario and Onorio fought off the Tomassoni swordsmen as they went down the street. Caravaggio jogged on unsteady legs to the corner. The last thing he heard as he turned into the dark side-street was the scream of agony as the Tomassoni gatekeepers raised Ranuccio.

■

He rode with his hand tight on the guide rope of his pack mule. The beast stepped easily under his few belongings and his painting materials. He pulled his hat down low to hide the bandage on his scalp and threw his cape so that it covered his chin. He went south past the cow pastures in the old Imperial Forum towards the San Giovanni Gate. The guards lounged in the shade. Pasted to the brown brick of the Aurelian walls was a wanted notice. It named Michelangelo of Caravaggio as a bandit for the murder of Ranuccio. Anywhere in the papal lands, a man presenting Caravaggio's severed head to the authorities might claim a reward. To signal the shame of his sentence and to persuade anyone who knew him that he was beyond aid, the poster depicted him upside down, hung by his feet.

The face shown in ignominy on the notice was a simplified version of one he had painted himself: his self-portrait as a bystander to the martyrdom of St Matthew, glancing over his shoulder with pity, fleeing the scene of the holy man's killing. *The police employ art lovers to do their wanted signs*, he thought, with bitterness.

The horses' hooves echoed under the gate, and then he was out in the fields. Rome was behind him, and Lena as well. He hadn't asked her to join him in his flight. He had imperilled his immortal soul, perhaps already damned it. Contentment would be forever denied him. He didn't wish that she, too, should be endangered, shrouded by the malign shadows of his capricious spirit. *I can't take Lena with me, knowing that soon I'll invite another expulsion,* he thought. *And don't forget the Tomassonis in pursuit, after my blood. Too dangerous to involve her.*

He left Lena without explanation. He feared that if he had told her where he was going, she might have volunteered to accompany him to hell.

II
MALTA
A Name In Blood
1607

6

Portrait of the Grand Master

At the prow of the galley, Caravaggio squinted into the glare of the sun off the swells. His lungs filled as if he was drawing clear air from beyond the far horizon. Only now did he understand how fear had constricted him in the crowded streets of Naples, where he had spent the last year. Everywhere had been the untrustworthy shadows, the assassins stalking him. The backstreets of the Sanità proved that Baglione was wrong – darkness didn't cover up your mistakes; it laid bare your vulnerability.

The open sea brought a sense of safety. Here there were no suspicious echoing footfalls, no soldiers rushing down from the new Spanish Quarter with bottles and daggers. He wasn't even concerned that those who waved them off from the quay had called out, 'God save you from the galleys of the Arab corsairs,' or that he had been ordered to carry his sword until they docked in Malta in case of attack. The pirates enslaved those they captured, but Caravaggio hadn't been free since he had killed Ranuccio.

Under his feet, two decks of slaves laboured at their benches. The splash of the oars was a soft tenor over the regular bass of their breathing. The loathsome odour of their defecations emanated from the hatches. The sea darkened emerald to olive. He cursed. He might as well have been tethered like the wretches below decks.

He looked along the length of the ship. Bigger than the galleys of Genoa and Spain and Venice, one hundred and eight oars and two massive sails, a shallow draught for raiding the inlets where the pirates had their lairs. *The Capitana*, flagship of the new Admiral of the Knights of St John of Malta: Fabrizio Sforza Colonna.

Costanza's son emerged from under the scarlet awning across the poop deck at the stern of the ship. He laid a brotherly arm over the shoulder of one of his red-surcoated knights and called out an order to the helmsman. His teeth gleamed like the waves in the sun. His skin was regaining its colour after his time in jail. Relaxed and confident like a host with his guests in his own hall, he passed among the sailors.

A few soldiers gamed with dice on the deck. Fabrizio threw down a coin and bent to read his numbers. He swore with good humour and enjoyed the laughter of his marines at their commander's loss.

He came to Caravaggio's side at the prow and lifted his leg to balance against the bulk of the figurehead. 'I feel as I used to when you and I would run out into the mulberry fields, just the two of us. No one to tell us what to do.'

'Freedom was an illusion then, too.'

Fabrizio pursed his lips. Caravaggio regretted his words. His friend had been in a condemned cell almost two years. He might be forgiven for feeling childlike in his sense of liberty.

'Not an illusion for me,' Fabrizio whispered.

Caravaggio heard the recollection of fragile memories in the new Admiral's voice. 'You're right that we escaped everyone back then – for a while at least.' The dry hills of Calabria striped the horizon a few miles distant. He squinted into the glare off the waves.

'We shall escape again, in Malta. Just as we did back then.'

Caravaggio's features sharpened. *Does he think I'll be in his bed again so easily?* 'I'm coming to Malta because I gave my word to your mother.'

'Then you are bound.'

'I am bound.'

The soldiers bellowed at the fall of the dice. One of them tumbled onto his backside, shoved by the angry loser. Fabrizio called out and the fight was defused. The game went on in sullen silence.

'Don't blame my mother, Michele. It's an opportunity for you. The Grand Master of the Knights agreed to take me on, in return for your presence on Malta. Your art will bring prestige to the new city he's building. I'm pardoned for killing the Farnese boy, and you'll get some good commissions. What else could Mama do?'

Caravaggio remembered the relief on Costanza's face as she explained the deal. She had called him to her chambers in the palace of her cousin the Prince of Stigliano, where he had lodged during his year in Naples. She had seemed younger by a decade, and Fabrizio was the cause. He remembered then how she used to glow when she came across the two boys in the gardens of her estates. *I had always hoped I was the source of the joy*, he thought. *Foolish of me. Fabrizio is her blood.* He glanced at the handsome, welcoming features of the man at his side. *I still wish it. But I'm like a pilgrim who competes with the Son of God for the Virgin's love.*

'You had commissions in Naples, of course. *Our Lady of Mercy* at the Pio Monte is a masterpiece,' Fabrizio said. 'But you were too much in danger there. The Tomassonis can't get you in Malta.'

Our Lady of Mercy. Another Madonna with Lena's features.

This time drained and grey-skinned, pouring out the compassion Caravaggio craved. 'Yes, Malta is so remote, it might as well be the Indies.'

Fabrizio's skin was smooth and fresh. He wore his confidence like the embroidered cape on his shoulder, loose and dashing. He pushed his hair, straw and gold, back from his brow and sucked at his lip. His hesitant eyes sought to meet Caravaggio's gaze. 'Do you think of him, Michele?'

'The man I killed?'

Fabrizio nodded, and his hair fell in a swoop over one eyebrow.

'He's more implacable than his vengeful brothers,' Caravaggio said. 'He pursues me everywhere. No doubt to Malta as well.'

'It seems sometimes a greater death to have survived my duel than to have been the loser,' Fabrizio said. 'Do you ever feel as though all your freedom and happiness expired with him?'

'I was cut off from freedom and happiness the day I left your mother's house,' Caravaggio said. 'There've been some times over the years when I sensed it again, but mostly I felt like a heavy man on boggy ground.'

Since that jab into Ranuccio's groin, every day and with every stroke of his brush Caravaggio had measured his soul's jeopardy. He reached for Fabrizio's shoulder. 'When freedom is open to you, you know only restriction. You end up taking a man's life, perhaps just to see if even that greatest of the Lord's commandments is yours to transgress with impunity. You and I are bound to the most sacred things by what we have done.'

Fabrizio snorted a sad laugh. 'A test from God?'

'No.' Caravaggio's voice was wondering. 'A gift.'

Fabrizio gripped Caravaggio's wrist and squeezed it.

Caravaggio flicked his eyes along the boat to signal the care they must take when together.

Fabrizio removed his hand. 'Scipione wants you to stay on Malta only so long as it takes to get the Tomassonis to agree to your pardon. The family still demands revenge for Ranuccio's life.' He craned his neck to check on the four ships in line behind them. 'On Malta, you'll be safe from the Tomassonis. But watch out for the knights, Michele. They're pledged to live as monks, except when they go forth to kill the infidel Turks. Some find themselves more given to killing than to praying.'

'What does that have to do with me?'

'These knights are all noblemen. A German knight needs to show four generations of nobility on each side of his family to enter the Order. A Frenchman must be free of the blood of a commoner in all four grandparents, and the Spanish and Portuguese knights have to demonstrate that they're untainted by Jewish heritage.'

'And you?'

'We Italian knights must be noble in all four lines for two hundred years.'

In the hold below, the lash cracked over the slaves at their oars.

'So they're not really monks,' Caravaggio said. 'They're princes.'

'Princes, and pirates preying on Turkish shipping. When they get back into port, their entertainment is whoring and the taverns. The senior knights exert slight control. Back in the Evil Garden, Michele, you could hit people on the head and Cardinal del Monte would get you out of jail. If you pick a fight with one of these knights, I warn you it'll be as though you declared war on the finest families of all Europe. The Pope himself thinks twice before he writes a rude note to a knight. Play the humble artisan. Stay clear of them.'

Fabrizio's voice was like the drone of a mosquito, so distant that it seemed almost to be a figment of Caravaggio's imagination, until, with a sudden crescendo, it was there on his skin and gone by the time he could slap at it. *The humble artisan.*

'What do you think I've been doing this last year in Naples?' he snapped.

Fabrizio wagged his finger. 'I told you not to argue with a prince.'

Two sailors came up through the hatch from the rowing deck. They carried the limp body of a slave. His skin was patchy and peeling with malnourishment. Excrement fouled his loincloth, and his thighs and hands were livid with sores from the bench and the oar. His tongue thrust from his cracked lips as though it might find sustenance on the air.

The whip had reopened old scars on the slave's shoulders. They bled feeble scarlet tracks down his sweaty back, as if his body barely had enough energy with which to die.

The slave groaned as the sailors jerked him onto the starboard rail. His neck rolled. The sailors dropped their burden over the side, timing the release so that the body didn't impede the stroke of the oars below. They gave a little cheer to celebrate a clean fall. The air cleared as though the man had been a bucket of night soil dumped into the water.

■

The façade of the Grand Master's Palace in Valletta was simple and stern. It extended along the square where the ridge dropped down to the hospital, the Knights' original vocation five hundred years before in Jerusalem. Beyond the gate, Caravaggio passed through a courtyard lush with palms and orange trees. A ramp rose to the Grand Master's chambers, so that knights might climb in their heavy armour with less effort than stairs would demand of them. The corridor to the Sacred Council chamber was paved in grey and russet marble. He awaited his audience.

The door swung open. The meeting of the Sacred Council was over. Out came the senior knights of the nationalities around which the Order was organized – of France, Auvergne and Provence, Aragon and Castille, Italy, and Germany – and a secretary to represent the few old English knights who had remained when their King Henry turned against the Roman Church. Their expressions were guarded, intense and subtle.

Caravaggio entered the Council chamber. Across the room, a fresco portrayed the arrival of the knights on Malta and the building of Valletta. A tall, gaunt man in the red habit of the knights examined him. His eyes were bloodshot and pale orange like shelled clams floating in a ragout. He squinted at Caravaggio and his red eyes were like two wounds on his face. Through such a filter, Caravaggio thought, a man would see nothing but blood. The knight had his hand on the hilt of the dagger in his belt. His beard was ragged and sparse, like pond scum on the disturbed surface of a pool.

'Brother Roero, you may leave us.'

An older man spoke from an enclosed wooden balcony framed by the fresco on the far wall. The younger knight passed close to Caravaggio, his nostrils quivering, as if he sniffed for some scent that would give Caravaggio away. He shut the door behind him.

Caravaggio took a step across the room towards the old man who wore the black doublet denoting the most senior knights. He was rugged and lined in the face, his white hair and beard clipped short. He fretted a rosary. Caravaggio made to kneel before him, but his melancholy eyes flicked along the Council room, signalling that it wasn't he who Caravaggio sought.

The Grand Master of the Order sat on his dais at the far end of the chamber. Alof de Wignacourt wore the vestments of his office, a doublet of woven gold and a cape embroidered with Our Lady of Liesse. His mouth was tight and his brow blotchy, as though some pressure pulsed beneath it. His index finger ticked at a large wart on the side of his nose and he watched Caravaggio's approach as if he were at the battlements reading the tactics in an enemy's formation.

'Your Serene Highness.' Caravaggio knelt on the step of the dais. 'Michelangelo Merisi begs to be of service to you.'

Wignacourt extended his hand. When Caravaggio brought down his lips, it was like kissing a glove of chainmail.

'Won't make any problems for me, will you, Maestro Caravaggio? Enough trouble with the Sacred Council. Don't give me cause for anger.'

The words of command were spoken in a tone of such loneliness that Caravaggio at first thought he had missed their meaning in Wignacourt's French-accented Italian. He glanced at the other knight, who had come to his side. The old man in black winked.

'Your Serene Highness shall witness how grateful I am to be given . . .' Caravaggio was about to say refuge, but he didn't want to acknowledge that he was so much at Wignacourt's mercy. 'To admire the feats of engineering carried out by the knights in building their new capital on this rock.'

Wignacourt flicked at his wart. 'Troublesome types, you artists. That fresco there, by Perez d'Aleccio. A bit like your story. Ran away from Rome after some kind of assault a few dozen years ago. Went to Naples, then came here. Can't leave. Isn't safe anywhere else. Vendettas, you understand. Us? Stuck with the decrepit old fool.'

Caravaggio jerked his thumb towards the wall painting. 'His art certainly isn't like mine.'

The other knight smiled.

'There's another artist. What's his name?' the Grand Master said. 'A Florentine, like you, Martelli.'

'He's called Paladini,' the Knight said.

'Paladini, that's it. Condemned to the galleys for a brawl in Tuscany. Ended up here. Twenty years now. Rough lot, you painters.'

'Like you knights.' Caravaggio caught Martelli's smile once more.

Wignacourt stood. Under his vestments, his knee rocked back and forth. His stocky frame was tremulous with tension. 'Always been an atmosphere of riot among the Knights of the Order. Previous Grand Masters tried to rein it in, faced rebellion. Me? Done a better job of it.'

Caravaggio recalled what Fabrizio had told him about the princes and pirates of the Order. *If the Grand Master aims to make these men behave like the monks they're supposed to be, his task is by no means at an end.*

'We'd like to pay tribute to the Grand Master's work,' Martelli said, 'by making a new portrait of him for the palace.'

Wignacourt tried to look grave, but the corners of his mouth flickered with pride. 'I acknowledge Brother Antonio's gesture. Commence with this portrait at our command, Maestro. Then I'll have a further project for you. Wish my knights to have more time for contemplation, fewer distractions.' The Grand Master caught Caravaggio's elbow. Brother Antonio took his other side. He was pinned gently between the two knights.

'His Serene Highness confronted the Turk at the Battle of Lepanto,' Brother Antonio said. 'I fought here in the Great Siege against the Sultan's army. Those desperate times gave us an understanding of life and death – and of the life to come. If we didn't live for God before those battles, we were His entirely after we survived them, by His Grace.'

'The novices of our Order should prepare themselves for the sacrifices of battle and of holy orders,' Wignacourt said. 'How? Contemplation of art, inspiration.'

'You might say that the proximity of death terrified the less worthy lusts and impulses right out of us older knights.' Brother Antonio squeezed Caravaggio's elbow. 'We wish for an equally inspiring terror to be instilled in our new knights – by you.'

Caravaggio said, 'What makes you think I know—?'

Wignacourt shook a dismissive hand. 'Want to read the letters the Marchesa of Caravaggio wrote to me about your fight with Signor Ranuccio? About his death? If the letters weren't enough, Brother Antonio here came through Naples recently. Saw your work there. Liked it.'

'I recognized what you depicted,' Martelli said. 'I saw your suffering and your hope for salvation.'

'Let our young knights see it, too, Maestro.' Wignacourt stroked at the buttons on Caravaggio's doublet and brought his face very close. 'Let them see it, and you shall be made a Knight of our Order.'

Caravaggio flinched in astonishment. The two old men watched him with a knowing pleasure, like merchants certain of an inflated price.

■

Caravaggio brought his materials to the palace for the portrait of Wignacourt. At the centre of the room allocated as his studio, he stared at the armour in which the Grand Master wished to be portrayed. He lifted the visor and imagined his own face looking out at him. He whispered a prayer with the fervour of a warrior before battle. To be dubbed Knight would release him from the threat of capital punishment. It would be a pardon for soul and body. He gripped the shoulders of the armour like an old comrade and regarded it with the firmness of a man entering the deadly fray. He would paint such works on this island that the knights would make him one of their own. He would be free. Saved.

Wignacourt came into the chamber with the gaunt knight named Roero. The gold chain of office around the Grand Master's neck looked heavy enough to moor the galleys in the harbour. 'Maestro Caravaggio, this is a day blessed by Our Lord. This morning I was able to persuade the landlord of another brothel to close.'

Caravaggio attempted to imbue his bow with admiration. He wondered what alley would now serve the whores who had been turfed out of their rooms.

'Our Maestro is an artist.' Roero's voice grated, dry like that of a man waking from sleep. 'Perhaps your news displeases him, Your Serene Highness. Whores would have no employment if it weren't for painters.'

Wignacourt affected to peruse Caravaggio's brushes.

Roero's infected eyes glimmered with suspicion through the glassy redness that shrouded them. *So the Grand Master brings his guard dog to goad me a little*, Caravaggio thought, *to test my temper.* 'You mean that painters use whores as models?'

'I don't mean that at all.'

'Oh, I see. Then I think you'll find a whore's main source of income is not artists, but soldiers like you.'

Roero dropped his voice, gritty and growling. 'Don't compare me to a common soldier, nor to a mere craftsman such as yourself. I am the Count della Vezza. My line is as noble as time.'

Caravaggio bowed low. *When I'm a knight, I won't have to listen to this arrogance any more. I'll be the equal of Costanza's sons – and of this bastard, too.* 'I humbly beg your Lordship's pardon.'

Wignacourt touched his beard. 'Brother Roero refers perhaps to reports from Rome – of your involvement with the ladies of the Evil Garden.'

'It was *against* a pimp that I fought the duel of honour for which I now suffer a price on my head.'

'Attend on me in the antechamber, Brother.' The Grand Master gestured for Roero to leave. With another hard glance at Caravaggio, Roero went into the corridor and shut the door behind him.

Wignacourt picked up a thick hogshead and brushed the bristles against his palm. 'Brother Roero is most solicitous of my safety. He has little respect for those who may not claim noble descent. Don't be perturbed by his zeal.' He opened the door. With his back to Caravaggio, he said, 'But don't be heedless of it, either. Tomorrow, begin the portrait.'

When he was alone, Caravaggio closed all the shutters and lit the lantern.

By late afternoon, the canvas was prepared. Caravaggio rubbed his eyes. They were tired and stinging. He wondered if Roero had passed on his infection just by looking at him. He was about to return to the Inn of the Italian Knights when a messenger entered.

Caravaggio rotated the lantern. The messenger raised his arm to cover his face from the glare of the light. Caravaggio let go of the lamp, his grip loosened by shock. Across the messenger's doublet was a black and white cross, each branch ending in a three-budded trefoil to represent the Holy Trinity: the coat of arms of the Inquisition.

The herald lowered his arm and peered at Caravaggio, as the light swung before him. 'Michelangelo Merisi of Caravaggio? The Roman painter?'

'Who wants him?' he whispered.

'Are you him?'

Caravaggio opened his arms and let them fall.

'Inquisitor Leonetta della Corbara commands your presence tomorrow,' the herald said.

Caravaggio knew better than to ask why. Whether he was witness or accused, he wouldn't know until he stood in the Tribunal Chamber.

The arc of the lantern grew shorter and faster. His heartbeat kept pace. He touched the grain of the blank canvas on his easel. The Grand Master would have to wait another day for his portrait.

◾

That night Caravaggio lay on his pallet, fearful of the Inquisition, staring at the high ceiling of the Inn of the Italian Knights. When eventually he drowsed, he dreamed of Naples. He had been on his way to the Pio Monte della Misericordia to sign the contract for *Our Lady of Mercy* when he had passed two jailers carrying a corpse out of the prison. The dead man's feet dangled, their bloodless soles ridged with filth. The jailers dropped the body on the steps of the law courts next door. They stretched their backs and squinted in the morning sunlight.

Naples was a dangerous place, not somewhere for passers-by to interfere with strangers. But Caravaggio had come out of the dingy mêlée of the street towards the jailers. 'You're leaving him here?'

One of the men frowned. 'Who?'

Caravaggio pointed to the corpse. 'Him.'

'Someone from his parish'll come to bury him.' The jailers moved away. 'Eventually.'

A scruffy brown dog gnawed at the thin calf muscle of the corpse. Caravaggio kicked it. The dog clamped its teeth to the bone and growled, as if Caravaggio were a rival who wished to feed off the dead man. Another kick and a shout, and the animal retreated.

Caravaggio squatted beside the corpse and closed its eyes with the side of his hand. He sensed motion on the man's face. He recoiled. Something touched his fingers. As his breath stilled, he saw the lice crawling in the dead man's beard. With a shudder, he brushed them from his palm.

At the Inn of the Italian Knights, he twisted naked in his

sheet, sweating through the sackcloth of his pallet, dampening the straw within. His dream passed now beyond his memory of the steps of the jail and into the unfathomable fictions of nightmare. The dog ripped at the corpse. Caravaggio chased it away. The lice itched all over him. They crawled across the features of his dead father. He knelt beside the body, waiting for someone to take it for burial. But no one came. His father's eyes opened. Each time Caravaggio shut them their lids lifted once more, as if his father wished to observe him. 'I'm still watching, Papa,' he sobbed.

Then his dream took him to the Church of the Pio Monte. He made a few final touches to *Our Lady of Mercy*, the highlights on the toes of the cadaver which was carried into the picture to represent the Christian duty to bury the dead. With each stroke of the brush, he squirmed, ticklish, as if the feet of the dead man were his own. The jailers came into the church and lifted him. He would have protested, but he could neither move nor speak. They dropped him into a plague pit. A woman stood in silhouette on the lip of the grave. She shovelled lime over him.

He jolted upright in his bed, coughing as if to clear the quicklime from his throat. Still thinking himself in a dream, he stared about his room. It had been Lena at the graveside.

Slowly, he understood where he was. The room was empty. He was sorry to have woken. He would rather have been dead and have her there with him.

■

Outside the Inquisitor's Palace, a Maltese man walked by in a tall hat he wore as a punishment from the Inquisition. The hat was painted with the image of a sinner kneeling before Satan. Egged on by demons, the Devil prepared to skewer his terrified victim with his pitchfork. The man paced slowly up the street to the amusement of those passing, his eyes lowered in shame.

A balcony over the gate bore the arms of the Inquisition, the only adornment to the façade of the palace. A Dominican priest led Caravaggio to the head of the stairs. He pushed open a low door and jerked his head. 'Through here.'

The door was built to enforce humility and to instil fear. Caravaggio had to bend double to enter the Tribunal Chamber. A notary sat at a low desk under a simple canvas of the crucifixion. Beneath two shuttered windows, the Inquisitor slouched on his throne. It was built into the centre of a five-man choir chair with a high oak back and a gold crucifix set above the Inquisitor's head.

Slumped to his right, his body formless in a black cassock, the representative of the Roman Inquisition raised his eyes, a signal for the notary to begin.

'You're Michelangelo Merisi, Roman painter?' The notary dipped his pen in the well. When Caravaggio answered that he was, the notary started his note-taking, translating into Latin as he went along. 'Come forward and face the Inquisitor.'

Inquisitor della Corbara adjusted his black skullcap. In the dim light, his skin was shadowed deep, as though a charcoal stick had shaded around his eyes, beneath his cheekbones, in the cleft of his chin. His lips were tight, round and ribbed, like a sphincter. He shifted as if to stretch his lower back. Then he reclined into his slouch.

'Undoubtedly you're the greatest artist to have reached these humble shores.' He spoke into his hand. He was slovenly and stealthy like a battered street cat. His breath wheezed out of one side of his mouth. 'I wonder why you'd come here?' He gave no opportunity for an answer. 'I have questions I would put to you. But they're not for the record.'

The notary shut his ledger and left the room.

A smirk progressed over the Inquisitor's face, like a cloud blotting the moon. It passed slowly as if some private puzzle were being resolved, a chess player seeing his victory five moves ahead.

Caravaggio had faced judges and even the possibility of torture many times before. Yet he had always done so with a sense of his own cunning and an almost theatrical pleasure in his performance. In front of della Corbara, he was disturbed to find his legs as unsteady as they had been when *The Capitana* rocked on the swells in the Straits of Messina.

The Inquisitor rose to his feet as though lifted by strings like a puppet. He slid his hands into the sleeves of his robe. 'Come with me.'

They went along the hall. Della Corbara's left foot was bent outwards. A broken shin must have been badly set. With each step, the foot landed a beat later than it should have. At the head of the main staircase, the walls were laden with the family arms of the eighteen Inquisitors to have preceded della Corbara in Malta. Beneath these were hung a collection of canvases portraying the deaths of the great Christian martyrs.

'Plenty of ways to kill a man, are there not?' The Inquisitor tipped his head towards the gallery. 'But then you know all about killing.'

'I'm no saint, that's true.'

'Good. Because you've painted enough martyrdoms to know what happens to saints.' Della Corbara turned down his lips. 'Anyway, what's death to us? We're all no further from meeting our demise than a cough or a sneeze or an encounter with a violent stranger. Like the martyrs.' He went along the hall, passing beneath the paintings. 'Here's St Sebastian, shot full of arrows, St Agatha, having her breasts cut off, and now St Lawrence, cooked on a griddle.'

'It's horrible.'

'Lawrence didn't think so. As he died, he joked with his persecutors, to show that he welcomed martyrdom. "Turn me over, I'm done on this side," he said.' The Inquisitor's laugh was a vulgar snigger.

Now that he was out of the Tribunal Chamber, Caravaggio relaxed a little. Perhaps he wasn't being investigated. He looked at the Inquisitor's lean, thieving features and reminded himself to be wary. *This one would prosecute you for your dreams*, he thought, *and God knows mine wouldn't pass the examination of the most kindly of priests.*

'I don't mean that the story is horrible,' he said. 'I'm guided by you in such matters, Father. I mean that these paintings are very poor.'

Della Corbara shrugged his head from side to side. 'They're not to my taste, it's true. I saw your *St Catherine of Alexandria* in Rome at Cardinal del Monte's gallery. It takes the viewer into the thoughts of the saint.'

'I'm gratified, Father.'

'Though that may be a heresy in itself. A saint should be more mysterious.'

Caravaggio forced himself to look away from the mediocre canvases, to concentrate on the man who stood in the shadows beside him. *Just because he used the word heresy in jest doesn't mean he wouldn't laugh at the flames while I burned. Beside him, I can almost feel the heat, as if he were the pyre.*

'It's in the eyes. Am I right?' della Corbara said. 'That's how you do it? Not with extravagant gestures or beatific faces looking heavenward, like this rubbish here. In your paintings, the eyes tell us all we need to know.' He stared into Caravaggio's face. 'When *you* paint a martyrdom, your saints think too much. They ought simply to suffer. The danger, you see, is that worshippers in the churches will start thinking too.'

The priest went into the light at the head of the stairs. 'What *are* they thinking about, though? Your saints, at the moment of their death.' He squinted into the sun. 'In del Monte's gallery I also saw some of your early canvases. The ones of buggered boys. Unlike the saints, who proclaim their martyrdom, your youths seem to cry out for something quite different. I imagine the Lords of the Knights of St John would enjoy such paintings.'

Caravaggio had been pretending to examine the canvases on the wall. His eyes snapped back to the Inquisitor. *Here's the trap.*

The Inquisitor's smile was faint and pitying. 'I hear you'll be asked to paint St John, the patron saint of the Order of Knights.'

'I don't know what you're talking about. I'm to paint the Grand Master.'

Della Corbara rubbed his eyebrows softly. 'The doctrine of the Church applies to images of the saints, not to portraits of blustering old soldiers – which means that such paintings may be judged heretical.'

Caravaggio's throat seized up. In Rome, Baglione had couched his dislike in the language of the art critic. It had led to the rejection of Caravaggio's paintings, but it had never been a threat to his person. Now an Inquisitor was interpreting his art. 'Heretical? Why?'

'As soon as you paint the saint, you'll be in my hands. It'll be easy for me to show that your portrayal violates the guidelines of the Council of Trent. I'll have other questions to ask you – about the habits of the Knights and their leaders. I'll expect those questions to be answered, if I'm not to pursue my misgivings about your art.'

Caravaggio felt a shudder of apprehension for Wignacourt and Martelli. And for himself. *If the Knights think I'm an informant for the Inquisition*, he thought, *it'll be my neck*. Della Corbara nodded, as if he were translating a trail of anguish crossing Caravaggio's face.

'The Holy Office would consider it a great prize to have more . . . control over the knights – to reduce their independence. It's a wealthy Order.' The Inquisitor descended the wide stairs to the first landing.

Caravaggio came behind him, unsteady, leaning on the smooth, carved banister.

'Of course, there may be something in it for you, beyond escaping the fires of heresy. You see, I report to the head of the Holy Office of the Inquisition directly,' della Corbara said. 'To Cardinal-Nephew Scipione.'

Caravaggio felt like a sheep shoved into a wolf's jaws. Was this why Scipione had sent him to Malta? To plant a spy within the Order of Knights?

'We all of us hang midway between the beasts and the angels, Maestro Caravaggio.' The Inquisitor took his hand and led him down the last flight. 'It's my job to lift those who drop too far. If I ask anything of you, it's only so that I may save the souls of those who've done wrong. The poet Dante showed us that God's justice is absolute. It's no use, he wrote, being a good-hearted man who sometimes sins. A sinner is a sinner, forever consigned to the Inferno, no matter what else he does right.'

Caravaggio stumbled. The Inquisitor held his arm. His strength was surprising and he smiled because he saw that the painter noticed it.

'Yet our proximity to the beasts dictates that the Inquisition presumes guilt. I investigate and, if that brings no result, I torture until the accused calls out "The guilt is mine." Then the presumption of guilt is removed.'

'Only by the confession of guilt.'

'Well, no one is innocent.' The priest squeezed his arm as they reached the bottom of the stairs. 'If you're a good Christian, you needn't fear me. Do you want to paint for these hooligans in the

Order the rest of your life?' He came close. His breath rustled Caravaggio's beard. 'You know something bad, I can smell it.'

'That's just linseed oil for thinning my paints.'

'It's the stink of secrets. But the reek doesn't have to cling to you. Purification can be through pain or through fire. But also by simple confession.' The Inquisitor pulled him down the corridor to a narrow doorway. 'The torture room.'

Caravaggio resisted the Inquisitor's grip.

'Don't worry, it's not for you,' della Corbara said. 'Not now.'

A pair of torturers held a manacled African. The notary was at his desk to record the questioning. On a stool in the corner, a doctor waited to repair the man's shoulders after the coming dislocation of the *strappado*.

The African stared at Caravaggio as though he expected rescue. When Caravaggio looked away, the man's chin dropped to his chest.

'I get a lot of Mussulmen like this in here, and Maltese witches. The Jews, of course, have money, so the knights keep them for ransom.' The Inquisitor gestured towards the torturers. 'I pay these Maltese to come and work for me. The doctor gets five *scudi*, too.'

'I'd have thought you could find people who'd torture for nothing. For the pleasure of hearing a man scream.'

'No doubt. But I prefer to know that the only one who relishes the struggles of the prisoner is Our Lord, so that He may soonest bring down the revelation of confession. Everyone else in here merely does his job, does God's work.' He signalled for the African to be lifted.

The torturers gripped the wheel and cranked the hoist. The African screamed to the Virgin as he swung off his feet.

'Who's after this one?' the Inquisitor asked the notary.

The clerk raised his voice to be heard over the African's cries. 'A Maltese whose neighbour says he saw him eat pork during Lent.'

The Inquisitor gestured for a further crank on the *strappado*. The African bawled. 'Good. If the fellow can afford pork, he can afford a little something for us.' Della Corbara twirled his fingers like a cutpurse and winked.

As he rushed away, Caravaggio imagined the exhausted face of Lena the way he had painted her as the Madonna in *Our Lady of Mercy*, looking down with resignation. The African could bellow to her all he wanted, it was Caravaggio she heard.

Wignacourt's eyes were restless, drawn to his blond French page, Nicholas, who posed beside him holding a helmet and a knight's surcoat. He seemed ready to reach out for the boy.

At his easel, Caravaggio watched from behind his curtain. He understood that the Inquisitor wanted him to testify that the knights were pederasts. *That'd give him the power to extract anything from these men – all their influence and wealth. Even to destroy them, as their Templar brothers once were.*

He told himself to concentrate on his work. This nervous wheedling face on the verge of a forbidden seduction wouldn't do for the Grand Master's portrait. *It'd be as if I gave evidence just as the Inquisitor wishes, and the knights would know it too. God help me if I cross them.* 'Your Serene Highness,' he said, coming from behind the curtain. 'Who are you? A Prince of the Holy Roman Empire. A noble of Picardy and France. A battle veteran of the naval confrontation at Lepanto. An administrator, a man of God. A warrior, a commander. Which?'

'All of these. What do you mean?'

'No, these things are *what* you are. I asked *who* you are.'

Wignacourt clapped his hands impatiently. 'Make yourself clear, man.'

'I may show *what* you are by the suit of armour, the baton of office, the knight's surcoat that your page Nicholas holds. But I may show *who* you are only by the expression I paint on your face.' He approached the Grand Master, his gaze locked onto the watery blue eyes. 'You must show me the man who inspires his soldiers. Imagine you stand before the knights in the moment of battle. Who's the man who leads them? What qualities do they see when they look at you? Why do they allow themselves to be led by you?'

Wignacourt raised his head and took a long slow breath. Stern and rough, inspired. Pompous, too.

That deals with the Inquisitor. Caravaggio took the Grand Master's chin between two fingers and turned it to the left. *And that takes care of the wart on his nose. Let's get to work.*

A Maltese kitchen boy from the Inn of the Italian Knights modelled the Grand Master's suit of armour. The boy's younger brother sat in the shadows grinding pigments.

The details of the metal would take more than a week – its glowing highlights, the curve of the breastplate, the overlaying joints. Caravaggio painted a glittering dash of greyish white light onto every tiny link in the chainmail over the groin between the hip plates. He was glad of the opportunity to work in silence, without having to comport himself before the Grand Master. If he made this man happy, he might be redeemed by knighthood. And beyond that, perhaps, he could be reunited with Lena. But until he was a knight he would be unworthy even of painting her. He was ashamed, fearful, lonely, loveless. *As a killer deserves to be.*

He threw down his palette. He waved to the kitchen boys that he was finished for the day. They started unstrapping the armour.

A killer whose every thought was of death, no matter how much he attempted to turn his thoughts to love. He saw Ranuccio, dead at the point of his sword. The stab wounds that killed Prudenza. Anna, expiring of syphilis. Lena, alone. What would have become of them if he had never entered their lives? *I'm like a rotten delicacy*, he thought, *seducing you with sugar on your tongue and then corrupting you from within.*

He stood before his painting of the Grand Master and felt scorn. It was well made, but distant from his own soul. There was only one thing he could paint, no matter who peopled his canvases. *From now on, it must be death*, he thought. *Until death is purged from me – or until it takes me.*

Wignacourt entered, flushed from the hunt. Martelli and Nicholas the page were at his side. Roero waited in the doorway with a hawk on his gloved hand. His sallow skin glimmered with a sickly sweat, like a man with a fever. The Grand Master bent to examine the helmet Caravaggio had painted in the page's hands. 'By God, it looks as if the boy's holding a severed head,' he shouted.

Caravaggio's features were stricken and aggressive.

'Made the lad into a blond Salome, Maestro.' The Grand Master pointed at Nicholas.

'Perhaps, Your Serene Highness, beheading is on our friend Caravaggio's mind,' Martelli said, 'subject as he is to execution in the Papal lands.' He laid a comforting hand on Caravaggio's back. The artist flinched as though stuck with a dagger.

'What d'you think, Nicholas?' Wignacourt said.

The young page glanced at Caravaggio. 'The Maestro has captured your heroism, Sire.'

The Grand Master's jaw firmed, stirred by his own image. He reached out absently to touch the boy's neck. His fingers lingered in his short blond hair. 'And you, Nicholas, see how handsome you are beside me.'

The boy dropped his glance to the floor. Caravaggio felt a

shudder of alarm. In the portrait, Nicholas seemed almost to be painted on a different plane to the Grand Master. Beside the stiffness of Wignacourt's armour, the page's clothing was soft, his lace cuffs delicate, his pantaloons rich as they dropped to his scarlet stockings. He stood out, as if he were the true subject of the work, carrying a message in his knowing glance.

I saw the danger, but I've still drawn too much attention to the boy, Caravaggio thought. *The painting is almost as clear as the evidence the Inquisitor asked me to give. You just* had *to show what you saw, didn't you, Michele.*

Caravaggio searched Roero's face. *I'm scared the guard dog won't like my work.* Roero was as still as the hawk on his wrist.

Wignacourt bounced on his toes with excitement. 'Martelli, what do you make of it?'

The Florentine's examination of the figure of the Grand Master was cursory. He ran his tongue around in his cheek, considering the painting of the page.

'Well?' Wignacourt said. 'He has me?'

Martelli folded his arms over the cross on his surcoat. 'He does, Sire. He has you exactly.'

7

The Beheading of St John the Baptist

On Fridays, as a token of humility, the Grand Master and his senior knights attended to the people they called Our Lords the Sick. Violent Mediterranean sunlight striped the main ward of the hospital through the high windows. Here the best and worst of the knights' pastimes were banned. There was neither gambling nor reading aloud. But for the groans of the dying and the ramblings of the delirious, the long ward was silent.

Martelli led Caravaggio into the hospital. At the head of the aisle, Wignacourt ceremoniously stripped himself of the tokens of his power with the aid of the noble knights gathered around him. He laid aside his chain of office and handed Fabrizio the purse representing the Grand Master's charity, as he took on the role of an ordinary penitent ministering to the patients.

Beside him, Roero rolled a trolley of broth and vermicelli. He filled a silver bowl and, with a grave nod, handed it to Wignacourt. The man whose titles included Guardian of the Poor of Jesus Christ carried the food to a wretch babbling under stained sheets, as every Grand Master had done since the crusading knights founded their first hospital in Jerusalem five centuries before.

Martelli took a dish and stepped towards one of the beds. Caravaggio lifted the patient onto his elbows. Martelli fed the soup through parched lips, his murmurs of compassion barely audible above the desperate slurping of the sick man.

'The Grand Master liked your portrait,' Martelli whispered to Caravaggio. He laid the invalid's head back on his pallet.

'I'm most gratified.'

'He has sent messages to the Pope requesting your pardon.'

Relief shivered in Caravaggio's chest.

'You see,' Martelli said, 'no one's beyond redemption here.'

The patient under Wignacourt's care choked on his soup and his face shaded a bright purple. The doctors from the Jesuit medical school rushed to the Grand Master's aid.

'Almost no one,' Martelli said.

Roero held out a pewter dish of broth. Caravaggio hesitated, then took it. 'That one over there,' Roero said. His bloodshot eyes wept pus.

Caravaggio went towards a young blond man who lay very still. His shoulders were bare, his chest bandaged all around. Martelli glared at Roero and Fabrizio muttered something under his breath, but the knight only dabbed at his eye and filled another bowl.

The man in the bed took in Caravaggio with a blank look. When he saw the pewter dish, he tried to rise and spoke in a guttural tongue Caravaggio didn't recognize. The patient dropped back onto his bolster and broke into a sweat.

'Who is he?' Caravaggio asked.

'A German knight.'

'Then the bowl is of the wrong metal. A knight must have silver.'

'Roero did it deliberately. The pewter is a signal to this poor

192

fellow. That's why you'd like to protest, Brother Jobst, isn't that right?'

The German's gullet worked in desperation. Martelli soaked up the man's sweat with a cloth.

'What happened to him?' Caravaggio asked.

'Wounded in a duel.'

He watched the man struggle. 'His opponent?'

'Was a French knight.'

'Was?'

Martelli cooled the German's forehead with water. 'But is no longer.'

'Then, the punishment—'

'To be tied in a sack and dropped into the sea – and to be shamed. Such matters of honour are more important to a man like Roero than life itself.'

The breath from the German's nose was slow and loud, as if it were squeezed from an empty wineskin.

'It's not for nothing that Roero chose you to serve this man,' Martelli said. 'Though Jobst is a nobleman, his offence strips him of all nobility. He's condemned as if he were a commoner.'

Caravaggio spilled broth on his wrist. He cursed and wiped it on his breeches. 'Roero wishes me to witness what happens to those who don't follow the rules of the Order.'

'Perhaps.' Martelli whispered a prayer over the German knight. 'I think it more likely that he just wanted you to see a man die.'

He closed the German knight's eyes.

Fabrizio paced the small grove of orange trees at the rear of his residence. For his two-year term, the Admiral of the Galleys was accorded this pleasant house down the hill from the Grand

Master's Palace. Five rooms deep and two wide, it was mostly given over to the administration of the fleet. For his private use he kept a tiny chapel dedicated to St Gaetano, where, that morning, he had prayed for a way to protect Caravaggio. He understood the threat to his friend in the cruelty with which Roero watched him when the German knight died.

The scent of the oranges in the heat shrouded the agitation of his spirits as if it were a foul odour. *Even the air I breathe has to be sweetened*, he thought. *Will I never be able to bear reality?* He kicked gently at the base of a murmuring fountain. *No, I know life with a clarity few attain. That's what makes it insufferable.* He had killed a man, run him through in a duel. That murder cemented his kinship with Caravaggio. They had shared so much as boys. Now they had partaken of the most dreadful mystery, the snuffing out of a man's being. But death had created their bond in the first place. The loss of Michele's father had brought them together, when Costanza took the boy into her household. It perturbed Fabrizio to realize that mortality had always been the link between him and his oldest friend. *What will break this chain?* he wondered. *Will it have to be another death?* He pulled an orange from the nearest branch and pressed its rind to his nose.

'It'll rot soon enough.' He tossed the fruit into the corner of the courtyard.

Glancing at the sun, he fretted that even the walk from the Italian Inn to the Admiral's house put Caravaggio in danger. Roero could pick a fight with him any time. He squeezed his fists together. Fabrizio had disappointed his mother in so much; he couldn't now fail to guard the man who had been like a son to her.

To guard him just as Michele had watched out for him. Fabrizio had been about nine that first time, an open guileless child. In the midst of a game with his older brothers, he had failed to see that the competition of hide and seek had transformed into a hunt with a vicious edge. His eldest brother Muzio had cornered him and thrashed him with a cane. The wickedness in his brother's laughter had been a betrayal much sharper than the pain. Michele came to his aid and assaulted Muzio, dragging him away from Fabrizio. Their father whipped Michele for his offence against the hierarchy of the household.

His eyes stung with tears of regret. *That's what you remember of your childhood*, he thought. *The feeling of loneliness in your own family home. And now you're alone again with the knights – alone, except for Michele.*

He straightened up when he heard footsteps inside the house.

Caravaggio came across the flagstones of the courtyard. He kissed Fabrizio's cheek and sat at his side on the stone bench.

'You know my duty to my mother . . .' Fabrizio hesitated. He feared Caravaggio would shut him down, as soon as he mentioned Roero.

'It's no less than my own duty to her.' Caravaggio raised a finger and smiled. 'Ah, you're anxious about this Piedmontese bastard.'

'Roero's a vicious character.'

'Are you worried for me? Or is it only that you want to please your mother, the Marchesa?' Caravaggio lifted his chin. 'I've no reason to fear Roero.'

Fabrizio shook his head. *Honour must be upheld, even between two men who are as brothers.* 'Be careful. You know why he contends with you.'

'Do I?'

'It's your birth, Michele.'

Caravaggio puffed out his cheeks. 'He's not the first nobleman to think me low-born.'

'And look what happened last time.'

Caravaggio stroked his beard. The gesture was meant to indicate his lack of concern, but there was tension in the fingers, as though he was about to rip at the hairs in despair.

'Come and live here,' Fabrizio said. 'You'll be safe and we'll be together as we were in our youth.'

'I'm happy at the Italian Inn,' Caravaggio snapped.

Fabrizio recoiled. *Does he think I want him in my bed?* 'You're at risk there. Here you have my protection.'

'I'll lock my door.'

'But the company you keep —'

'The knights? What's wrong with them?'

'They're killers.'

'Whereas you and I . . .' Caravaggio let his remark hang. Fabrizio clicked his tongue. For a moment, he had forgotten that he had done a man to death. Caravaggio laid his hand on his leg. 'You don't have the space here for me to work. There's another commission coming from the Order.'

This was what Caravaggio couldn't give up, and Fabrizio knew it. His painting would be the payment Wignacourt required for the knighthood, and this honour would free him from a death sentence. But in accepting the knighthood, Caravaggio would make himself a target of the noble knights who wished to preserve the purity of their Order. Fabrizio remembered the taunts of his brothers and the way they had enraged Michele when he was a poor fatherless boy. A man like Roero couldn't know what a profound sadness and rage he awakened in Michele. *Or perhaps everyone knows it, except Michele. He still thinks there's a way out of the trap fate has set for him on Malta.*

Fabrizio clasped his head. 'I'm sorry, Michele.'

'What do you mean?'

Fabrizio was exhausted by the new responsibilities of command, by his concern for his old friend, by the fear that he would let his mother down after she had secured his release from his prison cell. 'I'm alone, Michele.' His voice quivered, fragile and faint, like the light of a single candle in a dark hall.

'Not so. I'm just along the street.' Caravaggio rose and ruffled Fabrizio's hair. 'I have work to do. I'll see you soon, Admiral.'

The forced bonhomie in Caravaggio's words stung Fabrizio. It was as if he had exposed his feelings to a distant uncle, not a man he had loved. He watched him disappear into the darkness of his house. He frowned at the trees. He could no longer smell the oranges.

Wignacourt invited the knights to admire his portrait in the Sacred Council chamber. He wore a steel collar and shoulder armour. His cloak was trimmed with sable and a violet cap set off his sun-beaten face. He beckoned Caravaggio, who came to kneel at his feet and kiss his hand.

'A great adornment to our Order and our island, Maestro,' he announced.

The knights circulated before the portrait. Wignacourt acknowledged their admiration.

The Inquisitor pushed to the front. Staring at the portrait, he gave a knowing chuckle. He edged through the crowd of knights to Caravaggio. 'How do you do it?'

Caravaggio made a puzzled face.

'How do you get such a likeness?' della Corbara said. 'Is it pure genius? Did you wake up one day and discover that your childish sketches had become masterful representations of life?'

Caravaggio examined the Inquisitor's face for a hint of his true meaning. Della Corbara let his features open in a cartoon of innocence. 'I just want to know.'

'Well, I use a mirror to create the image on the canvas. From that, I trace the form of my composition.'

'A mirror?'

The amazement in the Inquisitor's tone drew Caravaggio out. It was rare that anyone bothered to enquire about his techniques. Either they told him he was a genius, or they condemned him for a charlatan. Almost no one asked how he actually worked. 'The mirror projects the subject onto the canvas, though upside down.'

'What kind of mirror? A speculum? A polished stone?'

'You speak of witchcraft, Father della Corbara. I use the mirror for a practical purpose. I don't bury it at a crossroads in the middle of the night with spells and incantations.'

'Nonetheless, I've heard that artists in Rome are experimenting with a camera obscura, a magical device to cast a moving image onto a canvas with the use of mirrors.'

The ugly feeling that he had been tricked into a confession overcame Caravaggio. Would a mirror be enough to indict him as a heretic, so that the Inquisitor might put him to the torture and demand information on the Grand Master's pleasures? *If I were tortured, what else would I confess?* 'Such implements are less magical than you suppose.'

'Certainly it's witchcraft and sorcery to project a moving image.'

'It's perfectly natural – a matter of science.'

The Inquisitor lifted his chin. 'You knew men of science at the home of Cardinal del Monte, didn't you? I remind you that science is the essence of witchcraft, because it seeks to explain the miracles of the Lord through means other than those laid out in the Holy Bible. Do you use a camera obscura?'

Wignacourt led the chief knights out of the hall.

'You're welcome to visit my studio. You'll find no strange devices.'

The Inquisitor held Caravaggio's arm as they followed the knights out of the Sacred Council chamber. 'You really think they'll grant you a knighthood?' He savoured Caravaggio's surprise. 'I'm well informed about everything, aren't I? Lineage is their lifeblood. Duke trumps count trumps marchese trumps knight.' The priest pushed his finger into Caravaggio's chest. 'Trumps you.'

'Who trumps an Inquisitor?' Caravaggio directed his finger upwards. 'Only Him?'

'Sometimes. Look, perhaps I can convince you that you have some other reason to collaborate with me. I can return you to Rome. Is there no one there for you? I heard of a woman named Lena.' The Inquisitor spoke the name in a low, insouciant murmur, as though he were with a girl in the night, brushing the syllables over her breasts.

Caravaggio glared.

Della Corbara's mouth pursed. 'Dine with me?'

Reluctantly Caravaggio gestured for the Inquisitor to lead on. Della Corbara's limp was pronounced. His right shoulder dropped into a hunch to balance the misshapen left leg. It was as though the proximity of so many tall, strong noblemen forced the Inquisitor to shamble closer to the ground. Caravaggio went after him with a feeling he was being placed under a spell, a charm that worked like slow poison.

They settled at a table in a hostelry across the square. The three Dominicans who attended on della Corbara sat with them.

'Let's see how the other half live, shall we?' The Inquisitor called to the waiter. 'Meat. Something Maltese.' He spoke with the forced conviviality of a traveller who wishes himself far away in a place less alien.

'The Maltese usually eat rabbit,' Caravaggio said.

'But not rabbit, in the name of Our Lord,' della Corbara said. 'I can't stand such peasant offal. Fish would be better.'

'There's no fish, Father,' the waiter said.

'An island with no fish?'

The waiter hesitated.

'Well, come on, boy. Why isn't there any fish?'

'The fishermen must work on the Order's galleys, Father. The knights let them go back to fishing at the end of the summer for two months. It's *lampuki* season, then.'

'What's that?'

'You bake it in pastry with onions and capers and garlic—'

'Stop, you're making me hungry.' Della Corbara grabbed his stomach and laughed. 'I won't listen. It's torture.' He slapped Caravaggio's arm. 'Like being hauled up on the *strappado.*'

The Maltese were leaving the inn as unobtrusively as possible. *A reeling drunk with a drawn sword couldn't clear a room as fast as an Inquisitor*, Caravaggio thought.

Della Corbara observed the exodus. 'There's nothing to be scared of, is there? Not now that you know me.'

Caravaggio twisted his lips as though he smelled something unpleasant.

Della Corbara's lean features quivered. 'Once in a while I think of a sinful thought someone has confessed to me and I wonder if it wasn't mine in the first place.'

'No doubt you hear what you want to hear.'

'Your paintings show all the great sinners, Judas and Salome, the murderers of the martyrs. You make them your own, because you've been a killer yourself. But you also look for something beyond death. You're trying to paint redemption. The only problem is you don't know what it looks like. I want to help you, and in turn that'll help me get promoted to a new post in Rome. If I don't make a splash here, I might end up burning witches in Calabria.'

'You'd enjoy that.'

The Inquisitor scratched his nose. 'Have you ever seen a body after a burning?'

'No. Is there a body left to see?'

'You think men burn better than mutton? The body's a husk, but it has the shape of a man.' He leaned forward and, as if he were grabbing a bird before it could fly away, he snared Caravaggio's wrist. 'On the Holy Father's life, I know you'll help me. We shall both go to Rome.'

Caravaggio stared at the pale hand on his cuff. The Inquisitor knew what troubled him as well as he understood it himself.

Della Corbara's expression passed from wheedling to aggressive, his teeth bared, like a man aroused and denied a seduction. 'I know what you want. I know it as if I had ripped your soul from your breast, flattened it against a lectern and read it aloud in my study. You don't know what redemption looks like? Take a look. It's me.'

Caravaggio pulled away. He smelled meat roasting in the kitchen. He wasn't like this Inquisitor. He would be a knight. *Otherwise, I'll forever be the boy taunted in the Marchesa's courtyard. Bitter like this priest.*

The waiter brought a platter of *bragioli*, egg and bacon rolled in a slice of beef, fried and simmered with onions in wine.

Della Corbara regarded the dish with distaste and excitement, as though presented with the severed head of a man he had disliked. He shuffled the cups over the table-top like a gambler. 'The devil plays a game for your soul. Can you be sure you'll outwit him?'

As the steam from the hot meat rose around the Inquisitor's face, Caravaggio felt certain he could draw Satan, if not fool him. 'Only with you on my side, right? No doubt an Inquisitor trumps even Satan.'

Della Corbara shoved his plate away.

Caravaggio hesitated on the steps of the Cathedral in the seething sunshine. Roero waited beyond the massive double doors and beckoned to him. A cross twice as tall as a man hung by the door. Roero extended a finger towards it. 'See that crucifix, painter?'

An olive-skinned Christ was painted on the cross. 'It's a fine work,' Caravaggio said.

'By a student of Raphael. You ought to recognize the style.' Roero came closer. 'It's by Polidoro from Caravaggio. Your great forebear.'

Though the church was cool, Caravaggio grew hot. *This is how the martyrs felt. Even if their end didn't come right away, they sensed its heat and felt it consume them. I'm marked for death.*

A cruel half-smile bent Roero's lip. 'Surely you know how Polidoro perished these seventy years past? He was murdered – in Sicily, while trying to get back to Rome, whence he had fled.' He drew out his words, vicious delight slowing his tongue.

Caravaggio turned away from the knight towards the hanging Christ. It came to him that all his violence had been rooted in fear. But what could he be afraid of? This nasty nobleman, sneering in the shadows? He shook his head. *I've more to live for than the opportunity to quaver before him.* 'Polidoro was murdered by a servant who stole his money belt. Such is the motivation of one who kills a genius.'

Roero's grin collapsed into outrage.

That was a little much, perhaps, Caravaggio thought, *but it's a good idea to meet haughtiness with even greater superiority.* He smiled to himself as he entered the Oratory.

Martelli motioned to him from the altar. His hand cleaved the sunlight angling from a high window. The old knight pulled Caravaggio to his knees. He whispered a prayer, made the cross over his breast, and gazed up at the bare wall behind the altar. 'Beneath the floor of this Oratory are buried the remains of the knights who fell during the Great Siege,' Martelli said. 'They were my comrades. I'd be there too, if Our Lord hadn't saved me for other purposes.'

'May God forbid it, Signore.'

'There're many accomplishments I could cite since those days. I was Admiral of our fleet and ran the infidel off the seas. I guided novices and young knights in the traditions of the Order.'

'With great worthiness you accomplish everything you set out to do, Signore.'

'The greatest achievement is in your hands.' Martelli slipped a letter out of his doublet and thrust it into Caravaggio's grasp. He came to his feet with a growl and a hand in the small of his back.

Caravaggio read the name of Cardinal-Nephew Scipione on the letter. 'Signore?'

'You've painted the Grand Master. It's time you contributed to our church.'

'You do me great honour, Signore.'

'The Grand Master wishes you to paint the martyrdom of St John – for this wall behind the altar.' Martelli took Caravaggio's arm. 'I told you I had something else in mind for you.'

Just as the Inquisitor predicted. Della Corbara will take my saint and pronounce the depiction in violation of the rules of the Church. Then he'll have me in his power. Caravaggio examined the massive wall he was to fill with his canvas. *What a painting it'll be, though.* 'It's dark in here.'

'You've painted in churches before. They're all dark.'

'These windows are so high and narrow. The place is like a dungeon.'

'How does the Bible describe St John's death? "The king sent a soldier of the guard and gave orders to bring John's head to him.

He went and beheaded him in the prison and brought his head on a platter.' Martelli put his hand to Caravaggio's shoulder. 'The Baptist was decapitated in a dungeon. So paint a dungeon for our dungeon here.'

Caravaggio scanned the massive stones. It would take him a long time to paint something big enough that it wouldn't disappear into the wall. He had portrayed St John as a young man in the wild. Yet the instant of death? He shuddered. He had lived that moment. Perhaps it was time he drew those few seconds out of himself, from the horror-struck place in which he had entombed them. He shivered again. The knowledge he had was irresistible. It would fill the wall, even if he painted it no bigger than a man's hand. *It'll terrify people or inspire them*, he thought. *Depending on how much guilt they bear.* 'I'm honoured, Signore.'

'Read the letter.'

Caravaggio unfolded the paper. The neat script of the Grand Master's scribe, its letters all of an even thickness and angled at the same sixty degrees towards the right.

Most Holy Father

The Grand Master of the Order of the Hospital of St John of Jerusalem wishes to honour a virtuous and deserving person who has the desire and devotion to dedicate himself to his service and that of the Order. He humbly begs Your Holiness to deign to grant to him the authority and power to adorn with the Habit of Knight the person favoured and nominated by him, despite the fact that he had once committed homicide in a brawl. He begs to receive this request as an exceptional favour, because of his great desire to honour such a virtuous and deserving person and to keep him. May the Lord protect you for a long time.

Wignacourt had signed the letter with a less sure pen than his secretary, the quill catching and spotting ink beneath his name.

Caravaggio was about to ask Martelli who this virtuous and deserving person was, but the old man caught his shoulders and shook him. 'You'll be a knight, my boy. As soon as the Holy Father sends word.'

Caravaggio slumped. It was as though the marrow of his bones was pure tension and his relief made him hollow and feeble. With this one letter, he might be saved from the man – whoever he was – who would kill him.

Martelli pulled him close and led him from the Oratory.

As they went out, Caravaggio looked up at the crucifix. One day, he would return to Rome, as the murdered Polidoro never had. He would go back as a knight, a free man.

Martelli walked Caravaggio to the Inn of the Italian Knights. The old man stopped outside the gate to talk to the *pilier* of the Knights of Castille. In the courtyard Roero paced around the well, fists clenched. *I recognize that kind of rage*, Caravaggio thought. *He tried to frighten me at the Cathedral and failed. He won't let it pass.* The kitchen boy went to draw water, regarding Roero warily.

Caravaggio cut left towards the stairs to avoid another confrontation. But Roero called out to him and followed Caravaggio into the cloister. 'Remember that your painting of St John is to be for the knights, not for a bunch of effeminate aesthetes in Rome.'

He knows about my commission. These knights are as hungry for my secrets as the Inquisitor.

Roero drew close. 'I've heard all about the pretty boys you painted for the cardinals and the merchants in Rome. I've seen you hanging around with this kitchen lad, too. I'm sure it's not just your pigments he's grinding.' He jerked his thumb towards the boy at the well. 'I don't want any poems written about your painting of our St John like the ones about your nancy-boy pictures. I don't want to hear that *he'll set you on fire.*'

He knows I'm to be a knight and he hates me for polluting the pure blood of his Order, Caravaggio thought. *Don't be drawn into a fight, Michele.*

Roero balled his fist inside his glove and struck Caravaggio on the shoulder. Caravaggio stumbled against the wall. Roero glared at him. Caravaggio rubbed his bruise. He knew that he asked too much of himself. His honour, like that of any man, was worth as much as his soul.

The knight drew a dagger from his belt. 'I'll cut your flesh away. Then I'll thrash your bones.'

Caravaggio's response was a reflex. 'I'll have your balls, you stuck-up clown.' Even as he spoke, he deflated, disappointed in himself. But it was too late.

They closed on each other. Caravaggio lifted his hands to grab at the dagger when Roero made his lunge.

A woman's voice came through the courtyard. 'My Lord Roero, he's unarmed.' Roero didn't respond. The woman called again. 'Signor Giovanni, no.'

Roero faltered. The two fighters looked to where the woman stood. She held the kitchen boy's hand. She was a year or two older than him, but the resemblance was that of a sister. In the Maltese tradition, all but her face was covered in a black wrap. Her eyes were deep, with long lashes like insect legs.

'An unarmed man, Signor Giovanni,' she said, gentle and scolding.

Martelli entered the courtyard. Roero sheathed his dagger. He looked with disgust at Caravaggio and went towards the girl. The kitchen boy stepped in front of him, but Roero shoved him aside.

He drew back his right arm. The girl didn't flinch. He slapped her so hard that the force of his blow took him two steps to his left before he regained his balance. The girl spun to the ground.

'You dare speak my name, you whore?' Roero said.

The girl rubbed at the blood from her nose. *She looks as though she could say more*, Caravaggio thought. *It isn't the only time Roero has touched her, I'd guess. She knows his first name, after all, and I doubt his caress is much gentler than the blow he gave her.*

Roero stalked through the gate. Martelli put a coin in the kitchen boy's hand. 'Take her to the apothecary.'

'Carmena, come.' The boy helped his sister to arise and took her away.

Martelli sucked in his lips. 'You'd better go armed for now, Michele. Honour doesn't prevent a knight like Roero from assaulting an unarmed man, as you see. You can't rely on his whore being around to shame him next time.'

Caravaggio went up the stairs to his studio and took his dagger from his trunk. He recalled the liberation he had known when he read the Grand Master's letter in the Oratory. *It seems I'm to be saved only by myself*, he thought. He slipped the dagger inside his doublet.

The dice rolled. Martelli tapped his counters around to the far side of the backgammon board, twisting a lapis rosary in his other hand. Caravaggio reached for the dice cup. The old Florentine didn't watch his opponent as he moved. In the lantern light his gaze was inward, reprising every wound and engagement with the enemy, every past encounter with God and the one that was to come. Caravaggio smiled with some bitterness. *I've never played with someone against whom it'd be so easy to cheat, and yet I find myself wishing to give him the victory.*

He imagined Martelli was recalling a similar game on a lonely watch during the Turkish siege of the island. That had been more than forty years ago and Martelli would have been about Caravaggio's age. *What has he seen coming out of the dark?* He drank a cup of wine, while Martelli had his turn on the board.

'You took great pains over the Grand Master's face in the portrait, Maestro Caravaggio?'

'No more than any other object on the canvas, Signore.' Caravaggio couldn't help the defensiveness of the professional who wishes every stage of his work to be credited.

'Come now, I observed you in your studio. I watched you circle his eyes for hours with many different tones. You sought to depict more than just the way the light fell on the Grand Master's face. You looked for an inner light.'

'It's there for all to see, Sire. The challenge is to portray it.'

'The essence of a man?'

'The essence.'

Martelli moved his pieces. To his surprise, Caravaggio saw that the knight had almost brought them all to their home.

'When I was a young knight, I learned all the most elaborate techniques of the swordsman.' Martelli held his right hand forward, en garde, though he gripped his rosary, not a rapier. 'The *cavazione*, moving the blade from one side of the opponent's sword to the other. Keeping always in *misura larga*, within lunging distance. Defending against the *mandritto squalembrato* with a *falso dritto*, so that when your opponent's sword strikes at the left side of your head you cut from the right to the upper left, and instantly deliver your riposte.' He mimed the moves as he spoke.

Caravaggio murmured his understanding. He knew the terms. He had practised the techniques.

'I based my swordplay on the chivalrous gestures of the courtier,' Martelli said. 'But once I'd been in a few skirmishes, I pared it down. In the Great Siege, I'd use my shoulder to knock the other fellow off balance, and I'd finish him with the most lethal blow there is.' He pulled Caravaggio towards him by the shoulder and shoved a hand into the side of his chest. 'A dagger in the armpit, like this.'

Caravaggio quivered, such was the sudden economy of Martelli's pretended blow. *Now I know why he doesn't have to guard against cheats at the gaming board.*

'On the seaward wall of our castle,' Martelli said, 'I took a blow from a Turk and lost my sword. He was about to finish me. I hugged him close, so that he couldn't swing his weapon, and I bit into his neck.' Martelli held Caravaggio and put his mouth beside his ear, whispering, hard and intimate. 'We tumbled down a flight of steps, but I kept my teeth in his vein until he bled to death.'

Caravaggio's breath stuttered, as though the force of the old man's memory drew him into the very combat of which he spoke.

'I almost choked on his gore. Not very chivalrous, but it worked. I delivered him to his death. I didn't try to make it appear nobler than it was.' Martelli winced and drew in his lips. 'A young man believes the world may be changed through his faith, through the way he wields his sword, even by the way he wears his clothes. But when you kill your first man, you know the world is as it is. Your illusions die with your opponent. It's all you can do to hope that after the death of that man *you* at least may change.'

Caravaggio felt himself soften as the old Florentine spoke. He seemed to have waited a long time to hear this voice. It was strange to feel joy when the talk was of death.

'I learned not to glorify anything – neither the way I parried nor riposted. In turn I told myself not to make idols of the saints. Their ends were deaths like anyone else's. The ultimate lesson is not to idealize yourself. Try to be a better man, but don't worry about being a perfect man.'

Martelli drew himself straight. 'When you paint St John, don't fake anything, Michele. Don't let it be an exercise in technique. Find the way to paint what's within.' He reached out and bumped his fist against Caravaggio's heart. Then he pushed the backgammon board away. 'My game.'

Caravaggio had four canvases sewn together to a width of six paces and a height twice that of a tall man. He fixed the size of *The Beheading of St John* after studying the blank limestone behind the altar in the Oratory from every vantage point. It had to be that big, so that the incident it depicted would be clear to worshippers at the back of the chamber. But not so big that the characters he painted would seem larger than life. *When the Baptist's head is cut away from his body, I want the novices to feel like spectators to something real*, he thought. *I want them to know what it's like to kill, and to fear death, as I do under its sentence.*

He dressed the surface of the canvas with animal glue, pushing the brush into the whip-stitching between the lengths of material, enjoying the way the canvas bounced on its wooden stretcher with each stroke. He laid down an orange-red ground layer into which he mixed a little yellow ochre and yellow earth. Over this, he put a second layer of darker brown made with charcoal black and red ochre. These layers would show through the final painting, their undertones giving life and light to the dungeon in which the saint's death would take place.

As he waited for his models to arrive, his energy was high. He had to walk a little of it off, or he wouldn't be able to hold his hand steady at the easel. He left the kitchen boy straining pigments through thin linen sacks and went into the street in his painting smock. He passed the Castilian Inn and entered the gardens where the knights practised their sword drills.

Across the harbour, the standard of the Order fluttered on the castle battlements. The white cross flickered against its red background. He wondered if that was the spot where Martelli had bitten into the neck of the Turk.

The agitation of the stiff wind seemed to make the colours on the flag mix. There were no clear lines. *If I painted that way, I might give the impression of motion, of an event unfolding*, he thought. *I could capture life itself.* It would mean less exact brushwork, because he would have to mimic the inability of the eye to nail down precisely where the flag stood at any moment under the surging breeze. As soon as he picked out the image on the standard, it was gone, fluttering forward or back, rippling like the surface of the harbour water.

The bite to the neck, he thought, *instead of the elaborations of fine swordsmanship.* Martelli had called it a pure, unadorned conflict. Caravaggio smiled broadly. He would make no show in this new painting. Everything would draw the viewer into the very moment of martyrdom – unfolding, in motion. He would go straight for the blood.

Caravaggio ran past Our Lady of Victories and into the Italian Inn. In the lower left of his canvas, he saw where he would place them. He could almost count the brushstrokes he would need. Someone entered the studio behind him. He didn't turn. He was transfixed by the scene he would paint.

De Ponte, the deacon of the knights, threw off his cloak. 'Who's going to be St John?'

The kitchen boy put down the yellow ochre he was straining. 'Maestro Michele says I'm to be the Baptist.'

De Ponte drew his knife and stroked the scar that ran white

through his beard. 'Come over here and let me slaughter you, then.' He slapped the startled boy's back and laughed. 'Don't look so scared, son. I'm to pose for the executioner.' The boy flinched and went back to his colours.

■

Two women, three men. De Ponte as the executioner, a Sicilian knight named Giacomo as the jailer. The kitchen boy was the saint, and his sister was Salome collecting the Baptist's head in a ewer. Their mother played an appalled bystander. They hovered in their poses, unused to the stillness Caravaggio required. He tried to persuade them to relax their muscles, but the scene displeased him anyway. The boy glanced heavenwards as if he were in one of the ill-done martyrdoms in the Inquisitor's gallery. The old woman raised her hands, imploring God's mercy like an actor in an old-fashioned morality play.

'Let's start before this.' Caravaggio came towards them. 'Relax.'

They shook out their aching limbs.

'Let's act out the story of the death of the saint. Begin with the arrival of Salome and her maid.'

He had them walk through the scene. The jailer issued the death sentence. The executioner shoved the saint to his knees, swung his sword to break the neck, and bent with his dagger to saw away the head. Salome lowered the ewer to receive it.

'Again.' Caravaggio watched them repeat the sequence three times, directing their reactions as they went. He urged them to look within, to *be* the person they represented. 'It's happening here. Don't think about it. Don't act out what was read to you from the Bible. Just feel it. The story will let you in.'

De Ponte took to it right away and it was he who fixed the moment. He struck the Baptist's neck, and Caravaggio wondered if this might be the instant he would depict, the pleasure of the kill. Then he saw an unexpected flicker of regret on de Ponte's tough features. *That's my scene*, he thought. *When I recall the way I killed Ranuccio, it isn't the absolute conviction and hatred that comes back to me. It's the guilt and contrition I felt when the dying man looked at me. He passed on all the monstrosity of the world to me, even as he went to his peace.*

Caravaggio drew them towards that instant. Another three run-throughs, each starting closer to the moment he had chosen. To the kitchen boy he said, 'You've been cut down. What would your last thought be?'

'That the Messiah is coming?'

'No, no, not as St John – as you. You're butchered in a dungeon. The last thing you see is the dirt floor.'

Anguished acceptance passed across the boy's face. It was the material Caravaggio needed for his art, but it was also the devastating face of his own shame. His excitement shuddered through every limb. He called out, 'You have it.'

◼

Fabrizio came to the Italian Inn to see what progress Caravaggio had made with *The Beheading*. 'You've changed your style, Michele. This is different from the works I saw in Rome.'

'It doesn't stop at the brush,' Caravaggio said. 'I've changed myself.'

Fabrizio stood a long time, stroking his chin, his face puzzled and then illuminated – stricken, then joyous.

Caravaggio, too, contemplated the scene. The Baptist was chest down on the ground. His executioner leaned over him with his fingers in his victim's hair. From Fabrizio's changing expression, Caravaggio understood that he had succeeded. He had depicted what went before and after this arrested moment. The painting was a whole episode, communicated in the swiftness of the brushstrokes and in the drama of the composition.

His face half-lit by the lantern in front of the canvas, Fabrizio grimaced at the dying saint. 'I think of that instant always, Michele.'

Caravaggio knew what he meant.

'I felt absolute justification, when I killed that Farnese.'

'I know.'

'When you killed Ranuccio . . .?'

I stepped into another world, Caravaggio thought.

Fabrizio twirled his hand as though signalling the passage of time that seemed to take place on the canvas. 'I often think of the moments before and after with regret. But the instant in which I killed him – I could never see it. Until now.' He put his hand on the back of a chair and leaned heavily, as if he were exhausted. 'You're so good at showing us the moment of death. You seem to know it so intimately. But do you understand what it's like to be alive? I've been pardoned for killing the Farnese. No one seeks my life. Yet when I look at your painting I'm suffocated by guilt and fear and foreboding. It must be terrible to be you, Michele.'

'Is that my fault?'

'Don't be angry, Michele. There's only one other time in my life that has meant as much to me as that instant when I became a murderer.' Fabrizio's pale eyes welled up, gleaming in the lantern light with an old longing. He reached for Caravaggio and put his hand to his neck, drew him close. Their lips met and the length of their bodies. Fabrizio moaned with the pure voice of a boy, all the raggedness of the man's throat soothed.

Caravaggio knew that sound from his boyhood. He recalled the feel of his friend in his arms. But he also tasted the fear that had come afterwards, the loneliness of leaving Costanza's house, the poverty of his first years in Rome. He had paid for the pleasure he heard in Fabrizio's voice.

He pulled away. Fabrizio held on, but he shoved him in the chest. 'Leave me.'

'Michele, don't.'

Who'll beat me this time? Caravaggio thought. *Who'll throw me out and tell me it's for my own good? While this man goes on being a prince.* 'I said, leave me.'

When he was alone, Caravaggio extinguished his lantern. He remembered Fabrizio's question. Yes, he knew what it was to be alive. Only an artist or a killer or God could know it, those who make or who destroy. *They're the ones who can tell the price of every breath.*

Caravaggio was at his prayers when he sensed the temperature in his studio dip. He shivered and opened his eyes. The Inquisitor was examining *The Beheading* with a look of glowing calculation, like a cheating saint.

'Is this how *you'll* end up?' della Corbara said.

Caravaggio recited another 'Our Father'.

'I think it more likely that your body will disappear and never be found at all,' the Inquisitor said. 'What's worse, do you think? To die like the Baptist in a dark dungeon? Or to be staring at the sky and the flowers and the sea when one's head is taken from one's body by a bounty hunter?'

'*Et ne nos inducas in tentationem, sed libera nos a malo. Amen.*'

'Amen.' The Inquisitor folded his hands over his stomach. It seemed a gesture he had borrowed from a better-fed priest. His own body was meagre and the cord of his belt threatened to slip over his hips to the floor. 'I hear you had a tussle with Brother

Roero in the courtyard downstairs. As a churchman, I'm not subject to the rules of vendetta. Perhaps I might intercede between the two of you, so that the rancour doesn't escalate.'

'Surely you'd have to side with the knight. He's a member of a holy order, just as you are.'

'Roero doesn't respect the Church. He carries out the will of the Holy Father in fighting against the infidels, that's true. But I don't count such murderers as true men of the cloth.'

'An Inquisitor ought not to talk so lightly of murder.'

'Before a man who profits from painting the slaughter of a saint, why not?' The Inquisitor paced in front of the canvas.

Caravaggio took up a dry brush to texture the ochre and burnt umber on the wall of St John's dungeon. The sibilant stroking of the brush was loud in the stillness.

'The Baptist on your canvas is dead,' della Corbara said, 'but you've yet to paint his blood. I wonder if you've finally reached the limits of your imitation of natural things.'

'What do you mean?'

'Perhaps blood is too close to home. Too close to your own, which may be spilled like that of the Baptist on the orders of a king.'

'The Pope is no king.'

'Greater than kings. Making your fate even more sticky.'

'I haven't painted the blood yet. So what? I'll get to it.'

'Your St John is certainly dead. Dead on the floor of a dirty courtyard, pale and lifeless. He isn't ascending to heaven, as the saints usually do in art.' The Inquisitor rubbed his thumb along his lip. 'If even the Baptist appears not to make it to the celestial paradise, you must doubt *your own* chances of salvation.'

'If I concern myself with salvation, that's proof I believe in God's mercy. If I didn't believe, I wouldn't care about my sins or my soul.'

'Then may He bless you.' The Inquisitor lifted his hand in benediction.

Caravaggio winced. He felt the man's gesture, not in loving absolution, but as an unwanted intimacy probing him. 'Why did you come here again? I'm not going to do what you want. I'm not going to give you information against the knights, even if you tell me this painting breaks the Church's rules.'

The Inquisitor examined his hands and slid them into the sleeves of his cassock. 'Duels, such as the one you fought with Signor Ranuccio, are under the jurisdiction of the Inquisition. I could have you extradited to Rome. Even the Grand Master couldn't stop me.'

'Then why don't you have *him* extradited too?'

Della Corbara whipped his hand from his cassock and slapped Caravaggio's cheek. 'Because I need a witness to his terrible crime,' he yelled.

Caravaggio tensed his fists, but held himself back. The blow had been out of rage, and Caravaggio knew it represented the Inquisitor's hopelessness.

Della Corbara lifted his hands in apology. 'Forgive me. The devil is more cunning than I am. He prepares traps for me.'

'I thought you were working together.'

The Inquisitor stepped close and dropped his voice to a rumbling whisper. 'You want to be the dog who's privileged to enter the great hall and eat scraps from the Master's table. But these knights will never let you in – because you're a wolf.' He pointed to his thin chest. 'And wolves hunt in packs. You'll need me in the end. Remember that.'

He left the studio. Caravaggio returned to the walls of the dungeon.

Caravaggio was painting the black lead teeth of the jailor's keys, when Martelli pulled back the curtain of his camera obscura. The knight carried a letter. He was immediately preoccupied by the canvas.

'You've painted the executioner's knife since I last saw this,' he said. A thick, white highlight marked the edge of the blade. The Florentine had been cut many times. He scratched at his scars through his doublet.

'You feel the executioner's touch?' Caravaggio smiled.

'I don't doubt I'd recognize it as my own. Actually I was thinking about you.'

'Thus far, it's I who has been the executioner.'

Martelli brandished the letter. 'You need be neither executioner nor condemned from now on. You're to be a knight.'

Caravaggio kissed the old man's hand. 'I feared that if the Holy Father declined . . .'

'We'd ship you back to Rome in chains? Well, I have some influence with the Grand Master and I'm a determined old bastard. I suppose the Holy Father realized we wouldn't let this go. Read it.'

Caravaggio unfolded the letter.

To our beloved Alof de Wignacourt Grand Master of the Hospitaller Order of St John of Jerusalem.
Pope Paul the Fifth.

Beloved son, greetings. The merits of your special devotion to Us and to the Holy See induce us to favour you by acceding to such requests as will enable you to show gratitude to those who pay their obedience to you or whom you hold in grace and favour. Wherefore inclining to the request submitted to us on your behalf, in virtue of this brief and by our Apostolic Authority we impart and grant to you authority to receive as a Brother of the grade of Magistral Knight the person favoured by you, who is to be selected and nominated by you, even though he has committed murder in a brawl, and to present to him the habit of Brother of the grade of Magistral Knight so that you may keep him.

Given at St Mark's under the seal of the Fisherman.

The letter felt hot in his hands. Caravaggio worried that he might set it on fire and burn it to ashes with the force of his feeling. He thrust it back to Martelli.

'As a knight, you can't be sent back to Rome. You'll have the protection of the Order.' Martelli folded the letter and slipped it into his doublet. He gripped Caravaggio's arms and embraced him. 'Michele, you'd be a knight even if this *St John* of yours were a lesser painting. But it's astonishing.'

Caravaggio scanned his canvas. Each stroke of the brush had seemed to liberate him. *Martelli knows*, he thought. *I made my work as direct as his description of killing a man.*

They shared a confiding silence. Caravaggio's fingers tingled from contact with the Pope's letter. A pardon. Perhaps he might return to the Pope's lands, to Rome, to Lena. It was all possible now.

At the bottom of his picture, the Baptist's gaunt face stared at him. It remained only to paint the blood flowing from the dying man's neck.

Caravaggio went to the Admiral's residence after the supper hour. As he dropped down the slope beyond the Grand Master's Palace, he fought to suppress his pride at his elevation to knighthood. *I'll be free of the sentence of death*, he thought. *I can return to Lena and work in peace.* But as he entered the empty offices of the fleet on the ground floor, he knew why his first urge had been to come and tell Fabrizio. *I won't be the servant of the Colonnas any more. I'll be the equal of any of them, a member of a noble Order.* A man like Fabrizio might now truly be his brother. He might bestow his friendship on him and on Costanza. It could no longer be demanded of him as a service due to their rank.

The sweetness of the orange grove was like scented skin in the evening warmth. He recognized it as the flavour of Fabrizio's kiss. He went up the stairs.

The Admiral's secretaries had gone to their inns for supper, so Caravaggio passed through Fabrizio's study towards his private chamber. The door was ajar. Beyond it, a pair of scarlet stockings spread over the brown flagstones.

Caravaggio halted. He heard a muffled grunt and a man's breathless laughter. He pushed the door open.

Fabrizio was at the bedside, his hose about his ankles and his shirt loose. He gripped the thin legs of Nicholas, the Grand Master's page. The boy's cheeks were flushed and a tremulous emptiness lay on his face.

The boy saw Caravaggio. He wriggled from under Fabrizio, gathered his clothing and ran. The pleasure on Fabrizio's face receded. 'I'm still corrupting young boys, Michele, as you see.'

Caravaggio looked about the room. It was little different from the chamber where Fabrizio and he had scrambled to consume each other. They had been the age Nicholas was now. *If this is Fabrizio's shame*, he said to himself, *then why is it I who feels humiliated?* The surge of pride at his knighthood, the closeness with Martelli, and the sense that Lena wasn't lost to him – it was gone, all of it. He was back in Fabrizio's chamber in the Sforza Colonna Palace in Caravaggio. He was thirteen years old, and his master's son held him to the bed and emptied into him all the guilt and lust on which his attempts to love had choked ever since.

There was a trace of hope and new lust on Fabrizio's face. 'Come on, Michele. What's the problem? Don't tell me you aren't doing the same thing with that Maltese kitchen lad you're using as your assistant. Or are you jealous? Jealous of the boy.'

Caravaggio slapped Fabrizio and fell on him, punching, gasping with tears, until Fabrizio got his hands free and rolled away. He lay on the bed, all his frenzy sapped. He wept, because he had wanted to tell Fabrizio of his joy. *The only thing he'll ever share with me is something he could as easily force on that page.*

He rushed to the stairs. As he went through the offices, he heard Fabrizio call him. *I'm to be a knight. When the Colonnas shout my name, I don't have to answer ever again.*

Late that night, the watchman whistled an oriental tune outside the Inn of the Italian Knights, his lantern swinging at his waist. Caravaggio shone his own lamp along the length of his canvas, swatting at the mosquitoes. He squeezed out an inch of burnt umber from a pig's bladder tube and dipped a medium brush in linseed oil to thin the paint.

He touched the shadowed ochre he had used for the flagstones of St John's dungeon and checked his fingertip for traces of the paint. It was dry, ready for him to lay a glaze over it. He twirled his brush in the umber and the linseed, and he lifted it to the canvas.

From a distance, the glaze would look as though it were the thin, transparent border of the gore pooling beneath the saint's wounded neck. But anyone who came closer would see what he had done. For the first time in any of his paintings, in the blood of the saint spilled by the same beheading that had for so long threatened to be his own fate and from which knighthood would soon rescue him, Caravaggio signed his name as a knight and a monk: *Brother Michelangelo.*

He felt as though all the gore he had seen in brawls and duels had soaked into him. It didn't bring death or pain: it filled him with life. It boiled inside him and spilled onto the canvas, his blood and the blood of the men he had fought and the man he had killed. He wrote his name in it, because he might bleed forever and his body would pump out yet more, hot and alive.

He dropped his palette and clasped his hands. He prayed that Lena would feel the blood surge in him and that it would connect them as surely as if they bled into each other's veins. *My God, let her live*, he murmured. *Let her be as full of life as I am.*

∎

As Caravaggio advanced through the black-cloaked knights in the Oratory, Martelli gave him a firm smile. Now he would be one of them. He mounted the steps to the altar with the unaccustomed weight of armour on his shoulders and chest. He spread his arms a little so that he wouldn't kneel on his cloak. Behind the Grand Master, his painting of St John's death ran across the wall. He read his name in blood and bowed his head.

Wignacourt recited the ceremony of investiture. He bound Caravaggio to follow a life of Christian perfection and social works, to dedicate himself to the Virgin and to St John. The Grand Master held out the white cross of the Order on a length of linen. Caravaggio kissed it. Had he been alone, he would have buried his head in the cloth, exultant. *Don't forget*, he told himself, *your joy is at least as much about escaping the death sentence as it is about your elevated status. You've joined the people to whom laws don't apply.* He looked at the

Italian knights beside the altar. Fabrizio turned his head, as if Caravaggio's gaze were a physical blow.

'Receive the yoke of the Lord,' Wignacourt said, 'for it is sweet and light and under it you will find rest for your soul. We promise you no delicacies, but only bread and water and a modest monk's habit of no worth.'

Wignacourt beckoned to the page Nicholas, who came forward holding a red cushion, a gold chain upon it. The Grand Master laid the chain around Caravaggio's neck and raised him to his feet. 'Giving you a gift of two slaves, as well,' Wignacourt whispered.

'Your Serene Highness is too generous.'

The Grand Master gestured over his shoulder towards *The Beheading of St John.* 'A masterwork, Brother Michelangelo.'

'You do me great honour, Sire.'

The Italians returned to their inn where Caravaggio would take his place as a knight. At the gate, Martelli welcomed him and requested that he sit on a simple carpet. He gave him bread and salt, symbols of a monk's ascetic life. As Caravaggio ate, Roero picked his teeth with the point of a dagger.

■

A Sienese knight named Brother Giulio took a long draught of wine. 'Here's a good one: The Duke of Brie, the illegitimate son of the Duke of Lorraine, is at dinner. A courtly French knight says to him, "Duke, you're divine, will you pass me the wine?" So the Duke gives him the wine. At the other end of the table, there's an ill-mannered German knight. He follows the Frenchman's rhyming example and says, "Duke, you're a bastard, pass me the mustard." ' He slammed his goblet down on the table and roared at his punchline.

Caravaggio drank off his wine and refilled it to the brim from the jug on the table. Roero watched him over his cup, his red eyes aflame.

Let him glare, Caravaggio thought. *He's not the first to give me a dirty look, and I've a new status as knight to protect me. I dine with these knights as an equal now.* He was glittering with the wine and the success of *The Beheading*, flushed like a boy tipsy for the first time. He toasted Brother Giulio's humour.

'You like a good joke, do you?' Roero said.

Caravaggio swallowed his wine. 'Yeah, why not?'

'You think it's a joke to make a painting for our Oratory with a naked kitchen boy and a Maltese whore?'

The knights along the table quieted. Brother Giulio coughed and tried another story. 'The Duke of Brie goes to hunt bears with a crossbow—'

'A whore in our church.' The shadows cut scars into Roero's face.

Even as he told himself to stay silent, Caravaggio opened his mouth and drawled, 'You're the one with the direct proof of the girl's profession, Roero.' *You couldn't help yourself, Michele. When they made you a knight, they restored all the stupid pride that leaked out of you with Ranuccio's blood. A little wine and a prod from this bastard, and you smash everything to pieces.*

'Come now, Brothers, which of us hasn't visited the whores?' Brother Giulio said.

'This Lombard pimp is a knight?' Roero said. 'I'm disgusted.'

Caravaggio felt the old stuttering pulse of adrenaline, and he knew the fight would happen. He was afloat on the whirlwind of pride and boastfulness in which men lived. 'You have two hundred years of nobility on both sides of your family, but your soul belongs to a peasant.'

Roero's laugh was triumphant. 'The closest you ever came to nobility, painter, was to stir the Marchesa Colonna's palette with your little pork paintbrush.'

A sudden motion and Caravaggio's dagger bit into the knight's shoulder. Roero went backwards onto his stool.

Brother Giulio staggered towards them. 'Why don't I finish telling the joke about the Duke and the bear?'

Roero unsheathed his rapier and lunged. Caravaggio parried with his dagger and punched him on the ear. Roero's impetus brought him forward and Caravaggio felt the point of his dagger enter below the knight's collarbone.

Staggering as if he had been struck with the battering ram of a galley at full speed, Roero frowned at the torn fabric of his doublet. A scarlet stain spread out of the black material into the white cross of the Order on his chest.

When they cast him inside, the moonlight illuminated the rock walls, sloping to a hatch in the ceiling. Now all was silent and cold and black. *At least I didn't bring Lena into this jeopardy with me*, he thought. He knelt in prayer and knew that he had made a mistake by leaving her in Rome. He had sought to protect her, but he had run from the one soul that might have soothed him. With Lena, he was sure, he would never have repeated his violence. She could have been his redemption. His pride in his knighthood had led him to this conical dungeon scooped from the rock of the Sant'Angelo Castle. It had destroyed everything – except his love for Lena. Even he couldn't wreck that.

The hatch lifted and Caravaggio blinked through the morning sun into the artful features of Leonetto della Corbara. *A strange Christ to raise this Lazarus back among the living.* The Inquisitor's eyes flickered, a minute deviation as if he were calculating the worth of the man in the hole beneath him. He made an impatient gesture and a ladder slid into the dungeon for his descent.

He held the sleeve of his black robe to his nose. Caravaggio pointed to the side of the chamber furthest from the slops bucket. Della Corbara sat against the wall, wincing at the contact of his back with the rough rock. 'Inside the infamous *guva*. It's almost like hell.'

'I could get used to it.'

'You mightn't have so long.'

From his sleeve, the Inquisitor slipped a paper. Unfolding it, he held it forward into the light from the hatch. 'A pardon. A blank pardon. Usually I sell them for a few hundred *scudi*, as you sell a painting. I'm offering this one to you free of charge.'

'Not quite free.'

'Well, you can have it – if you do as I wish. The knights are going to kick you out of the Order. There goes your protection, the pardon you thought you had. Tell me what I want to know about the way they live.'

Caravaggio gestured around him. 'I'm not at liberty to oblige, Father.'

The Inquisitor pulled up his bottom lip as if to suggest that the dungeon was a triviality. 'Don't you want to go home?'

'God is our final home and he'll lead us there.'

Della Corbara bellowed with laughter and wagged an appreciative finger at Caravaggio. The face of one of the guards appeared above, curious and disapproving. 'Don't quote St Augustine to me,' the Inquisitor said. '*He* was never imprisoned in the *guva* of Malta, Maestro Michele. Had he been so immured, he'd have advised you to rely upon your friends, not only on God.'

'Signore?' the guard called down.

'Father, to you.' Della Corbara made his expression harsh and the guard pulled back. 'Michele, you have no choice now. If you stay here, the knights will expel you for wounding a noble member of the Order. You'll be unprotected. They'll send you to Rome to be executed for the murder of Ranuccio. But I might be able to claim custody of you.'

Caravaggio shook his head. He didn't believe the Inquisitor could face down the knights. He felt sympathy for the priest's desperation.

Della Corbara displayed a momentary exasperation, like a tired father with a boisterous child. When he stood, the Inquisitor blocked out the light. His robe and the rock were black. 'I'm talking to you as a friend, Michele. If you get out of here, put your faith in love. We hope love is everlasting, but we know we can't count on it enduring. That's what makes its pleasure so intense.'

The Inquisitor had always seemed part of the prideful tide of the world, before which Caravaggio had to posture and push out his chest. In defeat, the priest showed him his weakness, and Caravaggio felt naked before it. The cold stone of the dungeon made him shiver.

In the Grand Master's Palace, the senior knights sat around a heavy oak table built in an open curve. As Admiral of the Galleys, Fabrizio took his place on the Venerable Council. He lacked long service in the Order so his chair was near the tip of the horseshoe. The *piliers* of each nation among the knights were ranked beside Wignacourt, who slouched on his throne, his hand cradling his chin, fingers disguising his troubled features. On his right, Martelli was upright and tense with a rage he seemed barely able to check.

The knights had heard the evidence of the investigators, but before they decided to expel Caravaggio from the Order Martelli had insisted that Roero recount the story of the fight at the dinner.

Wignacourt's page passed around the table with a taper, lighting the candles as the hearing went into the evening. When he set the flame to the candle before Fabrizio, his hand shook. Fabrizio smiled gently, but the boy hurried to illuminate the other candles. He cursed himself for what he had done with the page, for revealing the man he was to Michele. If he could have hidden himself all those years ago when he had first been with Michele, what pain would others have been spared? His mother, Michele, this page boy. He damned his father, who had been the first to lay his touch on him in lust, and he wondered when he would meet him and in which circle of hell.

Roero told his tale, a tone of horror in his voice. Fabrizio thought it a disgusting piece of acting. Roero had often done worse violence than Michele and joked about it.

The page threw the taper in the grate and took up his place behind the Grand Master. His delicate hand absently circled the rim of a chilled water pitcher on a trolley beside him. Fabrizio watched it, breathless. The boy brought the condensation on his finger to his lips, sucking it away. When he noticed Fabrizio's absorption, he snapped his hands behind his back. The disgust Fabrizio had felt for Roero passed now to himself.

'What started the dispute at the dinner, Brother Roero?' Martelli spoke low, more like a threat than a question.

'I criticized his painting,' Roero said. 'The *Beheading of St John* in the Oratory.'

'Your criticism was what exactly?'

'His model for Salome was a Maltese whore.'

'How do *you* know she's a whore?'

'What other woman would an artist consort with? Certainly she's not fit for the sight of our novices.'

Caravaggio was beyond protection. Even Martelli was powerless to stop the trial. Fabrizio wished his mother had been there to speak for her protégé. He clicked his tongue. How weak he was to require the strength of a woman in such moments. He recalled the desperation with which Caravaggio had wrestled him on the bed in his residence. Fabrizio had felt repulsed and embraced at the same time.

Roero's speech seemed interminable. Quietly Fabrizio rose. He looked for some command from Martelli, but the old knight's attention blazed at Roero.

Fabrizio went at a jog through the courtyards of the palace. *Let them sit up there in judgement. Michele is neither a knight nor an artist to me. I won't be constrained by their codes of behaviour. I judge him by another measure – by love – and in that he has never been lacking.*

The sound of a scuffle above him awoke Caravaggio. He wondered what time it was. When the hatch opened, the night was at its darkest point. *Roero has come to finish it.* He let his hands fall and relaxed his body.

'Michele, let's go.' Fabrizio slipped the ladder down to him.

He climbed out. The slaves given him by the Grand Master crouched over the body of the guard. One of them prepared to club the fallen soldier's head, but Fabrizio held him at the wrist.

'I told these two you'd grant them their freedom if they'd help you.'

The Africans watched Caravaggio like angry prey. They rolled the unconscious guard into the *guva* and shut the hatch.

'I'd advise you not to write up their emancipation papers until they've rowed you to Sicily. Otherwise, they might just drop you in the sea.' Fabrizio pulled him towards the battlements.

A grappling iron anchored a rope to an empty sentry post. Fabrizio signalled for the Africans to climb over the wall. They went quietly into the darkness below, their forms indistinct against the foaming water on the rocks.

'The Venerable Council is going to expel you from the Order, Michele,' Fabrizio said. 'The Grand Master will have no choice but to extradite you to Rome.'

'This rescue – it's a risk for you.'

Fabrizio averted his eyes with the resignation of a man for whom all perils were past. 'My mother has protected you all your life, Michele. I promised her I'd guard you in Malta.'

Caravaggio slipped over the wall and held the rope. He gave Fabrizio a searching look. The nobleman smiled. 'It's like the games we played in my mother's courtyard when we were children. Keep the memory of those times with you, even if our other intimacies are painful to recall.'

'I wanted you just as much. I've tried to forget that, but I can't.'

'Nothing is ever forgotten, Michele. It's the curse of the world.' Fabrizio gripped Caravaggio's wrist. 'Hold the rope under your arm. Push out with both legs at once. Lower yourself down a few stones at a time.'

Caravaggio sensed tenderness in the strong hold Fabrizio had on his arm.

'At the bottom, follow the slaves to the head of the point. There's a boat waiting there. One of my sailors will steer you to Sicily.'

'I shan't forget this, Fabrizio.'

'Neither shall Roero. Keep that in mind and let it inform your conduct. You'll have him in pursuit now, as well as the Tomassonis.' Fabrizio checked to be sure the guards of the watch weren't approaching. 'When I was in prison, I plotted an escape. I wanted to run away from death. You, Michele, seem to pursue it.'

Caravaggio's hands rubbed raw, as he measured the speed of his rappel. The sea in the harbour below seethed as if it were greedy for him. He made it down and followed the silent Africans along the edge of the water. Behind him, he heard the grappling iron slap into the water where Fabrizio had tossed it.

A high-sided wooden rowing boat bounced at the end of the walkway. The slaves glanced along the foot of the fortress to the barred caves where they had been captive.

Fabrizio's man prepared to cast off. 'Get a move on, in the name of Christ,' he hissed.

The slaves settled at the oars. The sailor shoved off and took up the tiller. Caravaggio craned towards the battlements for a sight of Costanza's son.

Within an hour, the lantern lights of Malta and all the knights and the works he had painted there slipped beneath the horizon.

III
SICILY and NAPLES
The Head of Goliath
1608

8

The Flagellation of Christ

In the Palermo dawn, he was alone. The early light glimmered off the tacks attaching his canvas to its frame. But no companion watched the sun cross his face.

He lay on his front, fully dressed and with his arms outstretched, like a man who had been assaulted by an attacker approaching unseen from behind. In the heat of the summer, he had sweated through the night, clothed and armed for a quick getaway in case his murderer should come. Shapes moved in the shadows and he tracked them, holding his breath. The shutters creaked as the wood expanded in the heat of the first sunshine. Their every click and rasp made his heart thrash.

Perhaps his killers would come today. *I'd almost welcome the company.*

He imagined the saints in the dawn of the day of their martyrdom. They had consolations unknown to him. They were certain of the fate of their souls. But when he pictured their deaths, he saw the bodies they left behind. Slaughtered, bloodless meat.

He leaned over his tray of pigments. 'Good morning, my only friends,' he murmured. The clay dug near Siena, filled with iron and making a yellow-brown oil, or burned in a furnace for the red-brown he loved to use; red ochre also from the Tuscan hills; St John's White, made from quicklime by Florentine monks; green earth quarried near Verona; and the most expensive, ultramarine blue, ground from lapis lazuli that was mined in the land of the Khans beyond Persia – he touched them all. They were like a cooling salve on a wound.

He descended the stairs to the kitchen. An old Franciscan monk laid a bowl of thin cabbage soup before him. 'How's our *Nativity* progressing, Maestro Michele?'

'Almost done.' Caravaggio had finished the canvas two days before. He lingered over it, fearful of what he might encounter if he were to leave his studio.

'God bless you, Maestro. Where will you go when it's completed?'

The minced cabbage in the soup was sparse. He noted the skin of a bean floating in the broth, but when he trawled his spoon through the dish he found no trace of the rest of it. 'I haven't considered that, Brother Benedetto.'

Only when he was working did he not feel as though he were heading downhill. He tried not to think about the future, because he knew the dangers and hardships he faced. He could hardly explain that to the monk. The Franciscans sought out mortification of the flesh among the poor. For all he knew, Brother Benedetto had skinned the bean and thrown away its meat when he made the soup. 'Wherever I go, Brother, I'll miss your cooking. Where else will I find these sumptuous delicacies?'

Benedetto laughed. 'You're an odd one, Maestro Michele.' He leaned on his knife to cut through a loaf of cheap spelt-flour. The bakeries gave the bread to the Franciscans when it was too stale even for a pauper to dip in his gruel. 'Brother Camillo said you raged at him the other day, because he suggested you wash your clothes.'

Caravaggio slurped his soup.

'You told him *they* might come to take you while you were naked. Who're *they*, Maestro?'

'Innkeepers who wish me to steal your luxurious recipes for them.'

He slouched up the stairs to his studio. He had painted this *Nativity* for the Oratory of San Lorenzo, intending to give the Virgin the face of Lena. But when he came to depict her gazing at the naked baby on the straw, he had been unable to clear his mind of her pale, perspiring, suffering face after she lost their child. He had painted the features of the Maltese girl from the *Beheading* instead.

The few times he had been out into Palermo, suspicion had exhausted him. Every door through which he passed and every sentence he uttered seemed to be a trap, a means by which he might give himself away, make himself known to his murderers. He thought he had seen one of the Tomassoni brothers in the street. He chased after the man, but didn't catch him. Then he fled, when he thought he glimpsed Roero outside the Spanish Viceroy's palace. As he ran, he wondered if he had lost his mind. *It makes no difference. They'll come for me, even if I'm mad.*

In the middle of the day, he started to think that even the beanskin had been an illusion and that the soup had been nothing more than discoloured water. He touched the bones of his face under his beard and found them prominent. His ribs, too, pressed at his skin when he lifted his shirt to look. Hunger overcame his fear.

He went out into the street and headed towards the Norman palace to find an inn. After so many days in the darkness of the monastery, the sun seemed to penetrate his skull. Dizzy, he leaned against the wall outside a pie shop. His eyes blanked, everything was dark. The smell of the baking pastry made him desperate and weak. When his sight returned, the colours were bright and flat, like the first oils laid onto a painting before they were shaded.

A dog scampered out of the pie shop with a sausage in its mouth. The piemaker chased it and cursed. A look at Caravaggio and he was silent. Clearing his throat he returned to his shop. A woman passed with her basket, averting her eyes. Caravaggio squinted into the street. Smiling people quailed when they glanced at his face. *What do they see?* he wondered. *They're repulsed. As if they caught sight of a wounded cat run down by a cart. They know my fate, and they don't want to think about it.*

He followed the piemaker into his shop, laid down a coin, and took a filled focaccia. He stuffed the food into his mouth. His tongue rolled between the soft strips of calf's spleen and lung and throat cartilage. From the entrance of the pie shop, he glanced across the street through the passing mass of carts and people. He saw a man in the red surcoat of the Knights of Malta.

Roero was staring up at the Franciscan compound. Narrowing his protuberant eyes, the knight crossed the road and entered the Oratory.

Caravaggio spat the wad of bread and sweetmeats from his mouth. He rushed into the courtyard of the Franciscans. In his studio, he took up a small sack. Into it, he shoved his brushes and the pigments he hadn't yet ground. He strapped on his sword and took his money belt from the locked box of stamped Spanish leather where he had stashed it.

He leapt down the steps and ran through the gate. From the corner, he spied on Roero as he left the Oratory and went up the staircase to the studio. Thankful for the hunger that had driven him outside, he whispered a blessing for Brother Benedetto's thin broth.

At the port, the next boat was a merchant galley bound for Naples. Once aboard, he crouched behind a barrel, watching for Roero. The sailors avoided him as they prepared to cast off. Gulls hovered over the deck until they chased after the departing sun. The boat put out to sea.

■

The Prince of Stigliano's palace at the edge of Naples overlooked Chiaia and the ellipse of the bay out to the grottoes of Posilippo. For the past several years, the Marchesa of Caravaggio had lodged with her cousin the prince so that she might attend to affairs of property and inheritance around the city. Costanza Colonna sat on a stone bench beside the garden fountain, as Caravaggio waited upon her. She flicked her fingers against two letters in her lap. Her nails were pale and grey. Something in the letters tormented her.

'The Spanish Viceroy has heard of your arrival in Naples.' Costanza cleared her throat. 'He orders you to complete *The Flagellation of Christ* that you left unfinished.'

Caravaggio's assent was grudging. The picture for the Church of San Domenico had left him uninspired. He had been glad to drop it when he took ship for Malta.

'Everyone wants something from you, don't they?' Costanza said.

And you, what do you want? he thought.

She raised her hand, reaching for him, but the fingers clenched and she put her fist back in her lap. She stood and slowly rounded the fountain. 'Look at this balustrade. It's engraved with the crests of some of the most powerful families in the Italian lands. The Carafa, the Stadera, Morra, Capua, Orsini. These clans guard you, Michele, as a service to me, because I'm related to all of them.'

The fish darted in the brown bottom of the fountain.

'We'll get you back to Rome, back to Lena.' Costanza held one of the letters out to him. 'It's from her. When you reply, remind her that Naples is where Boccaccio met his love, Fiammetta. The poet said that to enjoy love it must be sensual, illicit, sweet and difficult.'

'He didn't know the half of it.' Caravaggio turned the letter over. On the back, above the seal, was Lena's name. His excitement mingled with suspicion. Few knew where to find him, and Lena was illiterate. The letter could be a trap. His hands trembled. *She's alive, and I may hope.*

'I need you too, Michele. As she does.' Costanza's neck flushed. 'For Fabrizio's sake.'

'And only for him?'

She twisted the wedding ring given by her long-dead husband. Her voice rose, scolding. 'You have always eaten the bread of my house. Do I now ask so much of you?'

'You ask nothing, my lady, though I would perform any service for you.'

'Brother Antonio Martelli writes to me from Malta.' She lifted the other letter as if it were a diagram of all the shame she had ever felt. 'A sailor was intercepted sculling back from Sicily in a wherry a few days after you escaped the knights' dungeon. He was a crewman of *The Capitana*, Fabrizio's flagship. The sailor was taken by a knight named Roero. He didn't last long under Roero's tortures, but while he lived he confessed that Fabrizio had rescued you from the *guva*.'

'Fabrizio.' He covered his eyes with his hands. 'What's to become of him?'

'If this knight Roero had gone to the Venerable Council, Brother Martelli says Fabrizio would've been suspended for a few months. But Roero took some of his friends to arrest Fabrizio. You remember a Brother Giulio?'

'A bit of a joker.'

'The joke's on him now. Fabrizio refused to go quietly. He ran Brother Giulio through with his rapier and killed him.' Costanza's voice shattered into a sob. 'My son languishes in the dungeon from which he helped you flee.'

Caravaggio remembered the penalty for killing a knight. The sack, sewn up and thrown into the sea.

Just as Lena came closer to him with the letter he held in his hand, his oldest friend moved into mortal jeopardy. 'All my prayers, my lady, shall be for Don Fabrizio, and all my works shall be for him too.' He strained his eyes towards the Sorrento peninsula, as though he might spy his friend's corpse borne on the currents from Malta. Out in the bay, the two jagged peaks of the isle of Capri were a hazy indigo.

In the street, Caravaggio felt mauled, as if the throng that packed Naples was blind and made its way by touch alone. A pair of women quarrelled at a vegetable stand at the crest of the hill leading to the Spanish palace. Children with their noses running and their red eyes streaming jostled around the vendors. Their knees were skinned and scabbed, and their bodies were daubed in filth as if some moralist had tried to paint clothing over their nakedness with mud. The people were feral, reacting to all movement and approach with fear, poised to strike out and bracing to take a blow. They moved like cats – a few quick paces, then they would search around for the next safe spot, hurry there, and assess the threats again.

I'm a murderer, Caravaggio thought, *but I may be the most innocent man for miles around.* He touched the letter inside his doublet. He knew at once where he would read it.

He went towards the oldest part of the city. Since his return to Naples, he had yet to visit the church which held the greatest of his works there. He entered the narrow streets, parallel blocks just as the first Greek settlers had laid them out, and crossed the Spaccanapoli, the long, straight scar that cut the city in two.

Outside the taverns, Neapolitans lifted long handfuls of *maccheroni* and lowered it into their mouths, their heads cast back as if they might feed it directly through their throats and into their stomachs like sword swallowers. The wailing of the *zampogna* cut through the noise of the crowd, a shrill melody and a low bagpipe drone that reverberated in his very ribcage.

He slipped into a pew before the altar of the Pio Monte. Lena gazed on him with compassion. She was *Our Lady of Mercy*, the Virgin he had painted surveying the crowded streets of Naples. He unfolded the letter and read.

> Dearest Michele,
>
> I write to you in the hand of your friend Prospero Orsi. I tell you this so that you may trust what I tell you, and you must not think that anyone but I speaks the words you read. Prosperino wishes you well, as he takes down my words.
>
> For a long time, I dared not contact you. I believed you did not want me. One day you were gone and, though Prosperino told me you had fled because you killed Signor Ranuccio, I knew you were ready to depart, whatever had happened. I do not say you killed Signor Ranuccio to have an excuse to leave me, but I do say it was not difficult for you to go.
>
> This week I heard from Cardinal del Monte's gentlemen as I worked at the Madama Palace that you have returned from Malta to the Italian lands. Perhaps

you do not wish to know me. In that case, destroy this letter. Still I must tell you that I wish you had not left and I wish to hold you in the night – Prosperino pretends to blush, and I blush too because I have never been a wanton woman and I have not become so in your absence.

I love you, Michele. If your travels have shown you that I am your love and that you were mistaken when you left me in Rome, then come to me.

I cannot leave Rome, or I would come and find you even though the road to Naples is dangerous because of all the bandits. I must look after Domenico, who is weak with fever, and my mother, who has gone blind and cannot move the left side of her body.

My own health is poor too, *amore*. My work is hard, because I must stand in the Piazza Navona with my vegetables and the Tomassoni women sometimes scorn me and beat me there. But Cardinal del Monte's steward assigns me easy work out of regard for you, which gives me hope that at least the Cardinal believes you love me.

Come to me, *amore* – Do not make faces, Prosperino – If you have forgotten me, Michele, do not write to tell me. But, also, do not return to Rome. I would not be in the same place as you and be without you.

I go often to Sant'Agostino and I stand before *The Madonna of Loreto*. You were right: no one now pays attention to Maestro Raphael's fresco. They come only to see your painting. Though I have stood there many hours, none has stopped to tell me that I look like the Madonna. My features are too tired perhaps, or these last few years have been unkind. But I think of those times when you painted me and when you showed me the finished painting and took me into your bed –

Prosperino! – I am your Madonna, and I will be with your spirit wherever your work and heart take you. Let it be the will of God that they bring you home to me.

Your Lena.

The girl had made a mark that was something like the letter L beneath her name. Caravaggio heard her voice call from the stiff paper, and he wept. *I wanted to protect her, so I left her behind*, he thought. *But without her I'm a mess*. He had to get to her. He had to get the death sentence lifted, so he could be with her.

The letter had a postscript. He wiped his cuff across his eyes and read on.

Prosperino, the painter of grotesques, greets his dear friend, the greatest of Rome's painters, Michelangelo Merisi of Caravaggio.

Michele, I do not tell the girl what I write here. She believes it is only a few words of friendship. She came to me just now to write to you, and I see that it costs her something to contact you. She is sure you wished to abandon her, though long ago I told her otherwise. But I have been in Venice on a commission and while I was gone others – the Tomassoni women and Fillide – tried to convince Lena that you never loved her.

Her health is poor, Michele. Her skin is grey, the colour of a chimney sweep's spit, and darker than grey beneath the eyes and around her mouth. Her lips are like lead, though I am sorry to tell you that they are also flecked with blood which she coughed out as she dictated her letter.

I know you have tried to overcome the sentence against you. Such things take time. Onorio remains exiled in Milan, awaiting his pardon, and Mario too is in Sicily. Ranuccio's brother is absent from Rome for the same reason. I hope for your sake he knows not where you are. I shall send this letter through del Monte and I shall not ask where it will find you.

I have begged del Monte to intercede on your behalf with Scipione. He was irritated by my request, because he says your case is constantly on his mind and the Cardinal-Nephew needs no reminder from a third-rate artist. I begged him to consider me no more than tenth-rate, so long as he maintains your interests.

I shall do what I can for Lena, Michele, though I am not in the money these days. I have been supporting Onorio's wife. She is most importunate, as our friend sends her no funds from his exile and she has five children to feed. Meanwhile, Baglione and his clique take all the commissions I might have had. You must come back to Rome, Michele.

Your friend who misses all the trouble you used to cause him,

Prospero Orsi.

Caravaggio looked up at his painting. The Virgin held a young Christ at the top of the canvas. He had given the boy Domenico's features, but he had thought there was something in him of the child he might have had if Lena's pregnancy had come to term. He dropped to his knees and pressed the letter to this heart. If he made a few more touches to her image, he wondered, would she step off the canvas, clasp his face between her palms and say, 'Why couldn't you have done that final stroke two years ago?' She could have been with him if he had been artist enough to command her presence out of the paint.

He got to his feet. *I will make her real.*

In the Carità, on the edge of the volatile district of the Spanish soldiers and their whores, he entered an inn called the Cerriglio. Woodsmoke burned his eyes. He sat with a flagon of wine and drank quickly. He turned to the drinkers nearby and raised his cup. He had a letter from Lena. He was loved.

He ate from a basket of dough balls, each one wrapped around a leaf of seaweed to give it a salty flavour and then deep-fried. He called for another jug of wine. The whores at the corner table turned their heads when they heard him shout. One of them rose to approach him, but she was distracted by music in the street.

A sad-eyed musician entered, playing a *tarantella* on a short pipe, his fingers twirling on the airholes. A blind man came behind him, beating six-eight time on a tambourine and singing hoarsely in a dialect Caravaggio couldn't make out. The whores got up to dance. They bounced on one leg. With the other foot they kicked the beat and tapped their clogs to the floor. The whore who had been on her way to Caravaggio's table took his arm. 'Come on, handsome.'

It was hard for him to pick out her features. The wine had struck him quicker than he had expected. The grey light from the windows caught her braid, tied across her head from ear to ear as Lena's used to be. She was the same height as his girl and she had Lena's heavy Greek eyebrows. He would be with Lena again soon. He would find a way to join her in Rome. He drained his cup, laughing, and stood for a dance.

They swept side to side, their arms above their heads. *Lena.* He drank another cup, his head spinning. *I'm loved.* The whore raised a leg and hooked it between his thighs, behind his knee, pushing her groin to him in the dance. Her breath was milky with mozzarella when she laughed. He drew back his knee to bring her towards him.

246

One of the whores brought out a *triccaballacca*, flicking her wrists so that its small mallets swung on their hinges, wood clicking on wood above the rhythm of the music. The dancers strutted and twisted, as if they were working off the poison of the tarantula, as the originators of the dance had done. Caravaggio sensed his body cleansing something he knew had been killing him as surely as a spider's venom. He threw back his head, called out Lena's name, and roared with laughter. The whore poured wine into his smile.

The night stuttered, cut into disconnected moments by the wine and the fervour of his liberation from fear and loneliness. He threw dice on a bench with a Spanish soldier and argued when they fell to the floor. He tossed down his cards in a game of Calabresella, cursing a fisherman for palming the Knave of Cups and bringing out a King of Coins from his sleeve.

He ate a focaccia which was so good he was compelled to bother the cook with such boundless encomiums about the recipe that the whore had to drag him away. Then he lay beneath her in her foetid room above the tavern, groaning and bellowing and grappling with her breasts. He wept and mumbled, not knowing why, as he wrapped himself to her back in sleep.

When he awoke, she was naked, plucking her hairline to keep it far back from her brows, as did all women who wished to be thought beautiful. She turned from the polished pewter plate she used as a mirror and smiled. 'Morning, handsome,' she said.

'What's your name?' His stomach swung within him when he reached for his drawers.

'Stella. At least you didn't ask what you're doing here.'

The snapping rhythm of the *triccaballacca* went on. He frowned, wondering how the *tarantella* could continue all night. Then he realized that what he heard was the pain in his head, so sharp it seemed to him like percussion.

'I don't need to ask *your* name,' the woman said. 'I'm going to call you *o'ntufato*.'

'I don't understand your bloody Neapolitan dialect.'

'It means "the angry one". You were up and down last night like the bit we call the "father of your children".' She mimed a penis engorging and deflating and growing once more. 'One moment you'd be all over some fellow as though you were friends from childhood; next you'd be cursing him and hurling your cup at his head.'

'Oh God. I can't believe it.' He put his legs into his breeches.

'There were some rough types at the inn last night. You insulted so many of them, you're lucky you came away with the nose on your face.'

'No one cut it off, so now I can lose my nose slowly to syphilis instead.'

She kissed the top of his head. 'Don't worry about picking up the French disease from me. You aren't going to be around long enough to die that slowly, *o'ntufato*.'

When he left the tavern, Caravaggio went down the wide boulevard laid out by an old viceroy from Toledo. A gang of Spanish musketeers grew silent at his approach. The tallest of them licked his lips and slapped his gloves against his hand. Caravaggio waited for them to come at him, without time even to wonder why they might attack him. They grinned with anticipation and relish for a brawl. Then their eyes flickered between him and something beyond his shoulder. In a moment he realized that they didn't intend to fight him. They watched for the spectacle of another combat.

He spun to the side. His cloak twirled behind him. His attacker's sword caught in its folds. He unlaced the neck of the cloak and drew his dagger.

Giovan Francesco Tomassoni untangled his rapier from the cloak. 'Lucky for you, fucker, that you always wear black. They won't even have to buy you a new suit to lay you out for your funeral.' He lifted the point of his sword and lunged.

Caravaggio parried with his dagger, gasping as the long blade shuddered past his shoulder. A quick step and he was in close. He punched Tomassoni under the ribcage.

The hilt of the sword came down on his head. It would have cracked his skull had he not twitched out of its path. He felt his ear burning and numb and he knew the blade had caught him there. Caravaggio reeled away.

In his eagerness to strike again, Tomassoni slipped on the manure in the street and went onto his backside. The Spaniards laughed and mocked him. One of them tossed a half-eaten rum cake, catching Tomassoni in the mouth. Furious, he jumped to his feet, spitting cake and wiping crumbs from his moustache.

Caravaggio shoved past the Spaniards and rushed into a narrow side street. He dodged between the children who played naked in the muck and the sacks of produce outside the stores. He cut left towards the safety of the Stigliano Palace. He heard the shouts of Tomassoni clearing the way behind him and the voices of children and women cursing the man in return.

He stumbled through a dark, vaulted alley, striking himself against unseen objects, scattering cats and rats. In the wealthy quarters of Naples and down by the port, the sun would be bright, feeding the bay with shimmering opal and splattering the limestone villas with a glow like a young girl's skin. But here in the Spanish Quarter the lanes were as dark as a gambling den.

Abandoned by the light, Caravaggio went faster into the alleys. At the end of the street, he scrambled into a courtyard. Beneath a squat bell-tower, three high arches led into a church. He sprinted for the darkness and hid himself behind the altar of a side chapel.

When he heard footsteps through the door, he lengthened each breath to calm himself. He flexed his fingers around the hilt of his dagger.

'You think I want to kill you, painter?' It was as though Ranuccio's ghost spoke in the church. The same accent, the timbre that brothers share. 'If I intended to take your life, you'd have been dead a half dozen times already today.'

Tomassoni moved around the nave. 'Next week, they'll hold the parade to the cathedral. The sinners will walk on their knees behind St Gennaro's blood, praying for it to liquefy again. You ought to join them, to atone for your sins. Ah, but that's not the forgiveness you want, is it, you godless bastard. Well, don't worry, I just got my pardon from the Holy Father for my part in the duel. Your *cumpà* Onorio is absolved of guilt, too. You're the only one still on the run.'

Caravaggio heard the bass slap of heavy material thrown suddenly back. *He's searching for me behind the tapestries.*

'My family wants the Colonnas to pay compensation for the death of Ranuccio, because you're their creature. I won't kill you until we get the money. That's not to say I can't give you a *sfregio*, a scar of shame.' A roar of frustration and effort, and a table turned over. Screaming with rage, Tomassoni called out, 'Where are you, you bastard?'

A monk appeared at the entrance to the church. With a Spanish accent, he addressed Tomassoni. 'You forget yourself. You're in a house of God, my son.'

Tomassoni sheathed his sword and placed the table upright. 'I beg your pardon, Father.' His voice was husky and ashamed.

'Leave a donation for St Mary Pilar and be gone.'

Caravaggio heard a coin fall into a metal plate and Tomassoni's footsteps through the door.

The monk approached the side chapel and waited. Caravaggio came from his hiding place and lowered his eyes.

'You'd better leave through the sacristy and go out the back of the monastery.' The monk scratched his tonsure and put his hands inside the sleeves of his white habit. It bore the cross of the Trinitarians, whose mission was to redeem slaves taken by the Moors. 'There's a man outside the main doors, waiting for you.'

'Perhaps I should just face him, after all. I'll be all right, Father.' Caravaggio went towards the entrance.

The monk held his arm firmly. 'I don't mean that thug. Another man is there, a knight.'

Caravaggio shivered. Roero had come for him.

'This way.' The monk led Caravaggio up a spiral staircase. As they passed along a gallery above the cloister of the monastery, he glanced out of the window. Below him, in the courtyard before the church, Roero leaned against a column in the red doublet of the knights.

Caravaggio felt a halting charge in his breast, as though a fist folded around his heart. He followed the monk to the rear of the monastery and went out into the streets.

■

He studied his unfinished *Flagellation of Christ*. Jesus wriggled before the great column to which he was bound as though merely being tickled. The two torturers, one at his side and the other at his feet, appeared no more involved in the infliction of pain than the reverent sponsor of the painting, one Signor de Franchis, who crouched on the opposite side of the suffering Saviour. Caravaggio

251

sucked on his teeth and frowned. The painting owed too much to the work of previous artists. It was as if he were noting things down in shorthand that every art collector would already know. Things that weren't true.

For several days, he had tried to change the tone of the canvas, barely moving from his studio. Roero and Tomassoni were both in Naples, so it was best to stay within the palace walls and work. He had succeeded only in compounding his aversion to the painting. He would have abandoned the entire piece, but there was a bare wall awaiting it in San Domenico close to the main altar and the Spanish Viceroy who ruled over Naples had ordered that he fill that space. The whole thing made him feel devoid of energy, constrained and bored. He wanted to be on his way to Rome, to Lena. His discontent made him reckless.

He tossed his palette down and shrugged his smock over his head. Pulling on his doublet, he shoved a purse inside and stuck his dagger in his belt. Then he went through the twilit streets to the Cerriglio Tavern.

'Hello again, *o'ntufato.*' Stella approached him from the table where the whores congregated. She had a graceless walk, her feet flat and splayed in her sandals and her hips stiff, so that she appeared to limp. Her arm flapped at her side as though she paddled through the air. A noblewoman's poised step would have had a fraction of the beauty that Caravaggio found in Stella's ungainliness.

'I couldn't work, couldn't concentrate.' Caravaggio called for a flagon of wine and something to eat.

'Want me to take your mind off your troubles?' She sat beside him, put her arm across his shoulders and pushed her breasts towards him.

'Even you'd have trouble working that hard.'

She grinned. Something was wrong about her face. He stared at her mouth. Her teeth were tiny and uneven.

'My baby teeth,' she said. 'They never fell out.'

The teeth of an innocent child in the painted face of a whore. He expected her mouth to emit the cry of a starving infant, but instead she gave a rough laugh and bit his neck.

The innkeeper brought a flagon of garnet-red *aglianico* and a plate of artichokes. He shared his meal with Stella. She raised her cup. 'Let the blood of St Gennaro run like this wine.'

The miracle, Caravaggio remembered, *the vial of dried blood from the saint's veins which liquefies three times a year in the cathedral.* He raised his glass with a doubting smile.

'You're sceptical, *o'ntufato?*' Stella said. 'If the blood doesn't turn into liquid, it's very bad for Naples. Whenever the miracle fails, Vesuvius erupts or some army invades or the crops fail or there's an outbreak of the plague.'

'Don't worry about it,' Caravaggio said. 'There's always blood when I'm around.'

A shudder of fear trembled over her face.

He put down a few coins, touched his hand to the girl's cheek and went to the door. 'If the saint's blood doesn't flow, you can take some of mine.'

The moon was the slightest of crescents. He tripped through a darkness that was close to absolute. He stopped to listen, in case he had been followed. It had been foolish to leave the safety of the palace so late in the day. He sucked the flavour of the wine from the end of his moustache and elected to make his way through the narrow streets of the Spanish Quarter. There would be fewer people and he would more easily notice if he was tracked.

He went uphill a couple of blocks and turned left towards Chiaia. A single torch burned a hundred paces ahead of him. He advanced carefully, feeling his way along the walls of the quiet buildings. In the torchlight the silhouettes of four men quivered. Angry voices resounded off the tenement façades.

As he came closer, Caravaggio saw that one of the men was bound and his shirt had been ripped away. Another man sat on his haunches by the wall, holding the torch. The other two manhandled the captive. They kicked him behind the knee and he stumbled. One of the men yanked at the rope around the prisoner's wrists and pulled him backwards. The man cried out in a language Caravaggio didn't recognize. It sounded guttural and breathy like the speech of the Maltese. *Arabic*, he thought. *He's a slave.*

The man who held the rope lifted his foot and shoved it into the small of the slave's back, pulling on the rope with one hand and gripping the man's long dark hair with the other. In his snarl was an intensity so demonic Caravaggio's teeth chattered with fear.

They laughed and taunted the slave. The man with the rope hauled the slave's arms up and pushed against his back with his foot. A cry of agony echoed in the street.

Caravaggio went slowly to the corner, confused and fearful. He would have put a stop to this, but there were three of them and he had only a dagger.

The second man struck the slave a series of blows behind the neck. With each impact, the victim's twisted torso jumped out of the darkness into the strong glow of the torch. The muscles of the slave's chest and belly pulsed in the light.

The man who held the rope handed it to his companion. 'My stomach's killing me,' he said. In the wavering shadow of a doorway, he pulled down his breeches and groaned through a noisy burst of diarrhoea.

His companion giggled and pointed to the slave. 'You'll be dead of the shits even before this heathen goes down to Hell.'

The man came to his feet and tied up his breeches. 'I may shit myself to death, but I'll be damned if I don't outlive this bastard.' He lifted the slave against the wall and pressed his hands to his neck.

Caravaggio felt his own throat constrict as if he were the one throttled. He pictured the *Flagellation* in his basement studio. What would he have done, had he been in the dungeon where the legionaries tormented Our Lord? Would he have risked himself to save Christ? Was this his moment to redeem himself?

He was about to come forward into the light of the torch, when he heard footsteps from the other corner of the street. A cloak billowed as the newcomer closed upon the group. His arm lifted, a rapier catching the orange glow of the fire. 'Leave that poor soul, you scum.'

Caravaggio recognized the anger and the arrogant tone.

'Get lost,' the strangler said.

Roero cut the man's hamstring with a neat motion of his wrist.

One of the thugs fled right away. The younger one, who held the torch, made to go. But Roero halted him, the tip of his weapon at his chest. 'Give me that light. Pick this man up and help him to walk.'

The young man handed the torch to Roero. He looked down at the slave, slumped against the wall, and at the man who had been his tormentor, writhing in the dirt, clutching his ruined leg, breathless with pain. 'Pick him up?' the young man said. 'Which one do you mean?'

'Let me make it easier for you.' Roero stabbed down with his rapier through the wounded strangler's heart. 'Clear enough now?'

Roero went towards the boulevard with the torch. The young man followed, supporting the shuffling slave.

If Roero hadn't been distracted by the violence against the slave, it would have been Caravaggio who lay dead at the point of the knight's sword. Relief carried him to the Stigliano Palace so fast through the dark he seemed barely to touch the mud and the cobbles. In his studio, he set to work right away.

He opened out the canvas, extending it with a fold that he had made behind the original frame to allow a little extra material in case he wanted to change his composition as he worked. He widened the frame by a foot and filled in the holes from the original tacks with stucco. It would give him room to add another torturer for Christ. He painted out the reverent, kneeling patron who had been on the right of the picture.

Caravaggio worked through the night and all of the next day. He concentrated the light on Christ's torso, calling up the shock he had felt as each blow landed on the slave in the Spanish Quarter. On the face of the torturer at the left of Jesus, he painted the frightening viciousness of the man who had died on Roero's sword. The second torturer shoved his leg against Christ's calf, compelling him to take a painful, off-balance stance, as the other pulled his hair and prepared the next blow.

In the last light of the afternoon, he sat on a stool in his studio, slugging wine from a flask. There were still many touches he would need to make, but he had it now. *The Flagellation* was awash with cruelty and pain. It stank like a killing in a backstreet. He stared at the malicious pleasure on the face of the man at Jesus's shoulder. He wondered if this was what people saw on his own face when rage overcame him. The thought shamed him.

9

The Denial of St Peter

Costanza brought a letter to Caravaggio in his studio. She found him reclining on his bolster, as if he were watching the oils dry on the *Salome with the Head of John the Baptist* he had been working on for a week. He intended to ship it to Wignacourt, hoping it would so please the Grand Master that he would order Roero back to Malta.

'Good news from Cardinal del Monte in Rome.' Costanza tried to read Caravaggio's expression in the half-light. She found apprehension there, pure and animal. 'You're to be pardoned.'

He blew out his cheeks as though he had feared to breathe until this message arrived.

'The cardinal writes that Scipione is to pay off the Tomassonis. In return, they won't seek your life.'

He took Costanza's hands and kissed them.

She felt the pressure of his grip as if he had touched her all over. She put her palm to his beard. 'You're not in Rome yet, Michele.'

'I'll be careful,' he said. He kissed her hand once more and ran up the steps to find someone who would be happy for him.

■

In the doorway of the Cerriglio Tavern, he touched his fingers to del Monte's letter tucked inside his doublet. He went through the first room and under the arch to the inner chamber of the inn, where distinguished people came in by a side door to avoid being seen entering such a low place. He went straight out to the rear courtyard whose walls were decorated with proverbs celebrating the pleasures of food and wine. Stella sat at the edge of the small fountain, bleaching her hair in the sun. Mahogany highlights shone in the long russet strands spread over the brim of her wide, crownless hat. She saw the joy on his face. '*O'ntufato*,' she said, 'I'm going to have to find a different nickname for you.'

■

Stella opened the shutter. The sun lanced through Caravaggio's eyeballs into the pulsating dryness in his head. He rolled onto his side in the bed, stifling a retch.

Stella was already in her purple gown. 'I'll go and tell Ugo to put aside a focaccia for you. It'll calm your stomach.'

He frowned at her. She shook her head. Her smile was touched with bitterness. 'If I had a ducat for every time I've seen that nervous "What did I do last night?" look on a man's face, I'd have a dowry big enough to make me a duchess.'

'I don't see you as new nobility. You're more the type to endow a convent.'

'You're still sarcastic. So you can't be too hungover. I see you're wondering, so let me fill you in: you didn't get into any fights last night and you fell asleep while I was undressing. I couldn't wake you no matter what I did. It was as though you hadn't slept deeply in years.'

He would have told her it was true, but he couldn't find the spit to lubricate his tongue.

'Come down when you're ready to eat.' She shut the door.

After he had dressed, his sluggishness left him in a moment and he was alert. Del Monte's letter was missing. He went around the room, wrenching Stella's few items of furniture across the floor, turning over the dresses in her trunk. It wasn't there. His nausea made him dizzy. He had to get some food, to settle himself, so he could think straight enough to find the letter. He went down to eat.

The focaccia tasted gummy and bitter. He sat back to chew it and hit his head against a big round of cheese, hung up to mature. The cook noticed his frown. He rolled out another ball of dough, sprinkled it with rosemary and laid it in the oven. 'Hard to get it down, right?'

Caravaggio rubbed his head and stared accusingly at the cheese. 'What's wrong with the focaccia, Ugo?'

'The sirocco blew up during the night. I could tell as soon as I awoke. It makes me feel a pressure in my ears. Drives me crazy. But it isn't only people who get irritable when the damp wind comes. It changes the way the ingredients in the focaccia react with each other.'

'You're kidding?'

'It's true. Watch out today, Michele. Everyone misbehaves when the sirocco comes to Naples – even my dough.'

Caravaggio drank a cup of wine and went out onto the slope in front of the inn. The clouds carried in by the sirocco seemed to press the sun down low. It glared off the roofs and the damp cobbles. He blinked and tried to get to the shaded side of the street. In the impenetrable Neapolitan dialect, every voice around him sounded like a threat. He was suddenly aware of his vulnerability.

The silhouette of a man approached him from his right. The man flicked his fingers off the tip of his chin. Caravaggio went for his dagger, but someone who had come up on his left grabbed his hand.

Two other men held him from behind. Their breath strained as he struggled. The sun dazzled him.

Something cold drew down his right cheek. A glint of sunlight caught the edge of a dagger. He had been cut. The men who held him kicked at his legs. When he dropped, they thrust their knees into his ribs, laughing quietly.

Another blow to his face. He didn't see the weapon, but he knew the wound was deeper. It rang through his skull. The blustery air entered the gash and froze the bone.

He remembered the letter, the freedom that was soon to be his. He searched for Roero or for Tomassoni – whichever of them led this attack. *Get him and the others will fade away*. The glare blinded him. He butted the man directly before him. The man went down, falling into the low shadows where Caravaggio could make out his features. Giovan Francesco Tomassoni snarled as he came to his feet, the point of his dagger at Caravaggio's gullet.

A terracotta chamberpot struck Tomassoni full in the face. The pot smashed to the ground and Tomassoni dropped back, out cold. The other men let go their hold and dragged Tomassoni away. They cursed at someone, though it wasn't Caravaggio.

'*O'ntufato*, you forgot your letter.' Stella leaned from her window on the upper floor of the Cerriglio with a parchment in her hand. 'Why did you drop it in my pisspot, anyway?'

Caravaggio sat in the street, wondering if he was dying. The girl came down to him. She pressed a cloth against the wound in his cheek.

'How bad is it?' he asked.

She hissed and grimaced.

'Bad enough to shut even your mouth, eh?'

'Let's just say, you've painted your last self-portrait,' she said. 'Unless you really want to turn people's stomachs.'

Cardinal Del Monte's hairline had receded beneath his beret since Caravaggio had left Rome. Good living coloured his face almost to the shade of his scarlet robes. When he stepped from his carriage outside the Prince of Stigliano's palace, he saw the wounds beneath the painter's right eye and turned away with a wince.

They climbed the steep steps to the Church of San Domenico, guarded by a half dozen men in the Stigliano livery. Costanza had forced them to take bodyguards from among the palace grooms who had been cutting the grass in the gardens to sell for hay. She was sure Tomassoni would attack again.

'In Rome, it was reported that you were dead.' Del Monte paused outside the door of the church to recover his breath from the climb.

Caravaggio scanned the piazza, the palaces of the Dukes of Velleti and Casacalenda and of the Prince of San Severo. *He's watching for Tomassoni*, del Monte thought. *Or someone else, for all I know. He never was short of enemies.*

'Did they send you to Naples to work a miracle and bring me back to life?' Caravaggio blinked, as if his eye were obstructed by some detritus.

'No one is likely to mistake *me* for the vehicle of Our Lord's wonders.' Del Monte went into the church and crossed the nave to a chapel beside the main altar. He stood before *The Flagellation*, his fingers in his white beard and his weight on one hip. 'The thought that you might be dead caused the Cardinal-Nephew to make haste, finally. As Scipione sees it, this sort of art –' he held

261

out his palm towards the tormented Christ '– ought to be in Rome, not in Naples. Actually it ought to be in his personal gallery, not in a church.'

'Does Lena think I'm dead, too?'

Del Monte felt himself taken up into the canvas. The life it depicted was so precarious that he sensed Caravaggio's desperation even before the man stepped towards him and took his arm in an insistent grip.

'Does she believe me dead?'

Del Monte hesitated. He was unwilling to admit that he had concerned himself with a maid who washed the floors of his palace and dusted his picture frames. She was Caravaggio's woman, which made her someone whom he reckoned into his plans, but his dignity prevented him from further contact. 'I sent her a message that I'd travel to Naples to investigate.'

'I made a mistake. I should never have left Rome. She's not in good health – she needs me. Take me back there, to Rome.' Caravaggio laid his fingertips on the wound across his cheek. 'Surely you see what'll become of me here.'

'If it was only your soul that was required to do penance, I might grant you an indulgence from the Holy Father and all your sins would be paid. But, as you point out, it's also your body that's in jeopardy.' Del Monte extended a finger towards the livid scar below Caravaggio's eye. 'Even a document from the Holy Father is no amulet against harm, unless all the political arrangements have been well made.'

Caravaggio's eye wavered, drifting to the side as though the dagger blows to his face had damaged some controlling nerve inside the socket. He cursed and cupped his hand over it.

Del Monte recalled the early days of Caravaggio's triumph after the *Matthew* canvases at the Church of San Luigi. The painter's rages had been filled with pride and contempt, but del Monte had forgiven these flaws. He had known them to be a screen for fear and loneliness. Now his protégé was stripped even of these defences. Caravaggio's arrogance had been voided, as though his years on the run had exhausted the gland in which it was produced and siphoned it away.

The cardinal examined the brushstrokes in Christ's calf, where the muscle strained as the foot twisted. 'It's a shame we can't just take this *Flagellation* back for Scipione.'

'Take me instead.'

'Some excellent art would be better received – as an appetizer, if you like. You can be the main course.'

'Then I've got something for him.'

They went back to the Stigliano Palace. In the studio, Caravaggio pulled away the cloth that covered a painting of a bald, bearded man, a woman and a soldier. The man turned his hands to his chest and pulled in his chin, denying some accusation. 'St Peter.'

Del Monte went close to the canvas. He glanced sidelong at Caravaggio. *The man makes so many bad decisions*, he thought. *How can he produce such judicious art, such insight into the way people are, and yet not be a saint?* 'It's so immediate, Michele.' He let his hands follow the lines of the brush like a musician conducting an ensemble. 'Peter almost looks as *you* might, when you're an old man.'

'I hope to live so long.'

Michele gave his own face to Peter at the moment of his guilty denial of Christ, del Monte thought. The saint pointed at his heart to show sincerity, but it was the lying manoeuvre of a desperate man. In his expression, del Monte saw that he was guilt-ridden. His eyes didn't quite rest on the face of the soldier interrogating him. They were distant, looking over the soldier's shoulder.

Del Monte turned to Caravaggio in surprise. *He's ashamed of himself.* 'St Peter overcame his guilt. Remember that, Michele. He went on to found the Church in Rome.'

'Where he met his death.'

In the dark studio, Caravaggio's face was shadowed. His wounds marked him as an insulted man. They glinted like silver highlights on black cloth.

The cardinal beckoned to his page and ordered him to roll up the *St Peter*. 'I'll take this to Scipione when I leave Naples. Write me a letter for him now. Promise him another three canvases like this. He'll be so relieved that you're alive, he'll want you back in Rome right away.'

'What about Fabrizio? The Marchesa's son, in jail in Malta.'

Del Monte saw the guilt in Caravaggio's face, just as he had read it in the depiction of St Peter. *Is it only the loyalty of a family retainer that makes him speak up for this Colonna? There's something else . . .* 'Unfortunately for Don Fabrizio, his talents are of a less decorative nature than yours. But I'll do what I can.'

'He saved me in Malta.'

Del Monte adjusted his beret. 'Let's just write the letter now.'

Caravaggio knelt beside a linen trunk for a desk. He scribbled out the letter as del Monte dictated. The pageboy removed the tacks from the edge of the *St Peter*. When the boy started to roll it, Caravaggio looked up. 'Not that way,' he shouted, 'God damn it.'

The page dropped the canvas.

'Roll it with the paint outwards.' Caravaggio's voice was savage. 'If you roll it with the paint in, it'll compress the oils and damage the work.'

Del Monte laid a gentle hand on the page's shoulder and spoke the final line of the letter. 'Your most humble, devoted and obliged servant and creature, Michelangelo Merisi of Caravaggio. Can you put your name to those words?'

Caravaggio glanced in apology at the boy. 'Humble, devoted and obliged,' he said, as he dipped the quill again. 'Your creature.'

Del Monte drew a paper from his sleeve. It was bound with a red twine and sealed with the imprint of his ring. He handed it to Caravaggio. 'Here's your safe-conduct to Rome. I'm going to leave it here with you. It'll get you through the port inspection when you arrive. Don't use it until I tell you it's all right to return.'

Caravaggio balanced the document flat in his hands, his features amazed and wary. To del Monte his touch against the paper seemed as delicate as a man caressing his lover's face.

avid with the Head of Goliath
Caravaggio pulled away as Costanza touched his wounds with the cloth. Tomassoni's dagger still hummed inside his head. *But I've beaten its summons*, he thought. He had the letter of safe passage from del Monte. He would return soon to Rome and to the one woman for whom it was worth living. He had signed his name to a humiliating letter for Scipione, but it would merit the humbling if it brought him to Lena. *Your creature.* He was tired of life in the basement of Costanza's cousin.

'Wait, Michele.' The Marchesa lifted the cloth again.

'You don't have to do this, my lady.'

'The wound has to be cleaned.' She went delicately along the scab that drew down from his eye to his lip. 'If it gets infected –'

'You're worried I might die?'

'An infection would . . .' She halted, hearing accusation in his voice. 'Michele, what do you mean?'

'I'm going to live. I'm going back to Rome.' His defiance was edged with resentment and frustration. *I've been forced into danger for this woman and she has kept me always servile, humiliated.*

'Of course you are, Michele.'

'I'll see to it that Scipione orders the knights to free Fabrizio.' His sarcasm was undisguised.

She threw the cloth into the ewer of water on her lap. Her face was thin and pale, like a sketch with a fine quill and watered ink. Concern for Fabrizio pared her down and sucked her from the inside.

'You don't have to deny it,' he said. 'You don't have to pretend to be worried about me.'

'That's an awful thing to say.'

'It stands to reason you'd be worried. You'd have nothing to bargain with if I was dead. It's only natural. You're Fabrizio's mother, after all.'

'And what am I to *you*?' Her voice was loud. Her body quivered. She raised the ewer and dashed it to the floor.

Her shriek punctured his anger. He thought of the young woman who had taken him in when his father died. She had been with him all this time. She had understood him with as little effort as Lena had.

She murmured, 'It's the least you can do for Fabrizio after what you did to him.'

What does she mean? he wondered. *Something that happened on Malta?*

She saw his confusion and added, 'When you were boys.'

She thinks I seduced Fabrizio. He was about to spit out the words he knew would hurt her – that Fabrizio had been the one who wanted *his* touch – but his throat closed up. He thought back to Fabrizio's chamber almost thirty years before. Who had reached out first? Perhaps his memory had shielded him from his guilt. *I always thought I sacrificed myself for him, that I allowed Fabrizio's father to believe I was the one who made love to his blameless son.*

267

The wounds in Caravaggio's face stung and his neck twitched. *Was I telling the truth? Is this all because of me?* He blinked. *No, surely that's not how it was.*

Costanza sucked her upper lip and squeezed her fists together in her lap. 'Forgive me. Yes, you'll return to Rome. You're right.'

He would leave her and she would be alone. *What's worse – to have a price on your head as I do*, he thought, *or to know that at any moment the boy who grew from your own body may meet his death?*

'Those who love you the most see you more clearly than you see yourself,' she said.

'I'm a painter. Who sees better than I?'

'A lover, a mother – or God. His sight is clearest of all. With Fabrizio, you were a boy and you behaved as a boy, but you felt a man's guilt. You can't allow yourself to be forgiven.'

'But Fabrizio —'

'If you don't know that he loves you, then you know nothing.'

He pushed the heel of his hand against his brow. 'We have sinned so much, my lady, Fabrizio and me.'

Costanza leaned close and kissed his wounds.

◼

The Baptist's plump foot rested on the log at the fringe of the canvas. Caravaggio edged the toes with a deep umber, filling the nails with grime. He stepped back from the painting, the first of the works he would take to Rome for Cardinal Scipione. The young St John reclined on a stump, his fleshy midriff twisting against his staff and a flowing red drapery. Beside him, the ram that was the symbol of the saint reached up to eat a leaf from a tree.

'He's a bit chubby for an ascetic who lived off locusts in the desert, don't you think?'

Caravaggio dropped his palette and brush. Spinning towards the stairs beyond the studio door, he unsheathed his dagger.

'A fat little saint. It's almost conventional. Back in Rome everyone's doing dirty toenails now, just like you. I couldn't even call that a typical touch of Caravaggio anymore.' Leonetto della Corbara grinned as he approached the canvas. Guiding the dagger back to its sheath, he embraced Caravaggio. He held on as the artist pulled away. 'But I imagine the painters who copy your style in Rome wouldn't be quite so poised to drop their work and take up their weapon.'

'Yes, I'm the real thing.'

The Inquisitor slipped his hands into the sleeves of his black habit. His beard, unshaven for a day or two, cut dark across his grey skin. His eyes were avid and hesitant, like a man unsure of a woman yet desperate for love. 'I was happy to hear from Cardinal del Monte that the reports of your death were as exaggerated as Maestro Baglione's reputation.' A nervous, failed laugh. 'Even so, infections can set in, when a man is wounded. I'm doubly pleased to see that you still live.'

'Perhaps I'm already dead. I seem to be meeting so many ghosts from my past. Del Monte, and now you.'

'Maybe you've gone to heaven.'

'I wouldn't expect to see you there.'

Della Corbara looked hurt. It was a tactic he had employed before, but Caravaggio was surprised to see the expression linger.

The Inquisitor went to a curved-wood chair. 'Sit down, Maestro.' The Inquisitor's face was grave and for once it seemed he didn't pretend. Caravaggio gripped the arms of the chair tight.

'Michele, Lena is dead.'

Caravaggio doubled forward as though a dagger gutted him.

Della Corbara laid a hand on his shaking shoulder. The

Inquisitor's touch was trembling and exploratory, like a rat seeking food.

'I don't believe you.' The wounds in Caravaggio's face seemed to break open and burn. 'How did she die?'

'She caught a chill standing in the Piazza Navona with her vegetables. Her lungs were weak, it seems. Within a few days . . .' The verminous hand crept to the back of Caravaggio's neck. 'But come now, Michele. She was twenty-eight years old. It's not such a young age for Our Lord to take to His breast a poor woman in lowly circumstances. Let's talk about how I can help you with Cardinal Scipione.'

'What do I need your help for now? Lena's dead. What is there for me in Rome?'

'Redemption. Greatness as an artist.'

Caravaggio shoved the Inquisitor's hand away.

'Very well, how about your head on your shoulders?' della Corbara said. 'Because it's clear that here you'll be dead very soon.' He jabbed his finger into Caravaggio's scarred cheek.

The artist yelled with pain.

'I'm skilled in torture, Michele, but I'm not merciless.'

Caravaggio felt as though his muscles were wasting by the second. Breathing seemed an intolerable burden. His face contorted as if he were an angry child trying to squeeze out a tear. 'She had a beautiful soul.'

Della Corbara's hand circled Caravaggio's neck, like a seducer drawing him in for a kiss. 'Come to Rome. It's what you want. For yourself.'

'I don't want anything anymore.'

'What about your paintings? What do you want people to think of when they see your works? Innocence and the souls of the martyrs? Or murder?' The hand was in Caravaggio's hair now, caressing. 'Come to Rome and rescue your paintings. Even if you think yourself not worth saving, your work must be.'

Della Corbara toyed with a mortar and pestle on the table. 'You work from nature. By showing what you see, you reveal the deepest meaning of your subject. But what if you were commissioned to paint the Council of Ten that rules over the Republic of Venice?'

'What do you mean?'

'By a quirk of the Serenissima's history, there are in fact seventeen men on the Council of Ten. If you painted the Council, would you show ten men, so that everyone knew it was the famous Council of Ten? Or would you paint seventeen men and allow everyone to wonder what it was that you had depicted?'

'You're trying to trick me?'

'I'm an Inquisitor. You may be assured that I'm always trying to trick you.' He rose stiffly. 'But as Leonetto, the merchant's son from Salerno, I want to warn you. If you think nature can be observed and painted on a canvas, you forget that people's secrets aren't so easily recognized. There's no chiaroscuro in the heart, no radiance emerging from the shadows. The soul lies entirely in darkness. Only God brings it to the light.'

He went to the door. 'After you left Malta, the Cardinal-Nephew called me to Rome to report on what had happened. I came to know Lena there. I told her stories about you. I gave her absolution before her death, Michele. She's in the company of Christ.'

Caravaggio felt his chest tighten. He saw the trap that had been laid for him. Not by della Corbara or Scipione, nor by Tomassoni or Roero. It was set by the Almighty and he felt its jaws about to snap on him.

'If you wish to enter Heaven and be reunited with Lena, you must redeem yourself in the eyes of the Church. Otherwise, you know where you're going.' The Inquisitor poked his index and little finger downwards – the sign of the devil. 'Finish the paintings for Cardinal Scipione. Then you may come to Rome and be forgiven before God. I'll be in Naples for two weeks on other business for the Holy Inquisition. Return with me to Rome. We'll pray together for Lena's soul in front of the portrait you made of her as the *Madonna of Loreto*.'

Della Corbara mounted the steps. He was out of sight when Caravaggio heard his voice. 'Meanwhile, I'll pray for you. You look about ready to die. But don't let my prayers be in vain.'

Caravaggio stared into the mirror, preparing for his self-portrait. His mouth hung open, as though he had just sprinted some distance and needed more than the usual breath. His damaged eye wavered above the wound in his cheek, the image in the mirror blurred, and he squinted in frustration. The horror of what he saw crept across his features. His father had watched death summon his spirit from the plague room – it was coming for him too.

He shambled across the room like a man woken too early. The basement felt like a dungeon. He needed air. He went up to the gates of the palace and leaned against the piers of the entrance, breathing hard.

A group of women came over the hill from the Royal Palace and the old quarters, dancing and singing. 'The blood of St Gennaro liquefied,' they called out. 'God bless the saint and his miracle.'

It's a sign, he thought. *You know what you have to do.*

One of the Stigliano porters came out of the gatehouse and watched the women go by. 'The blood of the saint flows. We're all saved for another year,' he said.

The evening breeze brought the scent of salt on the air from the bay. Caravaggio watched the women dance down to the incoming tide on the beach. 'Let us give thanks for the blood,' he said. He went back to his studio to write a message.

In the morning, Caravaggio went down to the waterfront. He strode with purpose away from the city, until he came to the narrow strand of Chiaia. The fishermen gathered around their small boats, chattering with the eagerness of men who spent their nights riding alone on the darkness of the bay. They argued the price of their catch with the women and pulled handfuls of grey shrimp and coral-pink octopus from their pails.

A man perched against one of the beached wherries. His stillness marked him out against the laughing fishermen. At Caravaggio's approach, he rose and threw back his cloak. The fishermen moved away when they saw the cross of the Order of the Knights of St John of Malta on his breast.

From the rocks above the beach, Caravaggio touched the skin beneath his good eye and pulled it down, the Neapolitan signal that asked, *Do you understand?*

Roero licked at his lips and bared his teeth. As if to show that he too had learned the gestures of the city, he lifted his hand, the tips of all his fingers meeting and an insistent little shake from the wrist. *Hurry up.*

In his studio beneath the Stigliano Palace, Caravaggio completed the paintings for Cardinal Scipione faster than he had imagined possible. Three canvases, side by side, filling out the figures on one as the paint dried on the others, then moving on to the next to lay in new details once the oils were stable enough.

The Inquisitor came upon him as he blocked in the body of a youth for the final canvas. The model, a kitchen boy from the palace staff, held a bag of apples from his outstretched arm and gazed upon it mournfully. 'What's this? A sad still life with fruit?' della Corbara said.

'It doesn't matter what he's holding.' Without coming from behind his curtain, Caravaggio adjusted the concave mirror he was using to project the boy's torso. 'I just want the weight of the fruit, so I can show the muscles of his arm working.'

Della Corbara twitched his lips, watching the light from the high lantern pale on the boy's thin biceps. 'I'm glad you came to see it my way.'

Caravaggio opened the curtain and lifted his chin.

'Cardinal Scipione will be most pleased with me. Del Monte, too.'

Caravaggio gave a low, graceful bow. When he raised himself, his expression was placid and implacable. The Inquisitor was unnerved. 'Carry on, Maestro,' he mumbled. 'We sail north for Rome in two days. I'll see you at the boat.'

'I can't wait.'

The artist's insolent tone made della Corbara halt. He regarded him with curiosity, then impatience.

◼

The young model held the sword at a gentle angle across his legs, while Caravaggio worked at the slash of light down its centre and along its outer edge. Costanza watched from the foot of the steps. Caravaggio hadn't painted this boy's features. The face she saw on the canvas was of someone else. She couldn't quite place the pursed lips and pitying eyes. At the end of his foreshortened arm, the boy held a head. It was, as yet, without detail. From the darkness of the background, it emerged as a mass of unkempt hair and a beard. The base colour of the face was already drying as a yellowish brown.

'It's *David with the Head of Goliath*, is it not, Michele?' she said.

Caravaggio went on with his work. 'Quite so, my lady.'

She had seen many Davids before, but never one like this. David was usually a triumphant figure, the helmeted warrior of old Maestro Donatello or the muscular giant by the divine Michelangelo which she had seen in a square in Florence. 'The way you've painted it, David looks so sad.'

Costanza tried to remember how Caravaggio had appeared as a child. *There's more than a trace in the painting*, she thought, *of the boy I took in so many years ago.* 'Is it you, Michele?'

He rounded on her. She stepped away in surprise. The wound on his cheek, the twitching eye, the lowered shoulders, his scars all threatened her.

'The boy looks like you used to.' She gestured towards the canvas with a quivering finger.

'You're mistaken, my lady.'

The model broke his pose and reached for the fruit in a bowl beside him. He tossed a grape into the air and caught it in his mouth.

'Keep still,' Caravaggio said.

He circled his brush on his palette to load the bristles. 'My lady, I must get on with my work. I'll be here all night as it is. I need to be finished in time to sail with Father della Corbara tomorrow.'

'Will the paint be dry by then? Surely there's no time.'

'My lady, please.' He shuffled his feet, seeming embarrassed to have raised his voice. 'There're ways to pack the canvases so that the work won't be damaged, even if the oils aren't quite dry. Now, please, your Grace.'

As she reached the step, he bent to build the highlights of the cloth draped from the boy's shoulder. She was sure this *David* would be a masterpiece. It would overturn the conventions by which the biblical king had so long been portrayed. She watched the muscles in Caravaggio's back move under his light smock.

She felt such love for this man, whose genius might even rescue Fabrizio. She recognized love, too, in the intensity of his labour. *It doesn't matter what happened all those years ago. My boys loved each other and that love endures.*

'Michele,' she called.

His head dropped back and he sighed with impatience.

'Thank you.'

His eyes were shadowed black by the lantern above him, but she was drawn to them. She wondered if he wanted her to enter those dark passages, to follow them right to the heart that had so often been hidden from her.

The boy launched another grape. He laughed as it bounced off his lip and rolled across the floor.

'Good night, my lady.' Caravaggio went back to his canvas.

Beneath the loggia of the Stigliano Palace, the cart was loaded with his few possessions. Caravaggio tossed a rolled canvas into the back and came over to Costanza. He was bent at the waist. His mid-section seemed to have collapsed into his hips. He looked as though completing the paintings for Scipione had expended an entire lifetime's energy.

'You have your safe passage from Cardinal del Monte?' Costanza took his hands in hers.

'I have it, my lady.'

'In a day you'll be in Rome, safe from harm, pardoned for – for that fight. A free man.'

The Pope might forgive me my sins, Caravaggio thought, *but it's to God and to Lena that I must make my most earnest supplications.* He bowed to Costanza.

She drew him close and touched her mouth to the scar on his

cheek. A dart of loneliness pricked at him.

'You have the paintings, too, for Cardinal Scipione?' she said.

He reached over the side of the cart and tapped his hand against the tan weave of the canvas, tied with twine. 'The *St John*, a *Magdalene*, and *David*. I'll pack them properly once we get to the boat. I'm in too much haste now to reach the port.' He swung up onto the seat beside the carter. As the mules lurched forward in the traces, he touched his hand to Costanza's shoulder. 'You'll see Fabrizio soon, my lady.'

'God willing. Then we'll never be parted again. I'll never ask anything more of you. Since you were a boy, you've made such sacrifices for me.'

He protested, but she held up her palm to stop him. 'I understand that you left my household for Fabrizio's sake. I can hardly know what it cost you. You've nothing more to pay.'

Soon enough that'll be so, he thought. His injured eye wavered and she was a flickering blur, her hands over her heart until the cart went out of the gate.

The mules turned down to the beach. Caravaggio watched the bay curve towards the sap-green haze of Posillipo. The water was a vibrant shimmer of gold. The sea held his fate now.

When the carter reached the bottom of the road, he made to turn for Santa Lucia and the port. Caravaggio held his wrist. 'Not that way.'

With a shrug, the man yanked at the reins and took him inland. They went uphill and skirted behind the Stigliano Palace and the edge of the Spanish Quarter. Caravaggio directed the driver to a gate in a long plain façade. He whispered a few words to the man, gave him a bag of coins, and jumped down. He went through the gate and crossed a sunny grove of mandarin and lemon. He murmured the melody of the old Bolognese song. *You are the star that shines. More than any other lady.* At the far side of the courtyard, four armed men leaned against the wall of a chapel. Their faces were stern and hostile. Above them, a red flag dangled in the humid stillness. The white cross of the Order of the Knights of Malta.

◼

In her study, Costanza wrote to the Grand Master of the Knights. She informed him that Caravaggio had returned to Rome under the protection of del Monte and would take up a position in Scipione's household. She wanted the man who held the key to Fabrizio's freedom to know that she had secured an influential ally in the Pope's retinue and that she believed her son must now be freed. *Most humbly I salute you and pray God for your every happiness*, she signed off. *From Naples, July 18, 1610.*

The interminable slope of Vesuvius rose to its daunting crater across the bay. The sun shimmered on the water with an intensity that made her feel so much more a northerner, alien to this southern madhouse of vivid colours and crowds. The distant town of Caravaggio, where she had spent her adult life, was small, its weather damp and misty most of the year. From the street below, the raucous, gabbling dialect of the Neapolitans rose up to her and she wished she were at home.

She went along the loggia of the *piano nobile* and down the main stairs. Without the company of the artist she loved, she was drawn to his studio. She recalled her days as a young mother when Michele and Fabrizio had brought so much life to her palace – before her husband had made them part.

On the steps of the basement, she stopped to fill her nostrils with the scent of his paints. She expected the room to be empty, but the air would carry the memory of his work, the sweetness of linseed. She would find his presence there, even though he was gone to Rome.

The basement was dark but not empty. She went towards the window, stumbling against a trolley. It overturned and she heard the clattering of brushes as they dropped to the flagstones. She climbed the step to the window and pushed open the shutters. The sun lit up a canvas on an easel. It was the *Magdalene* Caravaggio was supposed to have taken to Cardinal Scipione. She went closer. She knew the features of the woman he had painted, though she had never met her. Often enough in his works she had looked at the strong eyebrows, the straight nose, the gentle mouth. But he would never have left behind a picture of Lena. His materials, his preparations and pigments, his brushes and palette, his mirrors, his swords and armour and other props, were strewn around the basement.

She reached up to the next window and shoved at the shutter. Her breath was tight. Had he betrayed her? On the furthest easel, the light from the window fell now on another canvas. It was the *David with the Head of Goliath* she had seen him working on the night before. She caught her hand to her breast and cried out as though someone had been slain before her eyes. The massive head of the biblical giant wore the suffering features of the painter. Blood gushed from Caravaggio's severed neck. His eyes were open, his lips parted as if for a final word.

Shaking, Costanza dropped to her knees before the canvas. She hadn't been mistaken. The boy's features were those of Caravaggio too. He had painted his young, innocent self as the regretful executioner of the adult, the murderer, the condemned man. She stared at Goliath's mouth, his choking tongue. The giant spoke, even in death, she was sure.

On the blade of the sword, something was inscribed. She peered closer and saw the motto of the Augustinian monks. *Humilitas occidit superbiam*. Humility kills pride. Did it mean that arrogance had led Caravaggio to sin? For the wicked pride to be eliminated, would he have to suffer death, like Goliath?

She heard a carriage enter the courtyard and a man shouting. Footsteps sounded on the stairs to the basement. The Inquisitor entered the room, squinting into the shadows. Costanza reached out for the wall to support herself. The motion caught the Inquisitor's attention. 'Michele? In God's name what're you doing? Why didn't you come to the port?'

She dropped into the window alcove and he recognized her. 'My lady, forgive me. I thought you were—' He saw the canvas, saw Goliath's head. 'By Christ.'

'What has he done?' She knew this painting wasn't the work of a man on his way to freedom. It was as though Michele's spirit hovered on the canvas, on the edge of death.

The Inquisitor shook his head, his lips pursed in fury. He kicked at a pile of dirty rags. 'May he be damned for doing this to me.' He pushed his beret to the back of his head. 'Ah, but this is the best thing he's painted.'

Costanza hurried up the steps to the courtyard and called for her carriage. If Caravaggio hadn't gone to the port, perhaps he had chosen a different way so that he might avoid the Inquisitor. She would follow him by the land route and force him to take the canvases. He must have them, so that he could be free. She would save him.

A rider came through the gates. He jumped down from his horse. Costanza rounded her carriage to see him. *Is it Michele?*

The horseman looked about him. When he saw Costanza, he ran across the cobbles towards her.

Fabrizio grasped his mother to him and laughed.

She shook like a palsied old woman. He took her shock for astonishment at his unexpected arrival. 'The knights brought me to Naples yesterday. They kept me here at the Priory. Then this morning they set me free. I'm pardoned, Mama, can you believe it? Thank you.'

'My soul, you're here.'

'It must be because of you. Thank you, darling Mama.' He kissed her cheeks and neck. 'They must've let me go for your sake.'

For my sake. She trembled and shook her head. Her sight went black. From the canvas in the basement, Michele's severed head glided towards her out of the darkness. His features were possessed by Death, and though they had no words she heard them speak. *Michele had found a way to redeem himself. He's gone to the knights.* She would have Fabrizio, and those killers would have Michele.

The needle slipped in and out of the calico sackcloth. The fishermen on the small boat laughed viciously, spitting. 'Careful you don't stick him with that pin,' one of them said. 'Wouldn't want to hurt him.'

With each stitch, the sunlight through the opening of the sack narrowed. Caravaggio watched it become a single shaft across the darkness, such as he had often used to illuminate his paintings. At the prow of the boat, Roero turned away. The final gap in the sack closed. Caravaggio linked the fingers of his bound hands in prayer.

The men picked him up and dropped him over the side. He hit the water. All his rage left him like a fire quenched. In the darkness under the surface, his father floated towards him. He sensed his touch as he passed. The martyrs he had painted drifted by, hands raised in benediction. Absolute silence and peace enveloped his body. As the breath went out of him, he saw a diffuse light. It crowned Lena. She inclined towards him as she had done in his *Madonna of Loreto*. She reached out. When her hand cradled his cheek, he felt cool and ecstatic.

The Knight Prior of Naples, Vincenzo Carafa, waited for Roero on the quay. He glanced with disdain at the lumpy, damp sack in the well of the boat as the fishermen put in.

'Did you get his paintings from the Marchesa?' Roero asked.

'Mind your own business.'

'Be sure you send them to the Grand Master. They're to be his compensation for Brother Fabrizio's freedom. Don't think *you* can keep them. The Marchesa has her precious son back. She won't complain about losing a few canvases.' He stepped up to the quay.

The Prior put a restraining hand on Roero's shoulder and gestured towards the sack. 'I don't want him here. You've had your revenge, Brother. Get rid of him a long way from Naples – and not at sea. If he drifts ashore in a sack, people will know what it means. That's how *we* do it.'

Roero returned to the boat. He commanded the surly fishermen to row back out into the bay.

AUTHOR'S NOTE

For several centuries, critics scorned Caravaggio as a ruffian whose work lacked depth. But his influence on painting is immense. Rubens spread his style across Northern Europe. Velazquez took his aesthetic to Spain. He's central to the style of contemporary artists, photographers and film-makers like David Hockney and Martin Scorsese.

Yet his death is an enigma, usually explained by art historians with a tortuous tale of mistaken identity, missed boats and a malarial beach in Tuscany. Some say it's not so unusual for a man who died 400 years ago to have simply disappeared from record, but look at it this way: Caravaggio is the most important of all the historical figures in this book – all my characters are based on real people – yet his end is the one mystery among all these lives. Even the deaths of the historically insignificant people in this book can be accounted for. Onorio Longhi died of syphilis in Rome in 1619. Mario Minniti lived until 1640, producing banal but remunerative religious canvases at his Syracuse workshop. Giovan Francesco Tomassoni, Ranuccio's brother, became military governor of Ferrara and died in 1628. Fillide Melandroni died in 1618 at the age of thirty-seven. Because she was a courtesan, the Church denied her a Christian burial. Her friend Menica

Calvi lived to fifty and bequeathed her sister property and other investments. Lena Antognetti died in Rome at twenty-eight, just a few months before Caravaggio disappeared.

There has never been an explanation which didn't pose as many questions as it resolved, however, for the death of the greatest by far of all the characters in this book – Caravaggio.

This story is my answer.

THE PAINTINGS

This is a list of the paintings mentioned in my story. You can look at them on my website (www.mattrees.net), but if you want to view them in person, here's where you'll find them (in the order in which they appear in the novel):

The Calling of St Matthew, Church of San Luigi dei Francesi, Rome

The Martyrdom of St Matthew, San Luigi dei Francesi, Rome

St Francis in Ecstasy, Wadsworth Atheneum, Hartford, Connecticut

The Musicians, Metropolitan Museum of Art, New York

St Catherine of Alexandria, Fondación Thyssen-Bornemisza, Madrid

The Gypsy Fortune-Teller, Capitoline Museum, Rome

Judith and Holofernes, Palazzo Barberini, Rome

Love Victorious, Gemäldegalerie, Berlin

The Martyrdom of St Peter, Church of Santa Maria del Popolo, Rome

Martha and Mary Magdalene, Institute of Fine Arts, Detroit

Portrait of Pope Paul V, Palazzo Borghese (private collection), Rome

The Madonna of Loreto, Church of Sant'Agostino, Rome

Rest on the Flight into Egypt, Galleria Doria Pamphilij, Rome

Death of the Virgin, Musée du Louvre, Paris

The Madonna with the Serpent, Galleria Borghese, Rome

Our Lady of Mercy (Seven Works of Mercy), Chapel of the Pio
Monte della Misericordia, Naples

Portrait of Alof de Wignacourt, Musée du Louvre, Paris

The Beheading of St John the Baptist, Co-Cathedral of St John,
Valletta

Nativity with St Lawrence and St Francis, formerly in the Oratory
of the Compagnia di San Lorenzo, Palermo (stolen)

The Flagellation of Christ, Museo Nazionale di Capodimonte,
Naples

Salome with the Head of St John the Baptist, National Gallery,
London

The Denial of St Peter, Metropolitan Museum of Art, New York

St John the Baptist, Galleria Borghese, Rome

David with the Head of Goliath, Galleria Borghese, Rome

■

You'll find more works by Caravaggio in these same galleries and
in other museums in London, Vienna, Potsdam, Moscow, Messina,
Florence, Syracuse, Genoa, Cremona, Milan, Dublin, Fort Worth,
Kansas City, Cleveland, Barcelona, Nancy and Rouen. *The Nativity
with Sts Francis and Lawrence*, which appears in the Palermo
section of my story, was stolen in 1969 and never recovered. If you
know where to see *that* one, let me know.

ACKNOWLEDGEMENTS

Brother John Critien is the sole Knight of St John who now lives in Sant'Angelo Castle in Malta. He was gracious enough to guide me around, though the fortress isn't open to the public, and to exchange theories about Caravaggio's time there. Philip Farrugia Randon, the president of the Knights in Valletta and an authority on Caravaggio, and his assistant Nadia Chetcuti were extremely welcoming. Joan Sheridan showed me around the Grand Harbour towns with great enthusiasm.

In Rome, Patrizia Piergiovanni generously accorded me access to the magnificent Colonna Palace. Only partially open to the public on Saturday mornings, it's well worth a visit.

My friends Ugo Somma and Marcella Tondi were great companions on my visits to the finest sights in Naples and some of its more squalid and shameful ones, too. Marco de Simone allowed me access to one of the Colonna family's Neapolitan palaces – and to his excellent restaurant in Chiaia, da Marco, which is almost as good a reason to visit Naples as the works of Caravaggio.

I'm grateful to Dr Raz Chen-Morris, professor of the history of early modern science at Bar-Ilan University, for introducing me to the extensive recent research about Caravaggio's likely use of a *camera obscura*.

To be better able to describe what Caravaggio did, I tried to pick up some new skills. I learned oil painting with the guidance of Yael Robin, filling my office with my own copies of Caravaggio's works. At the Academy for Historical Fencing in my home town of Newport, Wales, Nick Thomas gave me the benefit of his practical expertise, teaching me to fight with a rapier and passing on insights into swordsmanship in Caravaggio's era.

My wife Devorah was full of enthusiasm and intuition as we hunted down Caravaggio's art and the places he touched. I'm grateful to our friends Miriam Silinsky and Danielle Ceder for taking our toddler Cai on his own tours of Rome (he likes all the fountains) while I conducted my research. Cai composed a little song about Caravaggio which he sang to me as I wrote this book. I'm humming it now.